NO BETTER ALIBI

This book is a work of fiction. All the names, characters, places, incidents, and events in this book are the product of the author's imagination and used in a fictitious manner. The characters in the book, the views, attitudes, and opinions expressed by these characters and their actions are all fictitious. Any resemblance to actual events or persons, living or dead, is entirely coincidental.

The one exception to this is the inclusion of historical figures related to the nature and development of the eugenics movement. All the historical information used is readily accessible in the public domain.

A catalogue record for this book is available from the British Library.

ISBN 978-1-0686614-0-2 (Paperback edition)
ISBN 978-1-0686614-1-9 (eBook edition)

Typesetting and cover design by The Book Typesetters
thebooktypesetters.com

NO BETTER ALIBI

Andrew Donaldsson

Acknowledgements

I would also like to thank a number of budding authors for their positivity, encouragement, and helpful suggestions. My thanks to Kelly Arnstein, Jo Caulkett, Fran Cottey, Jean Holden, Carolyn Jones, Hazel Meredith Lloyd, Silvia Sovic, Lorna Stevens, and Carolyn Young.

Inspired by a quote attributed to French philosopher and author Albert Camus (1913–1960)

PART 1

When the Time Comes

Chapter 1

The sound of banging on the door followed by raised voices was more than enough to jolt the young man out of the dream world and back to reality. He rubbed his eyes and lay listening to muffled sounds, straining to hear what was being said. For a brief moment everything went quiet and then he heard the front door open and shut followed by his mother's raised voice as if she was calling to him to get out of bed and come downstairs. Her tone sending a message that something was very wrong.

He pulled on his jeans and quickly made for the stairs.

As he made his descent a woman looking smart and efficient in her tailor-made blue jacket and pencil skirt stepped into the hallway to confront the new arrival. On seeing the young man stop on the stairs in front of her she beckoned to one of her muscle-bound associates drawing his attention to the developing situation.

"What are you doing, what's going on?" The young man directed his question at the woman who was clearly in command.

The woman and her two male companions had been ransacking the house. All three dressed in matching blue suits. His mother had been protesting to the man who was restraining her, holding her away from the other two as they all went from room to room, emptying drawers and clearing shelves, determined to cause as much disorder and disarray as possible and enjoying themselves in the process.

"Nothing to get worked up about. Let's keep calm and join everyone in here for a bit of a chat shall we. Be sensible and no-one need get hurt." She looked to be in her mid-thirties, clearly very fit, her face set in a stern yet concerned expression. Her two associates were thick set and rather mean looking. Playground bullies that had never grown up to be anything different, never been shown the error of their violent and cowardly ways.

There was a momentary bemused stand-off before the woman turned and strolled back into the room where his mother was being gripped tight by the second man. He moved forward and stepped cautiously into the room to join them, assessing the situation, running through the possible options and outcomes in his head. The woman spoke before he could come to any decision about which he should take.

"Let us have what we want, and no-one needs to get hurt. You understand." From the tone of her voice and the look on her face they were going to take whatever they wanted regardless. The smug smile she couldn't hide told him she had no intention of leaving them unharmed.

"You leave my son alone. Just take whatever you want and get out." He was quite taken aback by how strong, calm, and controlled his mum sounded.

"JJ, stay cool ok."

John Jefferson Lang affectionately known as JJ to his family and friends was twenty-one years old. He was one of a disillusioned generation, isolated, devoid of all hope. A generation left empty like discarded beer cans at a bar-b-que. A generation living in a world where uncertainty drove anxiety. Ambiguity drove confusion. Frustration drove anger.

He had reached the point where he was just angry. Angry because he felt the best years of his life had been taken away from him. Angry because his dreams had been crushed like apples in a cider press.

"Yes JJ, you should listen to your mother. Now, which of those computers is your dads?" she asked looking straight at him and ignoring his mother completely.

He pointed to an old i5 computer they had thrown onto the settee. "That one I think."

A look of annoyance spread across her face. The boy was playing games. Her irritation was reflected in her tone as she followed up with another question.

"Think very carefully. Where does your dad keep any hard copies of his documents or any USBs he uses?" she said with a cold authority tinged with a hint of the threat of swift retribution for a wrong answer. "You need to understand the importance of my question. This is a serious matter of National Security. Your father and others like him pose a great threat to the safety and welfare of our society. You had better tell us or there will be serious consequences. Very serious consequences indeed. Right here, right now."

Consequences, he thought, isn't that what life is really all about. Every choice we make has consequences and every consequence ends with a choice. Each choice takes us down a different road. His choice right now was to comply or to not comply. He concluded the consequences of either would most likely be the same but the road to get there would not.

JJ thought for a moment longer then stared at the woman, defiance seeping from his every pore. He knew his father would, by his very nature, only seek to uncover the truth and that he would want to tell everyone, help them to understand what was happening in the world. Why would this make him such a threat to them?

With hindsight, with the world developing as it was, it was easy to see how naïve his father must have been but hard for JJ to believe it could be so. Surely his father would have considered the likely consequences of his actions. Would he have been aware that someone might come for him because of what he was doing? Probably, thought JJ. But aware or not, that particular morning, someone had.

"Where's my dad?" JJ asked. His challenging tone registering half-way between assertive and aggressive as he clenched and unclenched his fists in sync with his words. He wasn't afraid, he had been taught how to stand up for himself and was more than ready to do so. "He's done nothing wrong so just let him go."

"Let's see." The woman paused for a moment as if amused by it all. "Yes, he has, and no, no we won't. As for where he's going, well he's off to join a few of his like-minded friends for some special treatment. Perhaps you'd like to join him?" she said coldly and with real menace.

The woman shook her head slowly, muttered something to her two companions and gave what seemed to be an order to one of them to take him outside. He tensed and waited for their next move. The taller man on his right seized him by the arm and manhandled him towards the door.

"We need to talk to your mum in private" he snarled, "Get back upstairs if you know what's good for you."

Across the country other similar scenarios were being played out. It was announced on radio and TV that the Prime Minister would be giving a live update later in the day. He would confirm Parliament had been dissolved indefinitely after a number of its' Members had been found to be 'significantly undermining the Government and inciting unrest'. They too had been subjected to early morning wake up calls. The homes of MPs, scientists, economists, academics, and journalists had been raided. Their houses ransacked. Laptops, phones, and papers removed. Some of them were beaten and left to bleed. They were the luckier ones. Others, not so lucky, were loaded unceremoniously onto trucks and driven away for special treatment.

Where anyone had offered even the slightest resistance they had been forced to watch as their families were dragged out into the street and their houses set alight. Neighbours were called out to watch and encouraged to cheer as homes burned. Incited to vent their anger at the monstrous heretics. Many of the evicted were beaten in the very streets where they had once joined together in friendship. Communities were being ripped apart. The very roots of society were being torn asunder.

Journalists employed by the Government and loyal to the

cause had been contacted in advance and were present to film and record the scenes which would later be aired under headlines such as HERETICS FACE JUSTICE and JUST DESSERTS FOR DENIERS. The scenes were flashed around the country with one intent, to provoke hatred and hostility.

Very soon the streets were filled with vigilante groups marshalled and encouraged by the Special Operations Security Service Community Law Enforcement Officers, known colloquially as Cleos. Left unchecked, the vigilantes attacked homes and dragged men, women, and children out onto the streets. Innocents suffering the full force of so many venting their own pent-up anger and frustration. The Cleos looked on, proud of their mornings work.

Chapter 2

Such serious consequences had yet to happen for the young man and his family. The village street stayed quiet. Nothing to be heard except for the hum of the vehicles parked outside their home. The same could not be said for what was about to happen on the inside.

They all heard the stomping on the stairs. JJ knew it was his younger brother Billy about to make an entrance.

Billy, 'Our Kid' as JJ liked to call him as a reference to the cowboy legend Billy the Kid, was two years his junior and six inches taller. He too had seen his life change but was more relaxed about. He had always taken a more laissez-faire approach to life than his older brother. Billy understood what was happening but dealt with it with a sigh and a shrug. At times, this just added to JJ's frustration. Billy played on it. Occasionally exaggerating his indifference just to watch his brother go crazy. Lately though it had become a little bit too easy. Billy realized JJ's anger was all too real and the mood had started to rub off on him.

As laid back as he liked to appear, Billy had a much shorter fuse than his brother. Once lit, he was quick to anger, quick to action, no longer the gentle giant but his Hulk-like alter-ego. JJ knew when Billy burst in it would give him the edge he needed. How Billy would react on seeing someone hurting their mum would come as no surprise to him. His brother didn't let him down.

The woman was watching on, smiling at what was unfolding in front of her as JJ and his mother were being manhandled by the two men. Smiling in anticipation of what was about to happen to the mouthy youth and his mother. Over-confident and celebrating too soon her smile was about to be wiped from her flushed face.

The sight of the six-footer bursting in caught the two men momentarily off guard, giving both JJ and his mum the chance to break free of their grasp. JJ grabbed his mum and pulled her behind him. In the same instance Billy stepped across to join his brother and the two now stood toe-to-toe with the two Cleos, facing them down.

Their mum glared out from behind a protective mountain of muscle. She knew her two boys, strong and quick, were quite capable of dishing out an avalanche of pain to anyone who threatened her. She herself, quite prepared to step in and unleash all the power that lies within a mother's protective instinct when her young are threatened.

JJ had steel in his eyes as he spoke, long and slow, an ominous warning directed at the two men standing in front of him.

"Leave now or we'll hurt you. Real bad."

"Real bad." echoed his brother.

Both brothers had confidence in each other's strength and

agility. Their father had trained them well. In the old order, there was a good chance either one could have forged a career as a professional sportsman. JJ glanced at his brother and wondered if their father had known this day would come and had made sure they would be able to deal with whatever was about to happen next.

The two men in their smart blue suits half turned as if they were going to leave. The brothers heard the woman laugh sarcastically, overconfident in the prowess of her two stocky companions. Then the room erupted, and all hell broke loose.

The man nearest to JJ lunged forward raising his right fist, intent on landing the first blow. JJ had seen it in his eyes and saw it coming a mile off. He stepped forward to reduce the length of swing which allowed him to easily block the punch with his left forearm. Simultaneously, he nudged the man backwards by pushing the palm of his right hand hard into the centre of the man's chest. Somehow, he had always known the training in traditional Shotokan was going to come in handy although his next act would be far more at home in a street fight.

As the man's head bobbed up and back JJ moved forward. Using all the strength in his powerful neck he brought his forehead down with a crashing blow onto the bridge of the man's nose. There was a dull crunching sound. The sound of splintering bone cushioned by the compression of soft tissue and nasal cartilages.

The man reeled backwards, blood pouring down onto his smart blue jacket turning it a shade of deep purple. The over-confident Cleo collapsed to his knees. JJ caressed his forehead and admired his handy work, pleased he had drawn first blood. Pleased that he had followed his father's first law of battle. When the only choice is hit or be hit, hit first, and hit hard.

At the same time Billy followed suit. Seeing the second man hesitate, he took aim and landed a huge left hook to the side of the man's jaw, breaking it in an instance, and knocking him to the floor next to his bloodied colleague. With the finesse of a ballet dancer, Billy pirouetted on his right leg and with all his weight behind it brought his left foot down hard onto the outside of the Cleo's right knee. Any sound from tearing cruciate ligaments was drowned out by the man's scream. Billy had followed his father's second law of battle. When you put your man down, make sure he stays down.

JJ turned to the woman, pointed to the two men now writhing at her feet and spoke calmly and slowly.

"You'd best collect your trash and get the hell out of our house."

She looked down. The one with the broken nose was struggling to his feet, trying unsuccessfully to stem the flow of blood with his right hand. She gestured angrily towards the prostrate figure writhing around on the floor and the two of them pulled him up onto his good leg. Together the three of them staggered towards the door.

She paused for a moment, turned, looked back, staring deep into JJ's eyes. The expression on her face was a mix of raging anger and pure hatred.

"That was a very big mistake." she snarled, "You're all going to pay for that. Big time."

She turned back and half pushed, half dragged the two men out of the door. JJ moved swiftly across the room, followed them into the hallway and slammed the front door shut behind them. He turned back to face Billy and their mother.

"We'd best get somewhere safe and do it quick."

They had little time to think about what had just happened. They didn't need more than an instant to know what the consequences would be. Time was of the essence. All three knew it would not be long before a Special Operations Security Service squad of belligerent Cleos arrived to exact their revenge. The embarrassment and damage caused to their comrades at the hands of the two brothers would not sit well. Retribution would be swift and ruthless.

"I'm ok." their mother told them, "It's best that the two of you get yourselves away from here until things die down. I'll need to stay in case your dad calls, or they realize their mistake and let him come home."

JJ wanted to be optimistic too, but he knew that was just not going to happen. They had come for his dad for a reason and their intentions had been clear. There had been no mistake. Besides, after what had just happened the three of them were targets now too.

"No mum, you can't stay here it's not safe for any of us. Dad will be ok." He knew that was probably a lie, but they all needed some reassurance right now, "I'm sure Dad wouldn't be very happy if he thought we'd left you here all on your own. You need to go with Our Kid and get to Grandad's. Billy, take Mum's car and call me on your mobile when you get there. No land lines, always your mobile from now on. I'll take dad's car and don't worry I'll be fine. You know me, I've already hatched a plan."

Five minutes later two cars left the house. Their Mum made sure they had kissed and hugged each other before going their separate ways. Billy with his Mum turned right out of the driveway and headed south. Billy drove. He didn't have a driving licence but that would be the least of their worries if they were stopped by any cruising Cleos. It would take them about an hour and a half to get to Grandad's, but they should be out of immediate danger in about ten minutes thought JJ.

He stood next to the car on the driveway, got out his mobile and sent a short text message. He didn't bother to wait for a reply, he just got into the car, turned left onto the road, and headed on into town.

Chapter 3

The outside world was a dark and deeply troubled place. The impact of an economic recession was biting hard. The continual outbreak of infectious diseases had driven fear and apprehension deep into hearts and minds, pollution was turning the air toxic and making it unbreathable. Faces once bright and smiling were now hollow eyed, expressionless, and shrouded by masks.

A time for solace, a time when everyone needed hope had come and gone. The future of an overpopulated, undernourished world appeared evermore dismal and grim. The world had relied on hope, but then came the realization that hope was not a strategy. Nations turned to those that said they cared, turned to those that said their only concern was for the welfare of the people.

The Government congratulated itself on how much it cared. How it cared for its people, cared for humanity. Constantly praising itself for providing the world with the foundations upon which to build a future that would lead, ultimately, to the salvation of humanity. Expectations were raised and promises made. People were led to believe better days lay ahead, that their nightmare existence was coming to an end. They were told that thanks to their supreme effort and sacrifice the war was being won, victories on all fronts. But it was only carefully composed rhetoric. Promises as flaky as pastry: like pie crust, thin, delicate, and made to be broken.

As peoples' compliance with new laws grew, so the Government wrapped its long bony fingers ever tighter around the nation's throat and squeezed.

The Government's PR machine went into overdrive with the warm friendly face of Dr Caroline Bramney appearing regularly on radio and television. A figure familiar to the public, trusted and respected for her honesty and integrity. Dr Bramney had stated that the country must remain in a state of high alert. With the war raging on so many fronts she said it was not the time to risk sacrificing the gains made so far by engaging in any deviation from the established new behaviours. With so much still at stake, with the health and welfare of the people hanging so precariously in the balance, everyone must remain patient, everyone must have faith and trust in her and her Government to keep the world safe. Why? she asked. Because we care, she said.

The Government released an official statement condemning a small minority of the population for spreading false information and fake news and undermining the excellent progress being made. The effect of this subversion, it said, was an upsurge in the number of people, selfish, insensitive people, refusing to comply and hence putting others at severe risk.

To help to control this non-compliance, this immorality, the Government announced that Photographic Identity Cards were to be issued to everyone including children. Referred to as PICs, they were to be linked directly to census information, medical records, education, and employment histories. All personal data thus became immediately accessible to those with the means and authority to access it.

People were told not to worry because the personal data and photographs were only to be used to ensure their welfare and security. The majority were happy to comply. Only later did it become clear that the PICs were introduced to serve a more sinister purpose.

The face of the motherly Dr Bramney beamed out from TV sets across the country to provide further reassurance to a despairing populace.

'We care about all of you, your friends and your relatives.' she said comfortingly. 'We will make your world a better place and you must play your part too. We all need to care. We are all in this together. Together we must remain vigilant and stand united against those who would challenge the truth and the wisdom of our actions. We must all understand the reality of our situation. We live in a world where all our actions, all our behaviours, have consequences. It is foolish and irresponsible to pretend otherwise. Always remember we are at war. We are fighting for our future, for the welfare of humanity. Together we will triumph. Together we must show how much we really care. Follow the Law. Report the Heretics. Save Humanity.'

People complied and rejoiced in the belief the Government would save the day, would keep them safe, would save humanity. The Government praised itself for its leadership and its honesty. The die was cast. More new laws were passed. Laws made by the rich and the powerful, enforced by the brutal and the merciless, complied with by the weak and the poor. Freedoms once taken for granted were to be consigned to the realms of history. Consigned by those that claimed it was all for the welfare of humanity.

*

Lurking deep in the shadows, members of a secretive society established decades ago celebrated the coming of this dark and desperate time. Members of the Society for the Protection, Advancement and Welfare of the Nation, SPAWN. Spawners, as they called themselves. They had worked tirelessly over the years and finally their efforts were to be rewarded. The opportunity had presented itself and their long wait was about to come to an end. They had used the last five years to set the stage and now they were ready to rise up and seize the day. They knew they were unstoppable. At last, they could create their vision of the world, deliver their own Mandate for Salvation, and this time, no-one could possibly stand in their way.

Chapter 4

At eight o'clock on the night before the early morning intrusion, gatherings of like-minded people were being called to order. Patiently they sat waiting in anticipation. Waiting for the final call to arms. Waiting for the signal that would herald the beginning of a new world. A world built on their truth, on their wisdom, on their Mandate for Salvation.

The light was dim, the air stale and warm. The musty smell of cigar smoke and brandy seeped out of the dark oak paneled walls and up from the centuries old wooden floor. There they sat in semi-circular rows. The good and the great. Men and women at complete ease with the decadence of their surroundings. The portraits of their long-deceased predecessors looking down on them as if with expressions that had foreseen the future and given it their full approval.

In front of this particular gathering stood a tall, hooded figure dressed in a long flowing blue robe edged in gold silk and white fur. Eyes ablaze, head held high, and with his arms outstretched in a gesture choreographed to show he embraced them all. A figure of authority and control. A figure with position and power. A figure upon which all eyes in the room were fixed.

To one side of him and set slightly back stood a smaller, slighter figure dressed in a similar but plain, less ostentatious blue robe with hands clasped together as if in prayer. To his other side stood a small, thickset figure similarly dressed and clutching a small blue book as if it were his most treasured possession.

"We are Truth.", intoned the slight figure in a sweet, sultry chant.

"We are Wisdom.", came the deep, husky male voice from the right, holding up the small blue book out in front of him.

"We are Salvation." boomed out from centre stage to all those seated in front.

The wooden walls reverberated as every voice in the room chanted in complete unison.

"We are Truth. We are Wisdom. We are Salvation."

Thus, the ceremony began.

Taking a step forward, the tall figure slowly removed his hood to reveal the gaunt features and greying hair that had become so familiar to the public. He stared out into the wide eyes of the audience in front of him. Although it was too dark for him to see, he pictured adoration and exaltation shining back at him. He envisaged them like hounds at a hunt, like Pavlov's dogs, panting with the expectation and excitement of what was about to come their way.

His two lieutenants moved forward into the empty Queen Ann chairs positioned at each end of the front row. He glanced up at the large wood-rimmed clock on the wall in front of him. It was time. He took a deep breath and beckoned for them all to watch the large screen on the wall behind him as it flickered into life.

"Behold our great President. Our divine leader will speak to us with words of great truth and infinite wisdom and will show us the way. For the time is right. When tomorrow comes, we will move out of the shadows and into the light. Tomorrow the world our fathers and our grandfathers waited so long to create will become our reality. The new dawn will herald a new beginning."

An instant later the screen came alive and there before them sat their illustrious President. Some let out a muffled cheer whilst others clapped spontaneously. Seated in front of a banner that read 'Truth Wisdom Salvation' sat a slim, dark, hooded figure, face hidden deep in shadow. A figure shrouded in secrecy in a deliberate act to add mystery and allure. To preserve and protect the President's identity and in doing so create the figurehead they all craved. A figure that lived and breathed in their own imaginations, a figure assigned with immense power, power they themselves felt they could only dream of. A seductive figure to which they willingly devoted their hearts and their souls.

"Welcome my people from around the world." The President's hypnotic voice swirled around the room, beguiling them as if they were children listening to the magical music of the Pied Piper of Hamelin.

Although primarily directed at the loyal gatherings within the country, the speech was also being broadcast to specially selected audiences in other major cities across the globe. Since the very beginning SPAWN had always had an international membership. Its influence stretched far beyond this darkened room. However, it was those within it that would be the first to answer the call to action.

"My faithful Spawners the time has come. Circumstance and consequence have made ready the world. Only we can save our people. Now, at last, we must unite and move forward with our Mandate for Salvation. We have long-awaited tomorrow's dawn. You have all worked hard and used your positions of power and control with great purpose in pursuit of this, our true aim.

We have the power to ensure a lasting change. What we do, we do for the welfare of all humanity. We act out of our divine right. From this night forward, we will be praised for time immemorial.

We are the Saviours of all humanity. We will reward those whose belief has never wavered with the gift of wealth and power. For those whose lives we govern, our gift will be their eternal welfare."

The President paused for effect and then continued.

"Through our tireless efforts we have suppressed the human spirit, building hope with one hand then destroying it with the other. Together we have suppressed the will of the people. We have subjugated the people. We have taken away their individual and collective identities. We now control them and their behaviour.

People hide their faces everywhere they go. They have lost the power to show any physical or emotional expression. They comply, they have learned acceptance. Society is ours to do with as we see fit. We will do what we know needs to be done. Let no-one forget what we do we do for the welfare of humanity. Let no-one forget:"

The President took a deep breath.

"We are Truth. We are Wisdom. We are Salvation."

In the small, darkened room a chant went up in unison, replicated across the country, bellowed from the mouths of faithful followers:

"We are Truth. We are Wisdom. We are Salvation."

A few seconds passed to allow the fervour to subside a little and then the emphatic address continued.

"I must pay homage to all those of our members who have worked so hard to enable us to establish a culture of fear and panic, of despondency and despair, of hopelessness and surrender. I must congratulate you all for your efforts in creating a world where we alone control the social interaction and behaviour of the people. I praise all of you who have contributed so much, for so long, to bring us to this night, to the very eve of our new Mandate."

The President paused, brought both hands together and then, with palms facing outwards, moved them apart slowly and deliberately.

"A particular mention must go to someone who has already been lauded as one of the most influential people of our time. Since completing his studies at one of our most prestigious universities, he devoted his entire career to us in the staunch belief that one day our chance would come. Loyal to our cause, this brilliant man has worked hard to create this ethos, this culture. His influence has spanned the globe, his impact immense and unquestionable. Whenever a move back to the old normality was called for, he immediately presented a valid and coherent case for caution and restraint. Never once was he unable to find a reason to suppress the arguments, to suppress undesired action, to suppress the people.

He has always been and will forever remain a most valued member of SPAWN. He is our dear and trusted friend, he is of course, the renowned Fergus Butzemann."

In the centre of the second row a slim figure dressed in crisp white shirt and smart navy-blue trousers rose slowly to his feet, raised his hands, and turned a full 360 degrees to bask in his glory. Almost everyone in the room rose to their feet, clapping and shouting in delight. Those closest to him patted him on the shoulder and some bowed their heads to him as they did so, feeling unworthy to be in the company of such greatness.

At the far left of the back row, a disheveled unimposing figure with greying stubble sat hidden from view. Inconspicuous, his head was bowed to the floor. He wiped away a tear that was slowly making its way unnoticed down his left cheek. This was never what he had believed would happen. This was never what he had wanted. He had seen the signs but until very recently had always managed to convince himself he must have been mistaken. He had turned a hopeful blind eye. He knew by the time he had decided to act it was already too late. There was nothing he could do now except survive. He shed another tear but this time not for himself, this time for humanity.

The speech continued.

"We have convinced the world and the world reacted as we had expected. Frightened and panicked, people are only too ready to listen and to follow us, to willingly give us total power and complete control.

We took the timid and the fearful by the hand. We created a new reality. We tested their compliance and changed the very fabric of society.

We have turned their anger and their frustration towards the heretics that question our truth. We have broken the collective human spirit. Now we will continue on our journey. We will mend what we have broken. We will cleanse and purify with our divine hand.

We will give the world truth and with our truth will come light. We will give them wisdom, and in our wisdom, they will find belief. This is the dawn of the new civilization it was our destiny to create. From our truth and our wisdom will come salvation. This is our Mandate."

With arms spread wide, palms almost vertical, held flat with fingers fanned out in an altogether open and inviting gesture to herald in the future, the President paused to hold the moment and then continued.

"Yet, my friends, there is still much to do. The journey has not ended yet. Very soon the outcome will be irreversible. We must remain strong and true to our aim. We must never weaken our grip."

Two large figures in tight blue jackets stepped into view, one on either side of the seated President. Elbows bent. Granite fists raised to shoulder height. Statuesque. A performance perfectly timed to add effect to the words.

"The time is right. Bask in the power, feel it grow. Rejoice as our light burns the souls of all the heretics. We will cleanse the world for our future generations. Rise up from your seats for the world is at last ready for us. Rise up I say, for now the time is right."

Another split-second pause before the final rallying cry, said loud and with gusto.

"For We are Truth. We are Wisdom. We are Salvation."

They rose from their seats. They whooped and they cheered. The scene had been set and the time had come. Tomorrow's dawn would herald the new beginning.

*

In a small, terraced house in a small rural town, a young man had intercepted the broadcast and sat staring at his computer in disbelief. He quickly pressed an icon on the screen in front of him and then grabbed his phone. Breathless, he listened for a response.

"Sal, it's me Danny. Call me back. It's really urgent. I think something very bad is about to happen."

Chapter 5

The sun was just peeking over the village horizon when they came to call.

He had known he was on SPAWNs radar. He had estimated there was a high probability they would want to know how much he knew and who else was in the chain, so it was no surprise when the knock at the door came early that morning.

A light sleeper of late, he had sensed the arrival of the convoy even before he heard the sound of the car doors slamming shut on the road in front of the house. He quietly slipped out of bed and peered through the curtains. Without even looking he knew instinctively it was them. His first thought was for the safety of his family. His second was of annoyance. Annoyance that he had allowed it to happen here. The third was relief, relief that at least he had expected it.

He whispered softly to his wife, kissed her gently on her trembling lips, and went to meet the visitors. He knew his family's last vestige of peace and tranquility would end abruptly as the uninvited, inharmonious outside world burst in on them. He had brought this upon them. Now his only option was to put his trust in those he left behind to follow the trail of breadcrumbs that would lead them to him, wherever his journey ended.

As SPAWNs minions were making their way up the path, he was on his way down the stairs in anticipation. Sure enough, moments later came the unmistakable sound of a big fist banging on the door.

He closed his eyes, took a deep breath, and opened the door. Immediately he was knocked backwards as two muscle-bound men dressed in tight fitting blue suits burst into his house. Each wore a small circular badge on their lapel, signaling in some way their authority. He steadied himself and offered no resistance as he felt a strong grip on his left arm. It was pulled and twisted behind his back, thrusting his head and shoulders forward and causing a sudden sharp pain from his shoulder to his elbow. In an instance, the other man grabbed him by the hair and pulled his head back. They stood toe to toe, eye to grimacing eye.

"Not so smart now, are we?" the man sneered. "Time to go on a little trip with some of your buddies."

The burly blue suited Cleo hit him hard in the chest.

They shoved him, winded, out of the door and dragged him to the back of a large black van. A young woman probably in her late twenties or early thirties dressed in a well-tailored blue suit held open the door to the van.

"Get him in and get back to the house."

He saw the woman slip her hand into her jacket pocket as she gave the order. They hoisted him up and threw him forwards into the van. Inside in the gloom he could just pick out the shapes of bodies lying next to and on top of each other, dressed in what looked like their pyjamas. He could hear heavy breathing and the sound of people groaning in pain. He felt a sudden sharp pain in his back. His whole body shook and trembled as the electric shock from the taser passed through his body. Then everything went black.

Chapter 6

Danny was in front of his laptop, leaning back in his chair and staring at the poster of RuPaul on his bedroom wall. He had just watched the recording from the night before for the third time. He was struggling to understand what exactly had been set in motion last night. He had never been a supporter of conspiracy theories, but he knew what he had stumbled across went way beyond just theory. He was sure he had already identified that the Government, or at least one of their agencies, had been loading a tracker program on to the laptops and phones of anyone who had accessed Government, or certain other web and social media sites, to download or upload information, data, views, and opinions. Danny had sensed there was a high probability their surveillance went far wider than that.

Being the computer whizz-kid that he was, fortunately for him and his close friends, he had written and installed his own warning and detection program. Once uploaded to all his and his friends' devices, it identified and blocked any intrusive spyware.

He was very pleased with himself and for once he let it show. He was more than just a computer nerd who liked occasionally to dress up in drag, he was the one that had made sure they could communicate freely amongst themselves. Intuitively, he had been sure they would need to keep things to themselves.

Although he had not quite known why he was so sure at the time, now he was so pleased he had managed to convince them all. In particular JJ who had at least installed the scrambler onto his phone. He leaned forward, picked up his mobile and stared at it, willing it to buzz with a reply from Sally. Why was it taking so long for her to respond?

*

JJ had parked the car down a deserted side street in the centre of town. Driving in had been easy. He had seen only two other cars on the road, in part due to the route he took, in part due to the early morning hour. He knew it was safe to leave the car there as hardly anyone walked through that part of town now. He surmised that there was little danger of being caught on CCTV. The shops and the restaurant he had parked near had not been open for a long, long time so who would be looking anyway even if the cameras were still in operation. He allowed himself a smile. Even if they were looking, they would never recognize him with a mask on and his baseball cap pulled down to hide his eyes.

Following the introduction of the PICs, he had heard it was the eyes that the facial recognition software focused on. To keep us all safe and sound, he thought, who are they trying to kid. It had become a widespread belief amongst the under twenty-fives that the real purpose of the PICs was to enable swift facial recognition and hence provide the Special Operations Security Service with constant surveillance of everyone, everywhere.

He made a conscious study of the pavement as he cautiously made his way through the side streets until he came to a long row of terraced houses. Stopping at the corner, he looked around to check no-one was about before texting a short message.

Within less than a minute his phone buzzed with a two-word reply. He read it quickly, smiled and walked along the row, quickening his stride until he reached number thirty-one. He turned up the short path and pushed open the door which had been left ajar in readiness for his arrival. He stepped over the threshold and closed the door shut behind him.

Sally stood at the top of the stairs and looked down at JJ. She was dressed in tight blue jeans and a fuchsia pink T-shirt. JJ looked up at her. A welcome sight for his sore eyes that literally took his breath away. From the bottom of the stairs Sally somehow looked taller than her 5 feet 2 inches and more beautiful than ever. His hidden expression was a mixture of pleasure and pain. Pleasure at being there with her and seeing her again. Pain because of the thought of putting her in danger and the news he brought with him.

"Something bad is happening." Immediately, he caught himself regretting that he had jumped straight in without even saying hello.

"My dad's just been taken away earlier this morning by some of the Government's cronies. I have no idea why or where to, except that it has something to do with the things he has been saying and doing online. Me and Billy haven't helped either. We got in a fight with a couple of Cleos at our house who were hurting our mum."

He saw the expression of concern sweep across Sally's face and gave her the best reassuring smile he could muster.

"We're all ok which is more than can be said about them. They came off a lot worse which means they'll be looking for us now, I guess. Billy's taken my mum to our Grandads. I think what's happened to us has something to do with Danny's suspicions. Has anything been happening around here?"

Sally nodded solemnly and beckoned JJ to come upstairs. She put a finger to her lips as a signal to JJ that a silent approach was needed so as not to wake up her parents.

"Come into my room quietly," she whispered as JJ reached the landing, "My mum and dad are still asleep."

Words softly spoken that JJ had only ever dreamed of hearing, but this was not the time or place to get lost in wild imaginings.

As they entered the room JJ saw that Sally had already been busy and was aware things were happening. Sally's bedroom was a reasonable size and extremely well organized. The furniture consisted of a wardrobe, a set of drawers, a single bed, and two small desks. The desks were formed into an L-shape in the far corner of the room. Set out so Sally could swivel her chair between the two with ease.

On top of one of the desks sat a laptop, on the other a desktop computer. Both were on and their screens lit up the room, casting ghostly shadows on the opposite walls. The laptop with what looked like information, the desktop with moving pictures from what appeared to be CCTV cameras. JJ gave her what he thought was his warmest smile. Sally smiled back, pleased he was there, pleased he was close. The brightness in her eyes instantly gave him hope that things could only get better.

"Have you managed to find anything out about what might be happening?" he asked hopefully.

Sally and JJ had been friends for a long time. They had grown up in the same small village and first met each other at the local nursery although their recollections of that early time of their lives were a little hazy. It was at the village primary school where their friendship really began. JJ had been in the year above Sally. However, because the school had a particularly low intake in JJ's year, it had merged JJ and Sally's classes together so that year 4 and year 5 had become one.

They were both very sporty and had discovered a common interest in music. Out of which sprang a covert friendship. At that age, JJ was reluctant to be seen spending too much time with a girl from the year below. It just wasn't cool. So, despite how much he enjoyed her company, peer pressure usually got the better of him. Then they lost contact for a while when JJ went off to secondary school in town. Even the chance to bump into each other evaporated when Sally's parents left the village and moved to town a couple of years later.

Time passed and JJ progressed from playing the ukulele to being a very accomplished guitarist. He had become a key member of the school band. Sally had mastered the clarinet. It was because of their music that they met up again. It looked like romance was about to blossom. Then the world turned against them.

Despite what they perceived to be a determined effort to keep them apart, they kept in touch via text and then through chatting online as often as they could, but it was not quite the same as being together in person. They even took the risk of meeting up on the odd occasion, but the new laws had stifled any hope of a romantic relationship developing and their covert assignations had proved too stressful for them both.

That was not their only problem. JJ's lack of self-confidence didn't help matters. His somewhat misguided belief that Sally was too far above him compounded the already difficult social situation. His insecurity always got the better of him making it impossible for him to tell her how he really felt about her. Any signals Sally sent, he either missed completely or thought it was just his imagination getting the better of him. So, in the end, neither of them ever felt sure about how the other one felt.

He had become used to taking the safe option of assuming she just wanted to be friends. Sally just became totally exasperated with him. He had convinced himself his approach made sense, best to put his logic before emotion. He had rationalized the situation by telling himself that once they left the band, they would meet new friends, have different experiences, and ultimately follow different paths.

However, he could never deny to himself how he really felt about her. How, when he had seen her again for the first time since primary school he had been completely overwhelmed by a surge of emotion. How every time since just the mere sight of her sent his heart into overdrive. He always thought he hid it well.

He looked across the room as Sally sat down in front of her laptop. Such a combination, brilliant and gorgeous, he thought. His face flushed. He didn't really hide it very well at all. Sally waved him across to join her. He steeled himself. This was not the time for romantic thoughts and definitely not romantic gestures. Things were serious and to keep Sally safe he needed to keep his head clear and his mind focused.

Back under self-control, JJ perched himself on the small stool Sally had put out for him next to her chair. Sally turned to face him, as composed as always. Her expression was serious yet warm and caring.

"Danny sent this to me last night. See what you make of it. I'm sure it has a lot to do with what happened to you this morning."

Sally hit a few keys and Danny's recording sprang to life on the screen. They watched it together in silence. When it had finished JJ sat looking at the screen in some confusion and disbelief. Who the hell was that?

Sally closed the video and opened a screenshot she had taken about an hour earlier. It was a headline and associated text. It read EARLY MORNING RAIDS IDENTIFY HERETICS NETWORK. Sally scrolled down to the text beneath the headline.

"This was put up across the Government controlled media sites about an hour ago. I have already picked up loads of conversations about it online and on my phone. What they are all saying is really scary. You had better read the article. Putting this with Danny's video suggests something very bad is starting to happen. I think we're going to need to get together with Danny. Somehow, somewhere."

JJ read the article.

In the early hours of this morning a number of heretics were arrested by the Special Operations Security Service. This was the culmination of an extensive covert surveillance operation that had identified the sources of the publication and distribution of fake news and false evidence designed to undermine the great work and effort being made to keep us all safe. The Government has been horrified to see the depraved depths these dis-believers these heretics have gone to in order to undermine the fundamental truth. A spokesperson for the Government said that the dawn raids had been extremely successful and as a result of the action taken the world had become a safer place for everyone. Today we have won a victory over our enemies. Over those that set out to undermine our progress. But remember, winning one battle does not win us the war. The fight rages on. There is a long way to go before victory can be declared so we must all continue to do as we are asked. We must follow the rules. We must trust in the wisdom of our leaders. We must remain united against the heretics. We have today taken yet another small step towards Salvation.

JJ turned to Sally his face drained of colour.

"I think my dad is in real trouble. We need to find out what's going on. We need to get together with Danny. We should ask him to get hold of Obi too. Then we need to come together somewhere safe."

Sally nodded and picked up her phone. Danny, with some foresight had set up a secure WhatsApp group about a week ago. The group consisted of himself, Sally, and Obi. He had not included JJ as he still felt JJ was reluctant to admit there might be a need for it and because he knew of JJ's feelings towards Sally. He didn't want the conversation turning into some embarrassing online love story. It was hard enough to hide his own feelings for a member of the group.

Chapter 7

Obi was Danny's oldest and closest friend whom he trusted completely. Obi had not had a very easy time of it. From his first day at school, he had been picked on by a group of older bullies. A quiet boy who liked to keep himself to himself, he was subjected to the usual name calling and a bit of pushing and shoving in the playground. He knew they would get bored with him eventually and move on to the next new kid that was a bit different to them, so he decided to ride out the storm. His strategy worked. The bullies moved on.

Obi was the eldest of three children and so it seemed only natural that when his sister Jessie started at the school, he would take her whilst their mum took his youngest sister Katie to nursery school.

It was the morning of Jessie's third day as they ambled along holding hands. Jessie was chattering happily away to him about all the things she was going to do that day when Obi saw the gang loitering ahead of them by the shop on the corner.

The gang leader turned and smiled at Jessie.

"You're a pretty little girl." he said with a sneer. "Look, we've got some nice sweeties from the shop, would you like one? Come on missy don't be shy, we only want to be your friend."

The other four boys sniggered in unison and swung around behind their intrepid leader to form a barrier in front of Obi and Jessie.

Jessie looked up at her brother with wide, innocent eyes unsure what was happening and what she should do next. Obi smiled reassuringly, gently squeezed her hand, and then let it go.

"I'm taking my sister to school so just let us pass without any trouble. Okay?" Obi's voice was flat and emotionless.

"Trouble, who said anything about trouble. We just offered the little girl some sweeties, that's all. You upset because we didn't offer you any? Hey boys, little chicken shit here wants a sweety."

Two of the boys made clucking noises as they moved their arms up and down like chicken wings. The mimicry was cut short as the gang leader took a pace forward, a sign that the real fun was about to start.

"We're going to beat the crap out of you and then you can watch as we have some fun with your little sister." He talked big because he thought he was a big man.

Obi saw it differently. He guided Jessie behind him with his right hand, stepped forward stopping just out of arms reach and locked eyes with the loud-mouthed bully.

The bigger boy was shaken momentarily by such a direct approach. Flanked by his gang, he quickly regained his composure. Somewhat reassured by their proximity and their grunts of support, the bully's confidence flooded back. Enough at least for him to force out a rather nervous laugh.

"Looks like we're going to have us some fun boys. He thinks he's some sort of hero protecting his little sister." He pointed at Jessie. "Just you watch as I pound your stupid brother into the dirt."

Obi knew to land a punch the fat boy would have to take a small step forward or come at him fast. He prepared himself for both possibilities. The boy twitched and Obi knew the choice was made. The bully boy moved slightly forward and unleashed a haymaker towards the left side of Obi's head. Obi dodged the intended blow. Using his greater speed and agility he took a step to the side and punched his attacker hard on the right temple. As the bully reeled sideways Obi hit him hard in the back, right between the shoulder blades sending him sprawling forwards face first onto the hard concrete floor. The boy's head bounced up off the floor and then back down again with a dull thud. His friends stood paralyzed by the speed and ferocity of Obi's reaction. None of them moved a muscle.

Taking hold of Jessie's hand, he spoke slowly and calmly to the stunned onlookers,

"Make sure you and that useless dung heap stay out of our way from now on. Understand."

With Jessie on his outside, he strutted past the four shocked boys and never looked back.

Neither Obi nor his family were bothered again. Then when Danny was picked on at school it was Obi who stepped in to sort it out. This time there was no need to resort to a physical altercation. Obi's reputation was well established. No-one in the school was prepared to take him on. Danny and Obi became best friends after that. Danny considered them a great team. He supplied the brains and Obi the brawn. Although as Obi often pointed out he was also extremely intelligent and his reputation for fighting was only really related to one event, albeit now the stuff of legend.

No-one that really knew Danny would have been surprised that he had called Obi just after he had sent the message to Sally. Theirs was a special relationship and Danny took heart from the fact he had effectively put Obi on full alert. He was sure Sally would want to get together with the two of them. It was just a matter of time. Though Danny was growing impatient. Obi was happy just to wait for his friend's next call.

Chapter 8

It was 9.00 am on the morning of the intrusions. They were seated around a large oak table in the Prime Minister's recently refurbished private meeting room.

The Director General was standing with authority about to address the small gathering. He was the senior advisor to the Prime Minister. In some quarters he had been dubbed the puppet-master as it became very clear that whatever he advised was followed to the letter. Ruthlessly ambitious, he reveled in the military inference of his title. He felt like a General and after all, everyone said this was a war he was fighting.

The DG focused his gaze on the Prime Minister sitting opposite him, silent and subdued. Positioned around them sat the Deputy Director General; the Secretary of State for Health, Welfare and Security; the Secretary of State for Economy and Education; and the Director General's loyal secretary who was responsible for recording the meeting.

"Today we make history. I set out before you the roadmap that will ensure the welfare of our nation and the Salvation of our people. At 11.00 am this morning, you Prime Minister, accompanied by me and the Secretary of State for Health, Welfare, and Security, will hold a nationally televised emergency briefing that will go out on all media channels. In the briefing you will state that today you have been left with no alternative other than to dissolve Parliament and assume full control of the country under the Emergency Powers Act.

You will stress that this has been forced upon you and that reluctantly, you have taken the full burden of responsibility on your own shoulders for the safety, security, and welfare of the people. You will inform the country that swift action was necessary after a number of Members of Parliament had been found to have significantly undermined the Government. They had continually spread false information and were actively inciting unrest and civil disobedience across the country.

You will smile reassuringly when you add that order will be restored by the end of the day. Adding solemnly that a number of arrests have already been made resulting in a reduction in the risk to everyone's lives."

At this point, the Director General turned and nodded towards the Deputy Director General sitting on his right. Caroline smiled back at him, enjoying the moment. Everyone in the room knew and understood that she would carry out her upcoming role with great gusto. They knew she had the energy and enthusiasm for the job. Even so they still underestimated how much she would enjoy it.

The DG continued his instruction.

"So successful has been our program of social control and behavioural management that our actions today will go relatively unchallenged. Any challenge that does occur will be dealt with swiftly and sharply." He nodded towards his Deputy for a second time and motioned for her to leave. Her presence was needed elsewhere.

It was clear to those in the room that they had just witnessed the complete subjugation of the will of the Prime Minister. He sat in front of them a beaten man. His only remaining purpose was to do as he was told, to act the part as if his life depended on it. Through his own arrogance and ambition, he had ended up here. He was no fool and he knew he had no way out. Just like everyone else in the room, he knew he had no option but to obey the DG's commands because his life really did depend on it. There was nothing left for him to do. There would be no push-back from the dissolution of Parliament, no public outcry questioning his leadership, no voice of dissent. There was no-one left to come to his aid.

For many years, the Spawners had planned for this moment. Waited patiently and now the opportunity presented itself, they were ready. Like the DG, other members of SPAWN were positioned in places of power and authority across every sector, private and public. Around the world, their equivalents were prepared for the call to arms from their own offspring of SPAWN. They and their comrades were ready and more than eager to activate SPAWNs Mandate and bring their collective truth, their wisdom, and their salvation to the world.

Over the years they had collected detailed personal information on any outsiders who would prove useful to them on route to their goal. The Prime Minister was one such outsider. During his time at a distinguished private school, unbeknownst to him he had become friends with a number of young Spawners. Most of his new friends were third or even fourth generation members following the family tradition and inheriting the same ingrained beliefs.

Due to his overwhelming ego and pompous self-belief, he never once realized his life had been taken over and his destiny was being manipulated by SPAWN. He didn't even know they existed, but they knew him and had singled him out for great things. First though they needed to ensure that when the time came to show their hand, he would always be theirs to control.

"Hi there, you look a bit lost." said the smiling second-year university student. "I'm Fergus."

The target had been acquired and first contact had been made.

"We think we're in the right place, is this block B?" came the hesitative response hopeful of confirmation. "We're trying to find the politics lecture."

"That's where I'm heading so tag along with me if you like." Fergus scanned the group of five and settled his gaze on the smiling figure in the middle. "You have ambitions in that direction then?"

"Oh yes, one day I'm going to be top dog. You're looking at a future Prime Minister."

A thought flashed through Fergus's mind masked behind a friendly smile, indeed you are, you pompous oaf.

"We're having a party at our flat tonight would you guys like to come?"

They arrived bottles in hand and were greeted by an enthusiastic and slightly drunk Fergus.

"Get yourselves a drink and go mingle."

An hour later, Fergus sidled up to him, topped up his glass from the bottle of red he was waving around, put his arm around his shoulder and whispered drunkenly in his ear.

"You've hit the jackpot tonight, matey. See that girl over there, she hasn't taken her eyes off you since you walked in. Want me to introduce you?"

He felt Fergus squeeze his left buttock, turned to see him nodding and winking at him. No, he thought, I can handle this myself thank you very much, you just stand and watch a real man in action.

He looked across, smiled, and felt a warm tingle as she smiled back and slowly licked her lips with the tip of her tongue. He grabbed Fergus's wandering hand and gave a slight nod in her direction.

"What's her name?" he asked.

"Sophie." came the slurred response.

"Sophie. Thanks, Fergy old boy, I'll take it from here." He finished his wine, left Fergus with his half empty bottle for company, and sauntered over to where Sophie was leaning with her back against the wall. The closer he got, the more beautiful she became. By the time he reached her his heart was pumping at nineteen to the dozen. He was totally lost. Spellbound, he stood in front of her and all he could muster was an inane grin.

"Hello, I'm Sophie." she said, in a soft and sultry tone. She put her finger to his lips. "Shh, you don't need to tell me, I already know who you are."

Sophie took him by the hand and led him out into the hallway like she was taking an obedient toddler upstairs to be changed. She walked him into the bedroom and sat him down on the bed.

"Stay right there baby whilst I close the door, there's a good boy." She brushed the side of his cheek then moved her hand slowly down his body to caress the bulge at the front of his trousers. He reached out with his hands and Sophie smiled, gently pushing them back down to his side.

"Naughty, naughty. All in good time."

He watched her shapely form as she walked to lock the door. She turned, stopped to look at him, and began to unbutton the top of her shirt to reveal the black lacy edge running across the top of her soft pink breasts. He could contain himself no longer. He rushed across to her and slammed her back against the door, ripping her shirt open and frantically kissing her neck. She tried to resist but he was far too strong and too aroused for her to fight off.

"Get off me." screamed Sophie. "Get off me."

That was the last thing he remembered until he was shaken awake by Fergus.

"What the hell have you done?" shouted Fergus.

"What." he muttered, his head throbbing and his mind thick with fog.

"You've gone and killed her you fucking idiot." raged Fergus. "Get his clothes and let's get him out of here."

One of Fergus' friends stepped over to him and he followed him with his bloodshot eyes. A moment of sheer panic set in when he saw Sophie's body lying on the floor next to the bed. Her face was looking across at him, still and expressionless. He could see the blood around the corner of her mouth and bruising starting to form near her eye.

"What have I done? I can't remember, I can't remember." he whimpered.

The story Fergus told him was they had heard screaming and banging coming from the bedroom but in their drunken state thought nothing of it. It was a few hours later when they decided it would be a great prank to burst in on them only to be shocked sober by what they discovered. They were in no doubt, he had beaten and strangled Sophie. Everything, Fergus said, had been taken care of and he should have nothing to fear. They would stick together. It would be their secret. No-one would ever need to know what had happened that night.

Such was his character he closed his mind to all thoughts about Sophie. As far as he was concerned the matter was closed and he determined that the incident should never be mentioned again. SPAWN had other ideas. It was the DG in a former role that had shown him the photographs and explained the situation to him. He was their man now. His destiny now a foregone conclusion, he would rise to the pinnacle of an illustrious political career under the watchful eye of the Spawners. The man of the people was their puppet and when they whistled, he danced.

*

Out strode the Prime Minister as the bell chimed eleven, a disconsolate, powerless puppet. He was followed dutifully by the Director General and the Secretary of State for Health, Welfare and

Security. They took up their positions at the oak carved lecterns on the left and right side of the central figure. There between them, with his chest puffed out, elbows bent and unseen sweaty palms resting on the central lectern, stood the PM. As ready as ever to put on another great performance, after all, he thought, the show must go on. He looked down and shuffled his papers as if to remind himself of the content of the pages before positioning them carefully on top of the lectern.

Slowly and very deliberately he raised his head and looked to his left directly into the eyes of the Director General, searching for the approving nod from the tall, confident figure standing composed beside him. To those watching on, it was a simple exchange of pleasantries before the start of the briefing. To those in the know, it was another gesture of subservience and obedience.

"It is with great sadness and a very heavy heart that I have to inform you, the nation, that due to the actions of insurgents and lawbreakers and for the safety and security of all our loyal citizens I have had to take the regrettable decision to dissolve Parliament under the Emergency Powers Act and assume full responsibility for ensuring the welfare of you all.

I am sure you support my decision. You must understand that due to the impact of the reckless and unforgivable actions of a minority I was left with no other choice. We must remain vigilant to the threat posed to us by such minorities and we must be prepared to take every necessary action against their irresponsible attitudes and behaviours. Above all, you must remain faithful to the cause. For together, with your faith and your trust we will defeat our enemies and we will win this war. For together, we are the ones that really care."

The PM brought his clenched right fist down hard on to the top of the lectern with such force he almost knocked himself backwards. The two figures on either side of him nodded slowly, solemnly, and seriously, like guests at a wake.

"We must remain united in our determination to defeat our enemies." the PM continued. "Everyone must comply to keep us all safe. Anyone seen to be flaunting the law will be dealt with swiftly and severely. Should you see someone, be it a relative, friend or neighbour, failing or worse, openly refusing to comply, it is your duty to report them immediately for the safety and security of us all.

The heretics left amongst us must be driven out and brought under our control. We must always follow the facts not fiction. You must strengthen your trust in me to make the right decisions. We care and so we must stand together." The PM paused and held his arms out wide pointing at the two advisory figures standing stoically on his left and right, building steadily to a crescendo.

"We have wisdom and with your trust and your belief we will triumph. We are on the road to victory. We are on the road to Salvation. Remember:"

The PM paused, raised his arms in front of him and once again banged his right fist down hard on the top of the lectern for dramatic effect. He stared directly into the camera lens and proclaimed the mantra.

"Follow the Law. Report the Heretics. Save Humanity."

Chapter 9

Later that day the Government released another statement concerning the early morning abductions.

Following a number of house calls and arrests today the Government is pleased to announce that Operation Wake-Up Call has been a complete success. The heretics that have been spreading false and damaging information are now being detained at special centres around the country. They are guilty of serious breaches of the law and of inciting unrest. It is hoped that further questioning of those arrested will result in a greater cleansing of our society. We will put an end to the terrible lies and messaging that these evil monsters amongst us have been sending out. The detention centres will be managed by the Special Operations Security Service and those detained will undergo a facilitated program of re-education and rehabilitation. It is hoped that in time many of those taken this morning will become model citizens who can be reintroduced safely back into our society. This will be done slowly and cautiously. We remain totally committed and on course to keep everyone safe. Our roadmap to Salvation remains unchanged.

*

When he awoke, he was cold, wet, and face down on a concrete floor. The last thing he remembered was being thrown into the back of a van. His body stiff and his mind groggy, he calculated he must have been out for quite some time. Maybe zapped a few times for good measure or maybe even just for fun. Maybe drugged, he couldn't be sure which. He looked up and tried to focus through the hazy gloom. He could just make out the silhouette of a stout figure in a dark suit standing over him. What he couldn't see was that the figure was grinning from ear to ear.

"Welcome to our happy holiday camp." the figure said in a deep menacing tone.

He struggled to roll over realizing his hands were tied behind him. He twisted his body only to end up in a rather exposed and uncomfortable face up position. He felt pain in his wrists as the plastic ties dug deep into his flesh. The figure bent over, grabbed him under one arm and lifted him off the floor. Shoved hard against the wall, he was left sitting with his legs outstretched in front of him as his head cleared and his eyes adjusted to the murky surroundings.

The large muscular figure moved aside to reveal a slim middle-aged woman with long, dark hair standing behind him. She was dressed in a dark suit, which he assumed was the familiar blue in colour, over which she was wearing an unbuttoned long white coat. He knew by the way she was holding a medical syringe in her right hand she was making sure he could see exactly what it was. This is not good, he thought. He could just make out her face in the dim half-light and was surprised that under the circumstance he was calm enough to think she looked strangely familiar to him.

She moved forward slowly, with an air of assured superiority, calm and controlled. She bent over him moving her mouth close to his ear.

"You have been a very naughty boy, haven't you?"

The question was clearly rhetorical.

"What on earth did you think you were doing? Whatever possessed you to get involved in things way beyond your control? Your loyalty to your friend, admirable though some may think it was, amounts to nothing more than a basic act of crass stupidity. You really should have thought about what you were doing and what the consequences might be." She moved back a little so he could see her face.

"You and your kind are never going to change the truth we have created. You are never going to get even remotely close to challenging us. Surely an intelligent man like yourself should have been able to see what was coming. Such arrogance. Did you really think you could change anything? You? Get the better of us? How very sad, but never mind eh? Let's move on then shall we because we're so very glad you could join us now. I'm sure you will enjoy our hospitality. How about we start with a short tour of the facilities. For most this would be the experience of a lifetime. I know exactly who you are so I imagine you may have experienced this before on one side or the other. Either way, please, sit back and enjoy the ride. I certainly know our close association is going to give me the greatest of pleasure, for you, well perhaps not."

The sound of her voice triggered his memory. Now he remembered her. The wide eyes, the condescending voice. She was one of the many figures that had stood beside the Prime Minister, the people's favourite, that was it. She was Caroline Bramney. Always explaining the whys and the wherefores, quietly but firmly insisting on the need for compliance. What were her favourite buzzwords? That was it. Truth, Wisdom, Salvation.

The recall of his memories was short lived. He felt the prick of the needle as it pierced the skin on his upper arm and then everything started to blur.

"Just a little something to make sure you don't give us any trouble for the time being." she whispered softly in his ear.

Another ursine figure came into the room. The silhouetted man had already dragged him sideways away from the wall. The two men stood either side of him and lifted him up off the floor. Together they dragged him face upwards out of the door and along the corridor. He experienced the sensation that he was floating in the air. Moving effortlessly forward past bright lights in the sky. Oblivious to the scrapping of the skin off his heels as he was dragged along the rough paved floor.

He could just make out the sound of muffled voices and thought they were the voices of angels come to rescue him. How wrong he was. Angels they most certainly were not.

They untied his hands and sat him in a chair, securing his wrists and ankles tightly to its sturdy arms and legs. He was one of six men sitting equally spaced along the length of the room. Opposite them stood an array of high intensity spotlights between which were waist high tables with various instruments carefully placed on top of them.

Suddenly a blinding light filled the room and all six blinked and winced at its intensity. Then came a loud voice from behind the light that seemed to reverberate off the walls, high and shrill, malevolent with unmistakable undertones of menace.

"Welcome everyone, we really do hope you will enjoy your stay. I certainly will be having a wonderful time here with you all. Getting to know you better will be such a pleasure. Well, it will be for me at least. Shall we begin with a little bit of fun. A quiz perhaps to break the ice. Who shall we ask first?"

As he tried to turn his head away from the light, he felt his head gripped between two large strong hands, twisted forward, and held tightly as it was clamped into position. He felt a sudden jolt of pain as an electric current passed between the metal clamps that were pressed against either side of his head. The shock and pain stopped as suddenly as it had begun, leaving his temple throbbing and the sides of his face feeling numb. He heard a sharp cry of pain coming from somewhere to his left. It was followed by a slow whispering sound, too low for him to pick out the words being said.

One of the six had tried to shake their head free only for the clamp to be tightened further and the electric shock increased. Screams filled the room as the flow of electricity was ramped up. The screams subsided and turned to loud sobs.

A terrified voice was begging to know why they were doing this to him. As he listened to the cries of despair, the sour smell of urine mingled with the smell of burnt hair drifted up into his nostrils. Mixed feelings of pain, anger and regret swept over him. Anger at his own stupidity and regret because he should have been more careful and not put his family in harm's way.

All his senses told him things were going to get far worse for all of them but especially the screamer. Who was that poor guy, he thought, what did he do to deserve that?

"Oh dear, always someone who wants to make the most noise on the first day. Never mind, at least now we have a volunteer to do the main icebreaker for us. I recommend the rest of you try to stay as still and as quiet as mice. Moving about or crying out will only make your re-education longer and more painful. Be good and the quicker you can move on to better days. After all, you don't want me to enjoy myself too much, now do you?"

She chuckled loudly to herself rather than to them, turned and left the room. The large guy who had dragged him from his cell stepped forward, silhouetted by the bright light. His face was lit up by a broad smile, a sight somewhat wasted as none of them could make out his face. He turned and made a circular gesture with his hand. Gasps filled the room.

Clamped and tied in his chair, his hands curled tight into fists as electricity fizzed between the clamps, stopped, and then fizzed again. He lost count of how many times it ebbed and flowed. All power of concentration ebbed away leaving his mind lost in turmoil. The room filled with a sweet, sickly smell brought about by pain and fear.

When the shocks eventually stopped, the pain in his head made him feel physically sick. His groin throbbed from the involuntary erection brought on as the current had passed through his body. He retched involuntarily and a sliver of vomit ran down his chin. Whatever the rest of them may have done surely this shouldn't be happening, he thought. Not today, not in the modern world, not when the welfare of humanity was supposed to mean so much to everyone.

The fog in his brain started to lift and he remembered who he was. They're going to have to do better than this, he thought defiantly. Then it all began again.

Chapter 10

Just minutes seemed to have passed since the shocks had stopped. His body ached with pain. His muscles were tight with cramp and his head pounded and throbbed. He braced himself for the next round of brain-numbing agony, but it didn't happen. Instead, he heard a soft whispering voice, somehow soothing and comforting yet with a strong clear message.

"Oh dear, you have been naughty little boys looks like we need to clean you up. Let's see if we can make things a bit better shall we. Best get you nice and ready to go back to your nice warm room. You are going to have such a lovely time. Let's quickly recap the lesson so far. What must we do? We must learn to understand the truth. We must recognize the wisdom. We must always, always and without question, do exactly what we are told. I'm sure you'll all be very good boys by the end of your stay. Now how about a little bit of light entertainment."

The woman in the white coat appeared in front of them and the lights went dim. He could just make out her face, she was smiling broadly at them. She walked past each chair and looked the incumbent up and down before signaling to her thickset associate with a gesture to turn off the electricity supply. She moved back to the central position so that she could be seen by all six.

"Oo, what smelly boys you are. Time for a wash." She laughed and moved back next to the row of lights, passing her associate as he moved forward holding what looked like a fireman's hose. A wall of freezing water shot forward directed at each of the seated figures in turn, spraying them up and down and pushing them hard against the backs of the chairs. Once the last in line had been sprayed down the water treatment ceased.

Wagging her finger, she directed attention to the fifth in the line. A second figure emerged into the light and the two men began to unshackle the wet, slumped figure in the fifth chair.

He strained to his right to see what was happening. The two men came into view, between them hung a limp, pink mass, face down, feet dragging on the floor. They stopped in front of her and turned the figure over with legs outstretched in front. She calmly walked back to the table behind her and picked up what looked like a pair of curved blade surgical scissors.

The five others watched transfixed by the scene unfolding in front of them. Moving in front of the now conscious figure, she kicked apart his legs and stood between them grabbing a fist of hair and thrusting back his head. She spoke to him but loud enough so everyone could hear her.

"I had hoped we could have moved on without having to resort to this. You must understand that what I do is for your own good and for the salvation of all humanity. What you have all done was not and now you won't even behave and help us to put you on the path to righteousness. I'm pleased in a way because everyone needs an example to follow. Something to help their understanding of the situation and you my dear Henry are definitely the right man for the job." He looked up at her at the sound of his name. Now he saw who she was. He was always going to be her first choice, but he had no idea what she was going to do to him. The mere thought of what she could be capable of simply terrified him. Caroline smiled at him and in that moment, he saw in her eyes that she was capable of more than he had ever imagined possible.

"I think this might hurt a bit so take a deep breath and here we go."

Panic filled the man's eyes as she pulled down the front of his wet pyjama bottoms and cupped his testicles in her left hand. She held up the scissors in front of him so he could grasp her intent. He knew she was enjoying this and with sudden clarity he knew exactly why. He tried to wriggle free, but this only made them grip his arms tighter. He tried desperately to close his legs pushing them against her thighs, but she stood firm.

He lacked the strength to do anything except beg her not to hurt him. He was sorry, he whimpered. Sorry for everything he had ever done to upset her. He would believe in her forever if she would just let him be. Everyone in the room heard and understood what was really going on. He hadn't been picked at random, this was something personal between the two of them.

She smiled at him and for a fleeting moment he thought it had all been a bluff and she had never intended to go through with it. Then he screamed. A shrill high-pitched sound of intense pain as she began to cut away his testicles. The others looked on in sheer terror at what they were witnessing. She turned to face them, blood dripping from the two lumps in her left hand, held up high for them all to see.

"Please understand, you always have a choice on what happens next but choose wisely. As you can see, I really can hold you all by your balls."

She looked pleased with herself and laughed at her little joke. A harsh, maniacal laugh.

"Take him away to the Treatment Room. Then come back, clean up the mess, and take the rest of them back to their room."

She turned, tossed the man's severed testicles onto his chest, bent over him, and wiped her hand clean on the trouser leg of his pyjamas. The two men nodded dutifully. The man groaned as they dragged him away. She turned back, waved at the five remaining men still locked firmly in their chairs, swiveled daintily on her heels, and left the room.

*

The Director General believed appointing Caroline Bramney as the Deputy DG had been a masterstroke. There were two things about her that had made her the surprising yet ideal choice to head up the Special Operations Security Service. Her ruthless ambition and her hatred of men. Both of which he would be able to use to his and to SPAWNs great advantage.

She had never hidden the fact that she wanted the power she perceived was denied to her yet given to her male counterparts. She had though risen swiftly through the ranks. Politically astute, she had fostered strong relationships with senior figures, particularly from within SPAWN, and had been welcomed as a leading Government Advisor. She was delighted with her appointment as the Deputy Director General and had immediately gathered a hand-picked team around her.

She had built up a loyal following which consisted, rather bizarrely, of mostly men. Many she had captivated with her alluring charm. Many were equally ruthless and would happily do her bidding without question. Her power over them was absolute and she loved it. She was indeed phenomenal. She knew in her heart it had always been her destiny to become the most feared and powerful woman in the country. It was her ambition to make that the most powerful woman throughout all of history, past, present, and future.

As for her hatred of men, that began during her early days at medical school. On her first night the tall, slim, effervescent girl from the room next door had knocked on her door to make friends. Caroline had been immediately attracted to Julia's infectious smile and the sparkle in her eyes. They had become best friends. Caroline had hoped for much more. Then came that fateful night when Caroline lost her forever and her heart turned to ice.

Julia and Caroline had gone to a party together and were enjoying each other's company when a handsome young medical student from the year above them nervously approached Julia. The two of them hit it off from the moment their eyes met. They spent the night chatting, laughing, and completely oblivious to everything around them including Caroline. It was love at first sight. After that night, they were inseparable. Julia loved him with all her heart, truly, madly, deeply. Caroline hated him with a vengeance. Totally, utterly, intensely.

Julia and Henry were married two years later. Caroline didn't attend. With Julia's love and support behind him he had gone on to become a leading epidemiologist, a pioneer in his field. Always a crusader, he had joined an independent advisory group to provide debate and clarity over the information provided to the Government and the public in general. That, Caroline had thought, would turn out to be his biggest mistake.

She wondered to herself how Julia would feel should she ever find out. Find out that her once best friend had just cut the balls of her beloved husband Henry. She laughed out loud and sent a text.

*

The vibration of the phone signaled the incoming message he had been waiting for. The DG pressed his index finger to the screen. The phone lit up and he smiled to himself when he saw it was from her. He opened the text message.

> The process has begun. Holidaymakers arrived safely and are enjoying the scenery. The first dress rehearsal complete and everyone played their part very well. A star performance from one of our top entertainers. Genuine laughter all round. More rehearsals to begin again soon. CB.

The DG grinned and turned to face the select group

assembled before him. He was fighting hard to suppress his feelings of pleasure and excitement.

"Everything is going well. Nothing will stop us now. Our Truth and our Wisdom will go unchallenged. Our mandate will ensure the welfare of the people. We are Salvation."

The room erupted with cheers and applause. They raised their glasses of champagne and toasted their success. Like cigar smoke in a Victorian Gentlemen's smoking room, their conceit and arrogance filled the room with the smell of invincibility.

Chapter 11

An hour or so had passed since they had witnessed the horrific mutilation. He had been the last to be hauled back to the small dark room. As he was being taken down the wide corridor, he had caught a glimpse of what looked like a group of children being corralled into a large hall. A young girl had looked directly at him. When he saw the look of fear and bewilderment in her eyes, he wanted to reach out to her with some words of comfort but all he could muster was a half-smile and a message of hope that beamed out from his eyes. A moment later the girl had gone. The door to the hall was quickly slammed shut and one of his handlers punched him hard in the ribs.

"A chalet without a view. What more could a man ask for?" The two men chuckled as they threw him face down into the room, locked the door, and left. He crawled to the wall and struggled to sit up. He leaned back against the wall, his head still throbbing, his ribs bruised and his legs tingling. At least this time his hands were free. Through the hazy half-light he could make out four other figures. Two still slumped on the floor and two, like him, sitting with their backs to the wall in the semi-darkness.

He stared into the gloom, fighting the pain in his head that was trying to overwhelm him. He fought hard to calm himself. The sitting figure to his left shifted slightly and coughed as if readying to speak.

"Can anyone hear me?" came a hoarse dry whisper, barely audible above the heavy breathing emanating from the two in the middle of the floor. "I know why we are here and what we may have all done. I was an MP and challenged what was happening. What about you?"

He licked his lips, his tongue as dry as his throat and forced out a reply.

"I know why I'm here. The stupid thing is I even saw it coming." There was a calmness in his voice, an authority the others were too pained and panicked to hear.

"Oh God," came a voice from the far side of the room, "I'm a journalist. I challenged everything. I tried to get others to understand what was going on. I wrote articles for my paper. I even sent emails to all sorts of people. But surely that's not enough to warrant them doing this to me?"

There was a half scream, half whimper from a dark corner of the room. One of the slumped figures had come to and managed to drag himself into the corner.

"We're all done for. I remember now. When they grabbed me, I heard one of them say they'd got another stupid heretic. Then they laughed and one said something like I bet she'll have some fun with this one. Now I know what he meant. He was talking about that monster."

"So, what did you do?" asked the presumably now former MP.

"I managed to get on a radio phone in and questioned everything that was going on. I understand now why the presenter got really nervous, especially when I started to answer my own questions. I talked about what was happening to our world and what we were doing, asked whether the path we were following was the right one. I presented an alternative viewpoint, that was all. I never once considered it would drag me into this."

The man coughed and cleared his throat. From the sound of the emotion in his voice it was clear he was very close to tears. He stuttered and then continued his story.

"I then went on TV as a talking head thinking I could offer an opinion, another side of the coin so to speak. I thought people would appreciate what I had to say. I was after all a respected scientist. I wasn't denying anything. I thought I was just doing what the Government wanted and the people deserved. Facts not fiction. I guess they were the wrong facts. I guess my final mistake was to ask why they had introduced so many draconian laws, why did they need so much control over our lives, and when, if ever, would we be free again to make our own choices, run our own lives. Look where it's got me. How on earth could I have been so stupid?"

Listening to the others talk had given time for his head to start to clear. The fog was lifting. Things were clicking together in his mind. The power of reasoning was starting to return.

"None of you were stupid. I don't think the six of us were brought here at random. Look at who we are. A Member of Parliament, a journalist, a scientist, me, and the guy she knew personally. That accounts for five of us. I'm guessing our silent friend is something like a medic or a teacher. We're being used as examples, guinea pigs in some sort of experiment. We're the Winston to her O'Brien."

Before anyone could reply the door swung open. A big blue suited figure stepped in, kicked the man in the corner nearest the door and sneered sarcastically.

"No talking campers."

The room was equipped with two small hidden cameras. Every movement observed by a watchful eye, every word heard by a listening ear. Recorded for later reference.

Racked with fear, the man in the corner made a strange, suppressed gurgling noise as he involuntarily soiled himself. A man's last semblance of dignity taken from him for no reason other than he had cared. Now he cared no more. He would say and do anything they wanted; they didn't need to hurt him anymore. Sobbing and rocking from side to side, he murmured the single phrase, please don't hurt me, over and over again. A plea falling on deaf ears.

The man at the door murmured some foul-mouthed expletives, moved forward, and aimed a vicious kick at his ribs. Pleased with himself, he stepped out of the doorway to let his eager associate step in.

A jet of freezing cold water cascaded into the room, oscillating from left to right and back again. The water stung the bodies and faces of the five occupants, pinning them back against the walls.

"Let's get cleaned up, eh? You wouldn't want the nice lady to see you like this, would you? It's entertainment time you oh so lucky people. Shall we go celebrate happy hour together?

Cocktails all round, eh chaps?" His sarcasm was completely lost on the inmates, his sadistic nature was not. He continued to entertain himself, laughing uncontrollably at his own joke.

"After all, it is 5 o'clock somewhere."

No-one else saw a funny side to the situation.

PART 2

Darkness Descends

Chapter 12

The packed train pulled into the quiet East Coast station on that bright spring morning. It was packed with parents engrossed in their own thoughts, their children watching the world whizz by, over-excited by the prospect of a holiday by the sea. It had been dark when they had boarded the train and they felt they had travelled through time as the dawn broke, the weight of the world lifting from their shoulders as the sun rose and shone its warming rays through the east facing windows of the train.

Shiny coaches were parked outside the station waiting patiently for the holidaymakers to disembark from the train. Waiting for them to follow the directions of the blue suited reps to their drivers eager to load their suitcases and take them on the final part of their journey. All in a neat row glinting in the sun-light, a wonderful welcome to the seaside for the lucky families. They were the lucky ones because they had all received special invites. Invites to a pre-paid holiday for them and their children at a newly refurbished Holiday Camp by the sea.

Other camps were being built on special sites around the coastal areas of the country to provide many more families with the opportunity to relax and enjoy a break in the sunshine and a splash in the sea. The selected families would receive their special letter through the post, the invitation for mothers and their children to spend a week of fun and frolics at the camps. Just like the those arriving on the special train had received.

Their invites had followed a short advertising campaign. A two-minute presentation had been aired on TV during the previous week. It included edited clips of children playing happily on rides, slides, and swings, supervised by young girls in smart blue blazers. Mothers with smiling faces were shown relaxing together surrounded by young men looking very professional in their smart blue blazers and white summer trousers. It all looked too good to be true. Much too good to be free. Nonetheless, people wanted a future to believe in, they needed it all to be true. Above all else, they needed hope. They needed to know someone still cared.

The narrator declared the number of families invited would be very limited to start with. The familiar actor's voice continued to say that fathers should expect a letter in due course. The letter would contain the offer of the chance for them to either join their families later or for those unemployed to go to work on new construction projects and in new factories mainly based in the north of the country.

The first fortunate families were now within touching distance of the prize. There was a buzz of excitement as the younger children clambered off the train eager to feel the morning sunshine on their pale faces and to breathe in the seaside air, gulping it down and feeling it warm their lungs, fresh and clean. They yelped and whooped and jumped for joy. Their tired and exasperated mothers trying desperately to calm them down and herd them towards the waiting coaches, most managing a smile, some shedding a tear.

Buzzing with the frill and excitement of it all, Jessie and her younger sister were the first to scramble onto the coach and sat on the back seat next to the window whilst their mother shared the seat just in front of them. She looked at the young mother sitting next to her. The woman had such sad, sunken eyes, blank and soulless. God, thought Jessie's mother, do I look like that too. She turned and wiped a tear from her eye. Seeing the emptiness behind the woman's eyes was too much to bear, too close to home. Let's hope this sunshine break will help put some sparkle of life back into us all, she thought. For now, though, through some unspoken mutual agreement they both stared straight ahead in their solitude and silence.

Jessie let her sister take the seat nearest the window. Together they held hands and eagerly awaited their very first sight of the sea. They shrieked with joy as the coach turned onto the seafront and there, right in front of their very eyes, was a golden sandy beach and clear blue sea shining in the sunlight. The excitement levels on the coach rose exponentially. There were loud gasps and sighs. Some were so overwhelmed they just burst into tears. Mothers' eyes welled with tears at the muffled sound of their children's unbridled joy.

The coach stopped abruptly at the entry barrier to the camp. Jessie thought it odd that the men on the gate looked like soldiers, dressed as they were in khaki uniforms and holding what looked to her like some sort of guns. She noticed something shiny glittering on top of the wire fence and all along its length for as far as she could see.

A quiet hush descended throughout the coach. The mood changed abruptly. So much so that one or two of the very young children started to cry, sensing fear and worry as it swept from one to another. The air of excited expectation replaced by one of nervous tension, of confusion bordering on panic. Mothers close enough to the windows saw the guns and the razor wire shining menacingly in the sunshine. This was no picture postcard resort. The coach passed through the barrier and pulled up alongside the coach in front at the edge of what looked like a large parade ground. The intercom buzzed into life and the tour guide in her smart blue blazer told everyone to stay seated. The door of the coach swished open.

The woman stepped off to be replaced by an older man wearing a grubby white coat over what looked like the same style blue blazer. He walked down the centre aisle slowly, surveying the faces to the left and to the right. Jessie could see some of the passengers getting off the other coach. They were being herded together by two men in uniform like the ones at the barrier. Mothers grabbing hold of their children. She watched as they were forced apart and separated, the mothers in one group, the children in another. The look of panic in their eyes was plain to see.

Jessie clasped her sister's hand tightly and whispered to her to stay close and to not let go of her hand. If only Obi were here, she thought. Then came their turn to get off the coach.

As they disembarked one of the mothers at the front grabbed her children and started shouting at the man in the grubby white coat. In a fleeting moment one of the armed men stepped behind her and rained a crashing blow to the back of her head. There was a dull crack and she fell face forward onto the ground in front of her children. She lay there lifeless, blood oozing from a gaping wound on the back of her head. Her children stood in shock staring down at her. Too terrified to move a muscle, too petrified to scream.

"Couldn't you wait 'til we got them all off the coach?" yelled the man in the white coat. He looked down at the mother. Clearly seething with rage, he pointed at the body at his feet and then at the two children.

"Get this mess cleaned up and those two over there with the rest of them." He beckoned to the female tour guide.

"You get the rest of them off the coach. Do it now and do it quick."

Chapter 13

It did not take very long to empty the coaches after what they had just witnessed. Everyone was herded off without any resistance. Mothers meekly let their children go in deathly fear of the red-faced, white coated demon's raging anger.

Two large groups now stood facing the man and the woman on the parade ground. The mothers and children were separated by a row of uniformed guards. Jessie looked around her. There were no slides, no swings and definitely no rides. Jessie realized she was standing at the front of the group, gripping her sister's small hand tightly in hers. They were surrounded by other young children.

At fourteen, I must be one of the oldest ones here, she thought. High up in front of them she now saw a large board with large blue letters. She read it to herself without realizing she was muttering the words as if to help her understand their meaning. It read:

We are Truth. We are Wisdom. We are Salvation.

Underneath in bold capitals were just three words.

TRUTH. WISDOM. SALVATION.

Jessie thought she remembered hearing or seeing something similar on TV a few days ago but wasn't quite sure. She had heard and seen so many things like that recently. She wasn't sure what it all meant but knew something bad was happening. She shivered and her sister looked up with eyes wide, full of fear and uncertainty.

A young woman walked out in front of the children dressed in a white pleated skirt and a blue blazer holding a megaphone in one hand and a sheet of paper in the other. The badge on the pocket of her blazer was embroidered with the letters TWS surrounded by what looked like a coat of arms. The woman stopped in the centre of the group and turned to face the children. She smiled as she looked at the small faces etched with fear and on the verge of panic. This was just how she wanted them. Lifting the megaphone to her mouth she addressed the huddle.

"Hello children. Welcome to our holiday camp." Her reassuring tone seemed to do nothing to change the expressions on the faces in front of her. As she talked, she was joined by two young men, similarly dressed in blue blazers and white summer trousers. They positioned themselves on either side of her. She waved the piece of white paper from side to side as she spoke from a well-rehearsed script.

"We will be your camp guides during your stay with us and we will do everything we can to make sure you have a rewarding time. Please do exactly as we ask so we can get you to enjoy yourselves as quickly as possible. There is no need for you to worry, you are in good hands. As long as you do as we tell you, everything we be just hunky-dory. Please would all of you boys stay together and move off to your left and join our handsome Dan over there." She pointed to the tall young man who had moved off to the open space on her right. She spoke softly and slowly now.

"Now, please if you would be so kind, would all you lovely girls skip over there and join Sam and Kelly. Please no fuss, they really are warm and cuddly under those blue blazers." Another young woman appeared into view on her left smiling and waving at no-one in particular. She was joined by the man Jessie assumed must be Sam.

Some of the boys and girls started rather reluctantly to separate and move to their left and right respectively. Jessie clung to her little sister's hand, determined for them to stay together at all costs. Why did they need to separate the boys from the girls, she wondered? Must be to do with the accommodation, she thought.

A young boy about Jessie's age was standing to her right and holding hands with what looked like his two younger sisters, one on each side of him. Immediately she thought of Obi and how he would be protecting them if only he were here.

"We're staying together." The boy was defiant and clearly determined to keep his family together. Jessie could only watch on as he pulled the two young girls close to him. The woman seemed unperturbed by his outbreak almost as if she had been expecting someone to defy her request. Almost as if she actually wanted someone to challenge her.

She smiled and looked down at her sheet giving the impression she was searching for instructions about what to do next. She looked up wagging her finger at him and laughed. Putting the megaphone down on the floor at her feet, she casually stepped over it and beckoned to two men standing in uniform beyond the group to her right. The men walked forward with an air of menace to join her. Jessie saw that each of the men was holding what looked like a black baton, similar to the sort that the police used to break up rioting protestors. The three moved forward in unison and stopped just in front of the boy and his sisters. Far enough apart so that most of the children could see what was about to happen.

"We can do this the easy way or the hard way that's up to you, young man. Just for a while you need to let your sisters go over there and join Kelly who will take really good care of them, I promise." Despite the soft, reassuring intonation the boy stared her down and said nothing. The woman sighed and shrugged her shoulders.

"Okay, hard way it is then." Quick as a flash she lunged forward, grabbed the smallest girl, and tugged her free from his grip. A split second later, the two men moved in and flanked the boy. One grabbed his other sister and pulled her roughly to one side but was unable to break their grip. Their resistance was short lived. There was an audible gasp from the group of children nearest to the boy. They watched in horror as the other man raised his baton and brought it down hard on the top of the boy's head with a thumping great thwack. Both his sisters screamed in sheer terror as their brother fell to the ground, settling silent and motionless on the floor between them. The older of the two sisters kicked out and caught the man holding her on the shin. The man grimaced. He grabbed her by the throat and lifted her up, twisting her around so that she could see her brother's body lying crumpled in front of her.

"See what you made us do." He half-shouted, half-sneered in her ear. She tried to turn her head away as she felt his hot breath on the side of her face but his choking grip was much too strong.

"Oh dear, never mind. Do you think he could be dead, little girl?" he snarled nastily.

The woman intervened and with a voice like cold steel told him to put her down and take her and her sister over to where Kelly was standing. Clapping her hands and addressing the wide-eyed children in front of her, many sobbing loudly, she stepped over the small still body lying in the sunshine in front of her.

"Come, come, quickly now. Let's not stand around, nothing more to see here. Everything is fine so off you jolly well go. Boys over there with Dan and girls over to Kelly. Chop, chop." She was smiling again and looked every bit the warm and friendly holiday camp hostess. If it was her aim to give out the impression that what they had just seen had never really happened. It seemed to work. But not for Jessie.

Squeezing her sister's hand even tighter, so tight in fact she made her little sister squeal, Jessie was trying hard to stay calm and to keep them out of trouble. The last thing she wanted at the moment was for them to get noticed. After what she had seen so far, any attention could only lead to something bad happening. She looked down and whispered to her sister.

"It's okay Katie. I'll not let go and everything will be alright. Just wait and see. Now keep hold of my hand and stay as quiet as a mouse for me. Okay."

Together they walked across to join the back of the group of girls gathering in front of Kelly. Jessie had two plans in mind. Plan A was to wait and see what was going to happen to them next. Plan B was simply that whatever resulted from plan A she must not panic for Katie's sake. Maybe even after all they had just witnessed, they would be reunited with their Mum fairly soon.

Sam was walking along the line of girls at the front with a large cardboard box asking politely for any mobile phones promising they would be returned very soon. Jessie slipped her other hand into her pocket and caressed her phone. She let go of Katie's hand, smiled at her, and put her finger to her lips with a soft shush of reassurance. Deftly, she pressed her finger to the screen of her phone and in an instant was writing a text message to the only person she knew would never let them down. Whatever happens, she thought as her fingers did the talking, he would find us. Nothing will stop him. He's our brother and he will come for us. She pressed send and slipped the phone back into her pocket.

Chapter 14

The smell of antiseptic and various chemicals permeated the air, getting ever stronger on the approach to the source. Screwed to a plain white door at eye level was a wooden nameplate. On it in big gold lettering was written Treatment Room 1. Once inside the room opened up into two distinct sections. On the left-hand side was a row of twelve beds, each with leather straps dangling down on either side. They resembled the beds most likely to be found in an old psychiatric ward. In fact, that was exactly where they had come from.

The right-hand side was partitioned off to form a spacious laboratory area. In the lower half of the partition were solid panels, in the upper half large glass windows. Ideal for looking in, however more likely designed so that the inhabitants could look out at the row of beds and anyone unfortunate enough to be on one.

That morning the place was buzzing with excitement. They had heard that their first patient was on his way.

A stoutly built man dressed in a clean white coat covering a smart blue suit rubbed his hands together with pure joy. At last

Dr Sterbenson and his team could get down to business. Finally, they could work freely on healthy patients to perfect the treatment. Years of secrecy were about to be replaced by years of praise and glory. Years of dedication, a life's work, about to be recognized and rewarded. If only his mentor was here to see it.

It all began for him way back during his second year as a medical student. Dr Sterbenson was a student showing exceptional promise. One of the senior doctors, the highly regarded Professor Bramney, noticed his penchant for working with the terminally ill and took him under his wing. The Professor particularly admired how dispassionate the young student was. How he was able to remain emotionally detached from the patients and their families.

This was the protégé the Professor had been waiting for. He had hoped his daughter would be the one, but she was far too strong-willed and obstinate to work alongside her father. He thought maybe, just maybe, he might be able to bring the two like-minded youngsters together. What a match the two of them would make.

He was extremely pleased that his daughter Caroline had followed in his footsteps and trained as a doctor. It was when she moved away from genetics to focus on behavioural psychology that he felt their paths were diverging a little. Her saving grace was that she had followed the family tradition and would eventually take up her rightful place within the Society founded by her grandfather. The roots of which went back as far as her great, great grandfather who had attended the Galton debate in 1904. What had also pleased her father was that Dr Sterbenson had required very little, if any, persuasion to join SPAWN and rally to its cause.

The Professor had genuinely believed they would make a great couple. That they would grow together and go on to lead SPAWN to the fulfilment of its ultimate design. He had seen how his protégé had become completely smitten with his daughter and how his constant advances towards her had been dismissively rejected. Resigned to the fact his matchmaking had failed dismally he deemed it to be through no fault of his own.

Caroline was clearly carrying a torch for someone else and had been for a long time. Someone special to her he had never met. She had never discussed her feelings with him, a situation he had always been quite comfortable with. He finally broached the subject just once a few days before he died. All she told him with cold indifference was that the one person she loved had fallen for someone else. Don't worry, she told him, one day I'll be happy. That day had finally arrived.

That was the very day Henry arrived at Treatment Room 1 where Dr Sterbenson gave him a quick once over. There was a substantial amount of blood running down his thighs and rather oddly he was clutching something in a bloody hand holding it tightly to his chest. Dr Sterbenson beckoned to one of his male sidekicks to hold Henry down whilst he forced open his hand to claim the precious possession clasped inside. He couldn't help but smile as he looked down at Henry's severed testicles nestling in the palm of his hand. He knew instantly who the man in front of him must be. It was Caroline's old nemesis.

"I know exactly what we can do with these. A gift. A gift for a beautiful lady. A gift for my wonderful Caroline. What do you think to that my dear chap?"

There was no reply. Very close to passing out, Henry was becoming unaware of what was happening around him. The Cleos that had carried him there had taken their time, stopping occasionally to give Henry a few whacks with their batons just for the fun of it. By now, even if he had been aware, he was far beyond hope to care.

"Strap him in over there."

The instruction was short and crisp. Still carrying the prize in his dominant left hand, he entered the laboratory and spoke briefly to one of his white coated underlings who scurried off obediently. He went over to an array of glass fronted cabinets and squinted through the glass at the labels until he found what he was looking for. He took out a large plastic container chuckling to himself as he did so. On the label written in big black letters was the single word 'Formaldehyde'. Pickling fluid, the ideal preservative.

Minutes later his minion returned with a large glass jar. He guessed she had gone to the kitchen for it. Good girl, he thought, good use of initiative and quick with it too.

Moving over to the sink in the corner of the lab, chemical container in one hand, a pair of blood-soaked testicles in the other, he looked every bit like the mad scientist. All that was missing was the mass of unruly grey hair and the maniacal laugh. He rinsed the trophy under the cold-water tap, doused them in formaldehyde and plopped them into the glass jar. He filled the jar to the brim with formaldehyde and screwed the lid on tight. Extremely pleased with himself he held up the jar in front of him. He felt like jumping for joy but didn't want to risk dropping the wonderful surprise present he had just made for Caroline.

The arrival of two more patients dragged him back to the real task at hand. Placing the jar carefully at the back of the laboratory bench, he went out to greet the new arrivals. They were a woman and a young boy both alive but with serious head wounds. His first assumption was they were mother and son. In fact, their only connection was that they had made unfortunate choices that had resulted in serious consequences. It was of little significance anyway as no one in the room really cared who they were.

"Put them on the beds next to our friend over there."

He had already decided Henry was too far gone to provide any meaningful results, but it was rather fitting for him to be the first test case here in the new Treatment Room. However, the two newcomers would be useful in testing out the appropriate dosage levels for women and children. He smiled to himself and patted the left-hand pocket of his white coat. There was his precious little blue book. Safe and snug. How would he ever do without it. He smiled again as he thought of the fun he was about to have with his mutilated guest. Laughed when he thought about his gift to Caroline. What a woman. If only, he mused to himself.

Chapter 15

It came as some relief when Danny finally got the call. Sally spoke to him very briefly. No pleasantries, just a request for them all to get together and a question. Did he have any idea where they could meet up? Danny overheard JJ's voice in the background saying they couldn't go back to his house and laughed when Sally told him to shut up and be quiet. Danny said he would contact Obi and get back very soon.

A short while later, Sally and JJ were making their way to JJ's car. JJ leading the way, Sally following a few paces behind with her face so well hidden she could barely see JJ but that didn't seem to matter as she somehow sensed his movement in front of her. Each was carrying a bag containing the kit Sally needed to be able to work from what they hoped would be a safe house. Danny had sent her the address and they had agreed they should all get there as soon as possible.

It was Obi's house. Obi's family were away for the week and Obi was confident they could stay there in relative safety. At least for a few days whilst they found out what was happening and could decide on what they should do next.

Obi lived on a housing estate at the north end of the town. It had been designated a deprived area. Rightly so as many of the families were living hand to mouth with no change of fortune on the horizon. Of the adults that had been employed, most had now lost their jobs plunging the area deeper into despair. Despite the hardships, there was still a widespread feeling of unity and kinship throughout the community. Another good reason to set up a base camp there. JJ nodded his agreement as Sally had read out the message. It seemed that it was the best place for them to meet up face-to-face. Besides, no other suitable alternatives leaped into mind.

Danny was the first to arrive. He had decided to walk and had underestimated how far away it was, especially when laden down with two large kit bags. In one he had a change of clothes and a few bits and pieces. In the other he had packed his laptops, mobile phones, and the homemade plug-in devices he knew he would be needing. By the time he turned the final corner he was quite hot and breathless under his mask and beanie hat. Obi was waiting at the window and rushed to open the door as soon as he saw Danny come in to view down the street. He grabbed the bags out of Danny's hands and ushered him inside. He was very pleased now that his friend was safely under his roof.

"What the hell have you got in here?" he asked with a huge grin as he dumped the bags down on the floor.

"Careful with that you big oaf. Always knew you were like a bull in a China shop!" Danny stepped forward, reached out and hugged his friend.

"Thanks for letting us meet up here. Is there somewhere can I set up my stuff?"

Obi looked at the bulging bag on the floor, thought for a minute, then replied with more of a question than a statement.

"I guess the best place would probably be in here on the table. Then when the others get here, we'll all be able to sit together. We'll be a bit cramped, but it will make it easier to talk and to see anything you or Sally want to show the rest of us. I assume, genius that you are, that you have loads of stuff to enlighten us with."

"Absolutely." Danny nodded and they both burst into laughter.

Danny unzipped the bulkier of the two bags and pulled out his laptops and three mobile phones together with what looked to Obi like a mess of tangled cables, plugs and small black boxes. Obi watched on as his friend went about setting things up. In a matter of no time at all Danny had plugged that in there and this in here. With lightning speed, he had turned a spaghetti junction of cables into an ordered circuit of laptops, mobile phones and strange boxes. Obi applauded his friend's handywork, a genuine act of admiration for his friend's dexterity. Danny didn't take it that way.

"You do know that sarcasm is the lowest form of wit, don't you?" Danny saw the confused expression on Obi's face and realized his friend had actually been paying him a compliment.

"Don't just stand there watching me work. Make yourself useful and switch those on for me, just press the buttons by the red lights. Can you manage that?" He laughed and clapped his hands in a gesture of delight. Delight that he was with his friend and enjoying their moment together.

"What's that if it's not sarcasm? Not sure I want to help you now ingrate." They laughed together, happy to be in each other's company once again.

It wasn't long after that Sally arrived and was met with a hug from Danny and a nod from Obi followed a few minutes later by JJ who got neither.

"Okay now we're all here, what's got you so worried Danny?" The others seemed to accept it was only natural that Sally would take the lead. They sat down around the table and listened to what Danny had found out so far. None of it was good news. It had taken him a little time and a lot of skill to begin tracing the source of the strange briefing they were now all familiar with. His efforts so far had only resulted in a dead end. As yet he had been unable to identify exactly who and where it had originated from. With more time he was confident he could locate the source and uncover whatever secrets were to be found within. He had, however, had some success in finding out what was happening across the country.

The difficulty had been trying to work through the sheer volume of information that he had gathered via the huge array of social media sites and feeds he had tapped into. Many of which had been shut down only minutes after they had begun to tell their stories. Someone wanted to keep a lid on what had happened that morning, that was for certain.

What was clear was that a number of people had been visited in the early hours of the morning. Some had been taken away by members of the Special Operations Security Service.

"They were Cleos, described by many as thugs in blue suits.

No-one seems to know where they have taken the people to. I can find no explanation for why they were taken and there were some accounts of instances where other family members had experienced violence and intimidation when they had tried to intervene. It's got to be linked to that presentation." Danny reached the end of the sentence and his expression suggested it was the end of what he had to say.

Taking up the baton, JJ nodded and recounted his experience for Danny and Obi's benefit. He felt they needed to understand what was being described was real. It had happened to him, it was personal. They listened as JJ recounted the events of the early morning. After a short discussion, the consensus was that Danny should try to find out what sort of people had been taken. This, Sally suggested, would hopefully give them more of an understanding as to what was going on and why. Danny shrugged and looked at Sally.

"I'm not sure whether we can contact anyone directly. We need to make sure we stay hidden from any searching eyes. The fact some groups have gone off air almost certainly means someone is finding them and shutting them down. Either on-line or more worryingly, in person."

The look on JJ's face told the story. He was clearly tense and anxious to know as much as he could about what had happened to his father. This made him edgy and impatient. In contrast, Obi appeared to be calm and collected but that was soon to change.

JJ's response was curt, direct, and aimed at Sally and Danny.

"Between the two of you, is there any chance we might be able to hack into some government site or other. That might give us an idea of why and where they were taken too?"

Sally wasn't sure if she appreciated JJ's tone. She looked across at him and decided to let it go. She could see there was nothing to be gained by telling him to calm down and tread more softly if he wanted to get the best out of them.

At about the same time Jessie and Katie were being ushered into a large hall at the holiday camp. Jessie had only just managed to press send on her phone and had slipped it back into her pocket. Just over a hundred miles away Obi's phone buzzed.

The three watched on as Obi's face drained of colour as he read Jessie's message. He looked up. They could see the concern in his eyes. Danny could see and sense his friend's distress and immediately knew something was very wrong. Obi put down his phone and slid it across the table to Danny.

"Something bad is happening to my family. My mum and sisters went off early this morning to what they were told was a holiday camp by the seaside. They were expecting to have some fun by the sea. Jessie just sent me a message saying some awful things are happening. They need me. They need our help. We need find out where they are and when we do, I need to get there fast." He slapped both hands against the sides of his head.

"I knew I should have gone with them and been there to look after them."

Sally reached out and gently touched Obi's arm.

"We'll find them. I promise" she said softly. Obi looked across at Danny. He knew if anyone could find them it would be his friend. He also knew that when they did, he would have no choice but to go to them and no-one, no-one, should try to stop him.

Chapter 16

Cold and dripping wet, the five remaining men were hoisted to their feet and unceremoniously shoved through the door and out into the corridor. Standing in wait were another two burly men who looked every inch like they were enjoying, or most certainly about to enjoy, their job. Each held a long black baton in their right hands. Grabbing the first shivering victim that came through the door, the taller of the two men thrust him forward and sideways into the wall lifting his baton as he did so and giving him a hard thwack on the middle of his thigh.

"Come on and get in line behind this useless lump of shit." snarled the smaller, bulkier of the two men.

The five cold wet captives slumped against the wall. They were herded down the corridor and encouraged to move on by the occasional swish of air and dull thudding noise as one of them was hit at random by a hard black baton. The three guards had clearly found their true vocation. For them, they could think of nothing better than inflicting pain and suffering on someone else. What's more being paid to do it made it even more satisfying. They seemed to take special pleasure in seeing the look of the fear and terror in their captives' eyes.

They took them to a small room with no windows and told them to stand in a line facing the doorway. Battered, bruised and barefoot they stood as still as they could and waited for whatever torture was going to come next. There was a sickly-sweet smell lingering in the room. He thought to himself if he knew what a mix of burnt honey and vinegar smelt like this would be it. Now there were five of them. He was standing in the middle of the line. Not the best place he thought and then almost laughed out loud at the thought that anywhere in this line was definitely not the best place to be. Strangely, surrounded by two shivering, half naked men on each side of him, he smiled. Then she walked in.

It was difficult to tell in the dim light, but it looked like Dr Bramney had changed into a clean white coat. His smile had evaporated but he still couldn't stop himself wondering who picked up the laundry bill. She caught and held his eye for a moment. Just long enough for her to sense his defiance and for him to sense she felt no remorse. The words sympathy and empathy were evidently not included in her vocabulary.

Her eyes burned cold, colder than ice. Yet they were haunting and alluring. She turned her attention to the two figures on his left and spoke to them directly. Her voice was calm, almost soothing. It made them want to do their best to please her. They were to be saved from whatever would befall the other three. It gave them hope, hope that things were going to get better for them. Hope that their nightmare was coming to an end.

"I don't think we need the two of you to go back to my special room. You both look like you could do with a bit of the jolly old nice cop treatment, a spot of female company too perhaps. What do you say we let the other three enjoy the bad cop routine, eh?"

She turned to two of her underlings and beckoned for them to take the other three off to the room with the chairs. With a big grin, she stepped forward, turned her body to the side, stretched one arm forward and the other back in a gesture inviting them to walk with her. She led them back down the corridor the way they had just come, past their holding cell and out into a small quad. On the far side they could see what looked like the entrance to a large hall or perhaps a gymnasium.

As they hobbled across to the entrance, she told them to tread carefully and apologized to them for not having anything on their feet. Such concern seemed odd and out of character, bearing in mind what they had seen her do earlier. She told them to wait whilst she popped inside to check everything was ready for them. She took the remaining Cleo with her.

The two captives looked across at each other both wondering why she had left them alone. Things must be looking up as she was trusting them not to try to run away. They looked at each other. Each could see by the state of the other that running away was never an option anyway. So, there they stood waiting patiently for her to return.

Inside the small hall there was a rectangular podium two steps high positioned a few metres away from the entrance. Two ropes hung down from the ceiling in the centre of the podium, spaced exactly two metres apart. At the far corners stood two of the uniformed guards each next to a large open topped barrel. In front of them were the group of mothers from the three coaches, anxious and edgy, wanting to know what was going on.

A small group were berating one of the three guards positioned in a line behind them. Arms waving and eyes flashing, there was no doubting the mothers were getting very frustrated and very angry. Their biggest concern was the whereabouts of their children and when they would be reunited with them.

Dr Bramney quietly moved forward and onto the platform. The two guards in front of her looked up and acknowledged her arrival. She clapped her hands loudly to get everyone's attention.

"Ladies, please. Could I have your attention and I will explain what is happening."

The women crowded forward in anticipation, eager to hear her speak.

"Your children are perfectly safe as you will see shortly. However, before we can move on, we need to address a very nasty issue. One which I am sure will shock and anger you in the extreme. Hearing such stories before would most probably have left you feeling powerless to act, powerless to exact the justice perpetrators of such evil deeds deserve. Powerless to take the necessary action your anger and disgust demands. Well ladies, today is your lucky day."

She paused for the effect and to look out into the crowd in front of her. She was studying the rows of eyes staring up at her. How far could she push them? How far would they go?

The two men next to the barrels moved round the podium and out of the entrance where the two captives were still waiting, still and silent. Caught by surprise, it took but an instant for them to be bound and gagged and pulled into the hall by their shackled arms. Terrified, they were dragged onto the podium and suspended from the ropes. Arms pulled up above their heads, feet barely touching the floor. There they dangled. Wriggling and spluttering in front of the dumbstruck group of women. Pointing at the two petrified figures beside her, Dr Bramney continued with her account.

"These two creatures you see before you are two of the most hideous, heinous monsters you are ever likely to encounter. Between them, they have raped and murdered nineteen young children, some as young as just three years old. They kidnapped and tortured children just like your own. They subjected them to acts of such depravity I find it too difficult to even think of let alone describe to you. Your children sit playing happily in the sunshine just a few hundred yards from here. Safe and sound. These mothers' children suffered unimaginable pain and terror at the hands of these," she paused and pointed at the two men both frantically shaking their heads, eyes wide with sheer panic at the story of lies she was telling about them.

"These devils." she shouted, spitting out the words with as much venom as she could muster.

Her words were taking effect. She could almost touch the feeling of rage surging out from the crowd in front of her. One more push and they would be ready.

"Should we let these smirking beasts go unpunished? Should we set them free to rape our children, again and again and again? Should we let them taunt us and laugh in our faces? I say no. NO, NO, NO." She shook as she shouted the words.

"Why should we give them the mercy they never gave those

helpless children. Children who must have begged and pleaded. Children who must have sobbed and cried out for you, their mothers. Helpless terrified children who must have screamed in pain."

"No, we should not. Let us join together, here, and now. Let us seize this opportunity that has brought these creatures," she paused and pointed once again at the two terrified men. "Yes, these horrible creatures to us. Sisters, it is up to us to show them justice."

The room was ablaze with hatred. Hatred of the two men. Hatred at their missing husbands. Hatred at the loss of freedoms. Hatred for all the wrongs ever done to them.

Only a few stood silent and scared at what was happening around them. Unprepared for what would happen next.

Dr Bramney moved forward to the corner of the podium. The expressionless guard reached into the barrel, pulled out a wooden baseball bat and handed it up to her. She waved it in the air, walked back close to the first man, his head twisted towards her and his body squirming as he tried to lift one of his legs in an attempt to fend her off.

She smiled at him, swung the bat over her shoulder and hit him hard in the mid-drift. There was a sound more like a slap than a thud as the bat made contact, but no-one heard it above her shout of "Justice" and the screams of delight from some of the mothers. She pointed at the barrels on each side of the podium.

"Quickly, go, let's do the right thing, let's show them some proper justice!"

The men allowed three women from each side on to the podium, bats in hand, to join her on stage.

"Sisters, let them feel the pain of those innocent children, let them feel our retribution."

The women spread themselves out around the two men and unleashed their anger and hatred onto the men's bodies. The crowd roared their approval. After enough time for the beating to satisfy the lust for blood, the two men moved onto the stage and very carefully took hold of each bat in turn, pulling them free from the hot red-faced women's hands.

They ushered them off the podium leaving the two men dangling, floating in and out of consciousness. Keeping a bat in one hand the two Cleos returned to the stage and lined themselves up either side of the hanging men.

"Shall we ask our two friends here to finish the job for us?" Dr Bramney shouted.

She nodded to the men.

In an instant, simultaneously and without hesitation, they hit each man square in the face with all their weight behind the impact just as if they were hitting a home run. Blood and splinters of bone cascaded onto the podium floor. Some reaching as far as the faces on the front row. The sheer ferocity of the blows seemed to stun the group of women into silence.

Those that had stood frightened and bewildered throughout, found they had somehow been drawn together and morphed into a small group standing at the back. Like blinkers on a horse, their hands held over their eyes to block out the horror in front of them. In the middle of the group, eyes staring down at the floor, stood Jessie's mum.

Within moments things started to happen. Movements were calm and controlled, as if choreographed and well-rehearsed, yet the action was very quick. The women were separated into two groups, those that had been the angry mob and the small group of eight at the back that had withdrawn themselves and resisted the groupthink created so skillfully by Dr Bramney. The latter were herded out of the hall and down the corridor. The former squeezed together in front of the podium. The two men still hung there like trophies from a hunt. Between them and a metre in front stood Dr Bramney ready to give her final address to the crowd.

"My sisters. Lift your heads and be proud for today you have performed a wondrous act of justice. We have joined together to begin the salvation of ourselves and our children. No longer shall we let evil men such as these roam our streets. Today we have taken hold of the power to protect the innocence of our children. We cannot, we must not forget what we did here today. You are bound together by what you have done and now you must swear a sacred oath to the sisterhood." She scanned the back of the crowd. Kelly and another young woman in blue had arrived and were positioned at the back a few metres apart. She raised her arms up to the heavens as her voice boomed out from the podium.

"Sisters!" she shouted.

Both young women raised their arms and returned the call as loud as they could to encourage others to join in. By the time Dr Bramney's third rallying call came all the women were waving their arms and shouting back at her. She smiled to herself almost overwhelmed by the pleasure of it all. They were now hers to control and manipulate. It was all too easy. In her head she chalked up another success.

The women were taken off in small groups to an adjoining room where their names were recorded, and their personal items taken from them. The six who had wielded the batons were given smart blue blazers and white trousers. They were destined for supervisory roles. The others were issued with blue coveralls. They were told this was a temporary measure as it was necessary to sanitize their clothes and possessions which would be returned in due course together with their luggage. They complied willingly and were led away to a recently constructed accommodation block towards the south of the camp.

When the last group had left the hall a clean-up crew arrived to cut down the two men and to clean the podium and its surrounds. The limp, lifeless bodies were taken to the Treatment Room before continuing their journey to another recently constructed building at the north of the camp. Inside was a large refrigeration unit. One of the Cleos-cum-porters opened the wide door, wheeled them inside and unceremoniously laid them side by side next to Henry, his wide eyes staring at the ceiling and, not that he cared now, minus his testicles.

Chapter 17

Unemployment had soared to record levels. For the millions left with little hope and no income, any chance of work, whatever and wherever that might be, was to be grabbed with both hands. It was no surprise then, that when the letter arrived offering Obi's father Clive the chance to work on a construction project in the north of the country he was packed and ready to go within the hour. Together with the letter were the necessary instructions and a train ticket. By the same post, his wife Amanda had received the letter inviting her and their two young daughters to a holiday camp for a short break.

It was another twenty-four hours before they were due to depart. Clive heading north. Amanda and the kids on a short journey to the East Coast. Amanda was a little unsure about the invite. After some discussion and reassurance, Clive and Obi had convinced her it would be a good thing for her, Jessie, and Katie to go and enjoy themselves by the seaside. Obi would stay and look after the house. They all agreed this was the best solution, but they all had a sleepless night. Clive and Amanda because they were still very apprehensive and uneasy about it all. Jessie and

Katie because they were over-excited. Obi because he knew how much he would miss them all.

Clive stood on the station platform, checked his ticket against the departures board and headed for his train. Despite his unease, he was pleased that at the same time his family would be setting off for what he hoped and prayed would be a happy seaside adventure at a new holiday camp on the east coast. He wished he could be there with them to enjoy a family holiday together, but the chance of work was something he could not turn down.

He hoped his beautiful wife would be able to get a few days' rest from the stresses and strains they had been under for so long. It seemed to be for as long as he could remember. He could picture his two young daughters Jessie and Katie making sandcastles on the beach, probably the same beach he had played on many years before. He had smiled to himself at the very thought of them all finding some joy in these dark, depressing times.

As for his son, well he had grown up to be strong and independent. Obi was a young man now. Hit by a sudden feeling of loneliness, Clive hoped his family knew how much he loved them and how much they meant to him. He wished especially that he had taken the opportunity when Obi dropped him at the station to tell him how proud he had always made him feel.

We will all be together again soon he had thought as he boarded the train north. He re-assured himself that the time would come when he would hold them all in his arms once again. A time to say all the things that a proud father should tell his son. A time to tell his beautiful wife and daughters how much he loved them.

The train was a special express service. One destination, one stop. There were four coaches each full of men just like him. Men desperate for work. Men desperate for self-respect. Proud men who would once again provide for their families. Clive checked his ticket and walked down the aisle to his reserved seat. His eyes darted left and right to see if there was anyone he recognized. There was no flash of recognition. All he saw was the reflection of his own hope and expectation in the tired eyes that looked back at him.

The brief instructions in their letters had given them no idea why they had been chosen for the job nor what the job actually entailed. It didn't matter to them one little bit. They were going back to work and to them that was all that mattered. Clive sat down, nodded at the man next to him and thought about trying to strike up a conversation with him.

Just as he was about to speak his phone buzzed. It was a text from Obi just letting him know he had got back home in plenty of time to take Jessie, Katie, and their mum to the station. Obi confirmed the three of them had just left on the train to the holiday camp. Clive sent a short reply to say he was pleased they had got off okay and that he would text again later. He wanted to say so much more but couldn't find the right words. It wasn't the right time to get all soft and cuddly. Obi wouldn't be expecting it he thought so he just smiled as he pressed send. He put his phone away, settled back and closed his eyes. Within minutes he had found his way to the land of nod.

During the two-hour journey Clive had drifted in and out of an unsettling dreamlike state. A strange sense of foreboding had overtaken him in his dreams and manifested itself into reality. He turned to the man next him. He too had been sleeping and still had his eyes shut. His head forward with his chin resting on his chest. Clive looked down at the man's hands. Like his, they were the hands of a tradesman. Rough and calloused from years of hard work.

The train began to slow. He looked at his watch and calculated they had been travelling for almost two hours. They must be about to come into the station he thought. The man's head rocked backwards, startled he awoke with a muffled grunt.

It took a while for everyone to disembark from the train and onto the platform where they were met by a number of men in blue suits. Confident and curt men, who ushered them off the platform to a section of the station thoroughfare. The working men were corralled into a large group marshalled by the blue suited Cleos.

As they stood next to their suitcases awaiting someone to give them instructions, Clive sent a text to Obi just to let him know the train had arrived on time and that so far everything looked ok. A tall young man appeared and called for everyone's attention. He called out a series of names and instructed them to take the exit to the car park where they would be directed onto awaiting coaches. Clive heard his name called and joined the group heading for the car park.

The men were driven to a large construction site on the outskirts of the city. On arrival, they were asked for their names and their trade. They were then assigned to a port-a-cabin that was to be their bunkhouse for the foreseeable future. A bit like Auf

Wiedersehen Pet thought Clive as he dumped his suitcase onto the hard mattress on top of a low metal bed. There was half an hour before they had to report back in front of what he assumed was the foreman's office. He scanned the room. There were eight of them in total, all looking a little bemused.

Clive nodded and smiled across at the four men opposite him.

"The name's Clive." He spoke to break the ice.

We're all in this together, he thought. They're all hard-working, down-to-earth lads just like me. Still, he was relieved when the others followed his lead, nodded back, and said their names.

It seemed he had somehow managed to nominate himself as the head of their group just by that single action. The introductions were followed by a series of questions that no one could answer. Clive assured them it would all become much clearer at the meeting due to take place shortly. He reckoned it was sensible to assume they had been picked because of their skills for some sort of construction task. The room filled with a sense of optimism. It was work and they were confident they would get paid for it. That in itself was cause for celebration.

With Clive leading, the men reassembled in front of a small brick building as they had been instructed earlier. Flanked on either side by two blue uniformed figures stood a well-built man in a fluorescent yellow jacket. He was holding a clipboard so they assumed he must be the site manager. On the wall behind him was a large schematic blueprint and what looked like a map of the county. One of the men on his left shouted at the group to stop talking and to listen in.

"You are very lucky men." boomed the yellow jacketed figure.

"You have been given the opportunity to work on an important government project. You will be working the day shift as shift A and the other group of men you saw at the railway station will be the nightshift, shift B. You will be based here for your food and accommodation. You can see behind me a map of the surrounding area with a large, shaded area to the east."

He half-turned and pointed in the general area of the map. The men on the front row could just make out the area. Those further back squinted hard to see any of the detail, gave up looking, and returned their attention back to him.

"You'll be taken to that main construction site by coach, leaving here at seven every morning and returning twelve hours later. It is expected you will put in a solid day's work for which you'll be rewarded. Breakfast and dinner will be provided here, and you'll be given a packed lunch to take with you to the construction site. You'll be paid on completion of the project. You will all be expected to work hard, follow our instructions, and adhere to the required health and safety restrictions at all times whilst on this site. The project involves the construction of a series of electrical power plants that have been designed to provide green energy to the north of the country."

He turned again and motioned to the schematic behind him and to his left. None of the men bothered to look at it. He smiled. Look or not it made no difference to him.

"In a few minutes you'll be escorted to the supply hall where you'll be given two sets of working dress including safety boots. You will then be issued with a set of tools appropriate to your trade. You are responsible for all the kit issued to you. You will pay for loss or damage of any kind. You'll return to your bunkhouses, your bubble, where you'll remain until collected for the evening meal. Tomorrow, you will report back here at seven on the dot, ready and eager to get to work."

Chapter 18

It had been a full twenty-four hours since they had all gathered at Obi's house. The previous afternoon and evening had proved to be both edgy and tense. Sally and Danny felt they were walking on eggshells in the presence of the other two. As a result, they had concentrated all their efforts setting up their systems carrying out numerous security checks to ensure whatever they did next, they could not be traced back to Obi's house. They already understood how important it was to keep their whereabouts hidden. They knew they would have to be very careful not to attract unwanted attention as they searched for answers and reasons for what was happening around them.

Of the other two, Obi seemed to have been the hardest hit and had not taken the message from Jessie at all well. He had paced up and down, kicked a chair across the room in anger and frustration, and had not said a word to the others all afternoon. He had received another text. This time from his father which had seemed to brighten his mood a little momentarily. The uplift was short-lived as he now seemed preoccupied about how to reply. Obi decided to wait.

JJ's mood was not much better. Sally had managed to take his mind off the situation as best she could under the circumstances. She had got him running cables and connecting up all the little gizmos she and Danny had brought with them. Anything to keep him occupied until they had something more to show him and Obi.

By late afternoon Danny had managed to calm Obi down a little and proceeded to persuade him to go out to the supermarket to get some supplies for the next few days. Sally wasn't sure it was such a good idea. Obi was like a coiled spring. Full of pent-up anger and emotion, stored and ready at the slightest provocation to be released on anything or more than likely, anyone. Despite their reservations they let him go out.

By the time he returned most of the equipment was up and running with various firewalls and encryption being tested out. Danny was not impressed as he watched Obi stack a random choice of ready-made meals onto the shelves in the fridge. Obi unpacked the second shopping bag which contained soft drinks, bread, and fruit, placing them on top of the kitchen worktop. Sally felt a little happier. Did he buy that especially for me, she thought as she could easily live off a diet of toast and a piece of fruit if she was allowed to get away with it.

There was no doubt JJ would have preferred the odd bit of meat but appreciated Obi had been cautious and thoughtful in his choices in order to avoid any unwanted suspicion. Basically, he had stuck to what the supermarket staff had seen him buy before.

Nothing much was different about Obi's trip except that he

had noticed there were a number of blue uniformed security guards around the supermarket he had not seen before. He had almost bumped into one in the car park and had seen more on the streets when driving back. Cleos out on the town. He had used his mum's car as it was well known in the area and so would not be given any undue attention. He reported what he had seen to the others whilst they tucked into their dinner of cottage pie and baked beans. Sally opted for marmite on toast.

Later in the evening, the four of them were sitting around the table in a very animated discussion. Danny had identified a group on the millennials' web. A special protected site that had been set up by some extremely talented young people. From the content Danny had seen its purpose was to allow their somewhat persecuted age group to communicate safely on a wide number of issues, particularly about the way they were being treated.

Danny had initially bypassed their security and broken into their chat room. He had then realized he could join the group by creating his own invite and then revealing himself to them as a kindred spirit. He had since discovered a number of protests had been planned and were going to take place the following morning at eleven o'clock. There were to be peaceful protests in major cities and towns across the country. Those taking part would be mainly from the under twenty-five age group, but it was evident they would more than likely be joined by other protest groups demanding a return of their freedoms and their human rights.

Sally went to some lengths to point out that the protests would almost certainly be infiltrated and subsequently hijacked completely by the militant activist groups known to initiate riots and major unrest. Activists bent on causing mayhem and inciting the crowds to violence. The debate they were having was whether any of them should attend the one planned to take place in the centre of town.

JJ and Obi felt they had been couped up for far too long already and so were really keen to go along and take a look to see what would happen. Mainly, they argued, because they thought it would help their understanding of the current wave of feeling about the Government's actions and the recent briefings. They would get the chance to experience first-hand how the Government was going to deal with the protests. In truth though, it was also because they were bored from just sitting around whilst Sally and Danny oohed and aahed at the new information they were finding on the web.

Sally remained adamant going out and joining in was a bad idea. Arguing it could only lead to disaster and would serve no purpose in their pursuit of information about the whereabouts of JJ's dad and Obi's family. Danny had perched himself on the fence. Wavering between agreeing with Sally and letting his friend get involved.

He could understand why Obi wanted to go out but could see that staying together and safely under the radar was a more sensible course of action. Making a move when the time was right, when they knew what their best move might end up being, was how Sally had put it. He agreed with Sally but knew how stubborn and obstinate his best friend could be.

In the end they reached a compromise. JJ and Obi would go

but would stay well back on the fringe to observe the proceedings. At the first sign of trouble, they would split up and make their separate ways back to the house.

*

At 10.30 am the next morning they set off for the centre of town. They heard the noise of chanting and shouting well before they saw the large group of protestors crowded in and around the small square in front of the town hall buildings. The crowd was made up mostly of young people although they could see there was a smattering of older, more seasoned professional campaigners. Many were waving placards and banners. Most were hiding their faces. All around people were chanting and shouting.

Just as JJ and Obi arrived the chant of just one word rang out. Hundreds of voices old and young, deep, and shrill, coming together in unison, hoping, expecting to be heard. A single word echoing around the streets.

"FREEDOM."

The united voice of a few hundred people, a message loud and clear, driven by desperation and frustration. A plea for the return to freedom, freedom to choose to live life as it once was, as it should be again. A plea for a life worth living in a world that cared.

Out of the corner of his eye, Obi caught a glimpse of dark figures in blue uniforms emerging from the side street behind and to the left of him. He grabbed JJ's arm, pulled him towards him and shouted in his ear. Obi pointed in the direction of a well-drilled line of grim looking men and women forming up behind them.

The duo glanced to their right and quickly moved towards a large stone archway at the back of which stood a large glass door. Obi, adrenalin pumping, reacted quickest. He shoved JJ so hard he crashed into the door only for him to rebound back into him with such force it almost knocked him off his feet. For a spilt second Obi thought he saw a flash of anger in JJ's eyes as he turned away, grabbed the long vertical handle on the door and pulled it towards him. It swung open and they stepped inside.

Behind the reception desk they saw a young man no older than themselves. Somewhat in shock and looking at them with startled eyes above a bright, patterned mask. Just for a moment JJ pictured him without the mask and imagined his mouth to be wide open in a look somewhere between surprise and panic. The young man gathered his composure and started to speak. They never heard a word he said.

The sudden burst of noise made the glass door shake and shiver on its solid brass hinges. The deafening sound of automatic gunfire exploded into the foyer. All three young men jumped as if someone had just thrown a firecracker at their feet.

JJ and Obi, as much as they were taken by surprise, were quick to gain their composure turning to look out through the glass door into the street beyond. Obi turned to the young man. He was clearly very shaken and locked in that moment of fear and uncertainty. Obi shouted and waved at him, gesturing to him to get down behind the desk.

JJ had already moved to the side wall to the left of the door and was leaning out just a little so he could see a small section of the street. Obi took up position behind him close to the wall. An instant later, they saw the line of uniformed Cleos move past the doorway still firing down the street. Smoke was rising up all around them like the residue from a New Year's Eve firework display. These were fireworks of a different kind. Whatever was happening was not for the entertainment of the crowd.

It was impossible for JJ and Obi to see further down the street towards the protesters. They could only assume the shots were being fired over heads as a scare tactic. As soon as the gunfire ceased, they immediately realized how wrong they must be. They were totally unprepared for what they heard next.

Screams of pain and cries of terror came dancing through the rising smoke like a melody from hell. Images of a blood-soaked battlefield sprang into their minds, bodies twitching, flesh ripped and torn by the cascade of bullets. Images they were quick to suppress. JJ shut out the noise and shouted to himself in his head to focus on getting away from here and to do it quick.

It had been nothing short of a complete massacre. Uniformed Special Operations Security squads had materialized in three of the corners of the square. They had come out from the side-streets, formed up, and without warning or hesitation, they had opened fire on the crowd in front of them. Most of the crowd were facing towards the Town Hall buildings when the first hail of bullets hit. The protestors never even saw it coming.

Shot in the back, some fell to the ground screaming in pain and panic. Others fell silently, the pain of death come and gone in an instant. The rest of the crowd panicked and rushed forward trying desperately to avoid the bullets whistling all around them.

The realization that people at the fourth corner were getting away down the street caused a sudden stampede towards what they saw as a safe exit from the square. Pushing and shoving, people funneled forward forming a bottleneck that slowed their exit and left those at the rear exposed to the gunfire.

As people broke out into the open street they were running as fast as they could away from the square. Dodging and darting down the adjacent side-streets to supposed safety.

Those still in the square had become even more frantic in their efforts to escape. People were being knocked to the ground and swallowed up under the stamping feet of those climbing over them. Sheer desperation and the need to survive over-riding any sense of altruism.

A peaceful protest in a small town had just turned into a bloodbath. A scene of unprecedented carnage, of heartless slaughter. It was a sight beyond the comprehension of the souls that survived. Made more unbelievable for those that witnessed the whooping and cheering of the uniformed Cleos as they punched the air and waved their guns at the dead and dying that lay before them. They were too pumped up to turn and notice JJ and Obi as they slipped out of the archway, hugged the wall, and sprinted away in the direction they had arrived.

The two of them made their separate ways back to the house. Cautiously twisting and turning down alleyways and side-streets, masks pulled up high, hoods pulled low to avoid any risk of detection and identification. By the time they arrived back, Sally and Danny were in a state of high anxiety. They had been tracking every available news feed and all the sites on the underground social media channels in search of news. Danny had also been busy hacking into the Government systems and was still tracking the mysterious source of the disturbing broadcast.

The real time information was all about the protests and there seemed to be two distinct versions of events circulating. It was the version being posted by so many young people on the safe channels that had got them so concerned. They were reporting unprovoked attacks on the crowds at various locations around the country. It was beginning to look like no protest had escaped the attention of the Special Operations Security Service.

There were frightening reports of mass shootings accompanied by videos of the unconfirmed massacres. Gory pictures of the dead and dying posted all over the net. Both Sally and Danny hoped their two friends would have had enough sense to do what they had agreed the night before. To stay on the fringe, close enough to see what was happening, yet far enough away to avoid getting caught up in any confrontations.

As soon as they heard the key turn and the door open, they rushed into the hall. Standing there was a very hot and sweaty Obi. Red-faced, he looked at them both and saw the worried look on Danny's face ebb away as the sense of relief at seeing his friend was alright flooded over him. Danny moved forward with the intention of giving Obi a big hug. He just managed to stop himself in time as he remembered his best friend was not the most receptive to outbursts of emotion, probably even less so at that particular moment. Obi looked directly at Sally. He could see she was on edge, clearly desperate to know what had happened and that JJ was alright.

"JJ not back yet then?" asked Obi. The question was rhetorical.

Obi was about to give his account of what had happened when the door swung open for a second time and in stepped JJ much to the relief of the other three. This time Sally rushed forward and without hesitation or forethought wrapped her arms around the tall, handsome figure now returned safely to her. But for the mask still on JJ's face, she would have smothered him in kisses. She was so pleased he was okay and wanted him to know it. Obi raised his eyebrows and gave Danny a look of pure embarrassment. His eyes shot out a plea for Danny to move things on swiftly before it got really, really embarrassing for everyone. Danny took the hint.

"Shall we all go and sit down so we can catch up with what's going on out there?" he looked beyond the two entwined figures and waved his hand towards the living room door.

Chapter 19

The four of them sat staring at Danny's screen in sheer disbelief. Danny had scanned the web for news of the protests. He had carried out the easiest search first and found that the Government-controlled media had widely circulated an official version of the morning's events. The coverage had included a short video of one of the 'peaceful' protests filmed from above, a few photographs and most informative of all, an interview with one of the protesters. They had just finished watching a re-run of the interview.

"That's nothing like what really happened here." Obi protested.

"No. But that's what most people are seeing, and the way things are that's what they'll believe." Danny replied with an edge of cynicism to his tone.

The footage portrayed a scene of calm and orderly protest with people standing in a large open space surrounding something that looked like a well-known national monument. The helicopter view showed some of the people waving banners, but the angle made it impossible to see what was written on them.

There was some indiscernible crowd noise that meant it was impossible to conclude what the protesters were chanting. Dotted around the edge of the protest appeared to be a few uniformed men and women in bright yellow jackets chatting happily to the people nearest to them. It looked every bit like a peaceful, law-abiding gathering. Written in big bold capital letters, the headline read:

PEOPLE CALL FOR TOUGHER LAWS TO DEAL WITH HERETICS

The interview continued the theme. Danny clicked on a few icons. It was being widely promoted on other Government controlled social media platforms. Already the interview appeared to have tens of thousands of followers. Danny took his hand off the mouse and turned to face his friends. Obi was red-faced with anger and looked fit to burst. Sally was the first to break the stiff silence.

"I don't think we should be surprised. It's obvious they're not going to show what really went on. They are never going to admit they ordered the cold-blooded killing of innocent people protesting in the streets. We need to stay calm and try to confirm if it only happened here or whether more people were shot at the other rallies. Danny, start trawling to see what you can find out for us. Obi, you and I will look at your phone and see if we can use it to trace where your family actually are. If their phones are still switched on, I should be able to get a fix on their location. JJ, you go and make us some lunch." She turned and smiled at him with the hint of a mischievous sparkle in her eyes.

No-one argued. Danny scrolled, clicked, and typed away, instantly engrossed in his task. Sally and Obi sat in front of Sally's computer looking intensely down at Obi's phone. From their expressions they weren't being very successful. JJ watched them at work for a minute or so then wandered into the kitchen to make their lunch.

*

Just over a hundred and thirty miles south of the four young crusaders sat another very irate and agitated red-faced individual, the Prime Minister. A heated argument had been taking place across the large oak table between himself and the Director General. This time they had gone too far. Far too far and the time had come for him to make one brave last stand no matter what the consequences. Looking on in silence, sat the two Secretaries of State and the DG's secretary. The only absent member of the group was the Deputy Director General who was elsewhere dealing with other business.

The PM was so furious he looked on the verge of an apoplectic fit. The DG was trying hard to calm him down, pointing out that ranting and raving was not helping to explain events nor to decide what needed to be done next. The other three could see this strategy was having no effect on the PM's demeanor. They needed intervention. It came in the form of a buzz on the DG's secretary's laptop. It was positioned in front of the large screen at one end of the table so as always to be ready to operate the system. He pressed a few buttons and a few clicks of his mouse later the

Deputy Director General appeared on the screen.

"Sirs," called out the DG's secretary. "Dr Bramney is on screen and has a report on progress."

"Sirs." He repeated loudly and pointed at the calm, smiling face looking out at them from the screen. The two antagonists unlocked horns and turned to face the screen. The PM glared at Dr Bramney and spoke immediately.

"Before you say anything, I want to know what the hell happened this morning. Were they your people? Who gave the order to open fire? I want to know who is responsible. I want to know, do you hear?"

Caroline was never one to get flustered or nervous under pressure. In fact, she seemed to enjoy things even more when she was putting angry men with over-inflated egos back into their tiny boxes. Some people never learn, she thought to herself. Does he really think he has any control over what is going on?

She looked down at him from the big screen and tried very hard not to laugh. She settled on giving him a conciliatory smile. It worked. He spluttered on for a few seconds before yielding the floor to her. Calmly she began explaining what had happened and why.

She assured the PM that once he had the full facts, he would realize everything was under control and no harm had been done. In fact, she told him, the negativity surrounding the morning's events that had been reported to him had been over-exaggerated and it was his source who should be called on to justify themself.

The action taken had been warranted, she said, and had definitely not involved the unnecessary use of force. The response to the protests had been swift and fully justified. The streets were now peaceful and safe. Did he not want that? Why of course he did. Her tone and manner had become somewhat condescending by this point.

"We must remain strong and remind ourselves this war is not yet won. Difficult decisions still have to be made. We must take all the necessary actions to ensure the safety and welfare of our good, honest citizens. Should I need to remind you Prime Minister that we are responsible for the welfare not just of our people but ultimately for the welfare of humanity." She paused to allow her words to register before she added a veiled threat.

"All actions have consequences. You of all people should be aware of that. Please would you be so kind as to excuse me now. I have other very urgent business to attend to." Dr Bramney smiled and signed off. The DG picked up the thread and outlined what would appear in the news coverage of the protests. The PM, eyes red and watery, sat sullen and almost in tears, knowing he had just fought his final battle and lost. He knew his last stand was over. He was defeated and he had nowhere else left to go.

*

As Danny searched the free speech network, he found more and more reports of horrific scenes from protests around the country. There were videos of lines of uniformed Cleos opening fire on unsuspecting crowds, of widespread panic as people tried to flee the onslaught.

Video postings of the carnage left behind, posted from mobile phones, taken from what appeared to be first floor windows.

Graphic scenes showing the dead and dying. Some bodies still twitching in their last throes of life, cradled in the arms of a friend or a loved one hoping and praying someone was coming to help.

Behind Danny stood JJ watching the footage. Not knowing whether to shout in anger or cry in pain.

"Stop that one a second, Danny. That's here. That's what we saw. They just shot anyone in front of them. No-one stood a chance. They didn't even know they were there until they opened fire."

JJ turned away. He didn't have the stomach to watch anymore. He had been there for real and that was more than enough to deal with without the need to watch it all over again on a screen.

There was no doubt in the room about the reality of what had happened around the country. They knew the truth. JJ and Obi had been there to see it. Many innocent people had died. All they had wanted was their freedom back and to be trusted to play their part in the race to secure a safe future for their world. The four friends looked at each other as the seriousness of their situation hit home. Something very sinister was happening. Something bad, really bad. The question was written across all their faces. Are we alone in all this? No-one had an answer. No-one said a word.

They needed someone to break the stony silence. That someone was Sally who rallied to the cause and pointed at the sandwiches sitting on the table.

"Let's have lunch, shame to let the master chef's sandwiches go to waste." She looked at JJ and smiled. "Then we'll decide what we do next. I know there are only the four of us but there must be others just like us. Those brave people can't have died for nothing. History shows freedom is always worth fighting for. Somehow, we are going to have to take the fight to them." The others could see she meant every word.

JJ sat down opposite her and thought how much he needed to tell her the way he felt about her. At that very moment in time, he was so full of love for her he thought he would burst wide open. Sally looked across at him. Her eyes shone brightly. He thought for a moment she could see deep down into his soul. Colour flooded into his cheeks. He blushed bright red. Not in his soul, Sally saw what was in his heart.

PART 3

The Generations

Chapter 20

Still trying to understand what was happening around them, the group of young boys had been taken from the coach park to a large room and told to wait quietly. A couple of the older boys remembered being there before. The room they were in was on one side of the main atrium at the centre of what they had recognized to be the original holiday camp. Their memories were of happier times of noisy excitement, fairground rides and outdoor sports and games. They remembered having to shout to be heard over the loud pop music coming from the centre stage and getting ice cream to soothe their overworked larynxes whilst their dads drank beer, and their mums drank cocktails. Now just ghostly reminders of a bygone age.

The boys were told to ask if they needed the toilet and that some food and water would arrive soon. Time passed and they waited, hungry and scared. The older boys around Jessie's age started to talk to each other in whispers and agreed to look after small groups of the younger ones. Through some sort of natural selection, they formed into three groups, all sitting next to each other against the longest wall of the room facing the door. Supervised by a shift of men in blue suits, they spent the night huddled together trying to sleep on the hard wood floor.

Reveille came early the next morning in the form of a loud siren. The two boys wearing watches looked to see what time it was. It was six thirty. The others could only guess as most of them relied on their phones to tell them everything, not just the time of day but probably even what day it was. They had been forced to hand over their phones as they had entered the room the night before. Those that resisted had been persuaded by a hard slap around the face from one of the blue suited Cleos. Three of them now stood over the boys shouting and cursing them awake. Happily kicking and occasionally whacking some of the bigger boys with their batons and smiling as the boys cowered beneath them. They so enjoyed their job.

A smartly dressed woman in a tailor-made blue suit glided into the room followed by the older man still wearing his grubby white coat and looking every bit like he had slept in it. Behind them came the young woman who had first spoken to them on their arrival yesterday. The three of them walked forward and stopped in line a short distance away from the boys. They peered down at the frightened faces in front of them.

"Now pay attention." Commanded the young woman. "This is Dr Bramney. A very, very important person and you need to listen very carefully to what Dr Bramney is going to tell you. Do not interrupt or talk whilst she is speaking to you. Just listen. You understand?" She and the older man glared menacingly as they swept their gaze across the wide eyes looking up at them.

"Boys, boys, boys." Began Dr Bramney.

"You poor boys. First of all, I want to tell you why you are here. That should make things easier for you to understand, especially the older ones amongst you. Then we will discuss what will happen next. Oops, what I should say is then I'll tell you what will happen next." She half-chuckled, half-smiled to herself at her intentional slip of the tongue and then continued.

"So why are you here? Why indeed? You are here because no one cares about you. Oh my, yes, no-one cares." she paused for effect and to let them register what she had just said before she rammed the message home.

"Let's face facts. Your fathers left you and your mothers with no money, little food and most likely very soon no homes. Your mothers brought you here then walked off to enjoy themselves. They have just left you here with us. They are all having a good time by the way and so are the girls. Your teachers never wanted you boys back in school and if you had gone back, they wanted you permanently in masks and under complete control. What about the rest of society? Well, society says you are all bad and should be punished accordingly. You are boys. Boys do very bad things. Therefore, all boys are bad and should be punished. Doesn't it all make sense."

Caroline's tone of mock sympathy changed sharply.

"Look at you, you do know what you are don't you? You are evil and disgusting creatures. Why? Because you are boys."

I'm getting good at giving speeches, she thought to herself. Her tone softened once again.

"But I am here because I do care about you. I will look after you and see you get everything you deserve. Show me you are prepared to do as you are told. Show me that you are willing to work hard for me and things will be much better for you. That sounds fair, doesn't it? What do you all think?"

Another pause as she scanned her audience.

"Just hold on a minute though. I'm not so sure. Serious doubts are creeping in. After all, we can't trust you to do what you are told, can we, because as we all know, boys will always be boys. Isn't that the truth of the matter?" She raised her voice as she hurled her final question at the bemused faces in front of her.

"Well, can I trust you or not?"

Whatever the response she expected from the young boys in front of her, none came. They just sat in silence, staring up at her, any signs of emotion hidden behind their blank faces. Perhaps this was the response she had expected. She held her hands out wide out in front of her, palms upwards, and made a slow, sweeping gesture as if giving them each a warm embrace.

"We can trust each other, of course we can." she said softly. Some of the younger boys nodded in reply.

Earlier Dr Bramney and her two accomplices had been watching the boys on the CCTV system installed for just that purpose. They had singled out six of the older boys.

Dr Bramney talked whilst her two companions moved forward and beckoned to the chosen six to stand up and come forward.

"We have chosen some of you to be the leaders of the group. Please would you six stand up and face me. Four of you will be given responsibility and power over the rest of these boys, two of you will not. Which four depends on what happens next."

Dr Bramney gestured to one of the guards standing behind her to step forward. In his hand he was holding four black batons similar to those of the guards but slightly smaller in length. He placed them on the floor some three metres in front of the six boys on an imaginary line parallel to the rest of the seated boys. It was clear the intention was for them all to see exactly what was going to happen next.

"The challenge is a simply one. There are six of you but only four batons. Whichever four of you are left standing with a baton in your hand, those four will be given very special privileges and will have control of the others. The two losers will be taken off to join another group for some very special treatment. Are you ready boys? Ready? Then," she paused to allow the tension to build and for the boys to register what they needed to do.

"Let's play."

Five of the boys rushed forward in an attempt to be the first to grab a baton from the floor. The sixth boy didn't move. He just stood still, perhaps to slow to react or maybe just not wanting to engage. Either way it would prove to be costly. Three boys, batons in hand, were now watching the other two battling it out for the honour to join them. Fists flew and feet kicked until the bigger and more aggressive of the two claimed the victory.

He towered above his beaten foe who was trying to get up from the floor and just to ram home his superiority, he kicked him hard in the face with his right boot. He turned to the other three and waved his baton in the air in triumph. The other three whooped and did the same.

"Excuse me for interrupting but you haven't claimed victory

quite yet. Five of you are still standing." Dr Bramney pointed at the boy who was now shaking his head slowly in disbelief. The four moved in and between them viciously beat him to the ground. He offered no resistance and in return, they showed him no mercy.

"Well done boys. Well done indeed." she said. She was genuinely pleased with them. Pleased too, to see the look on the other boys' faces. Faces with eyes wide, staring at the two bleeding figures on the floor in front of them, terrified that they would be next.

"From now on all of you will follow orders from these four brave souls. Their first order is for you to sit here quietly until they return. Mandy here will stay to make sure you all behave properly."

Turning slightly to her right, she directed the attention of the baton boys to her male companion.

"Under the direction of Dr Katchory, Dr K as he likes to be known, you will take these two away and then go and get something to eat."

Dr Bramney nodded in their general direction. Walked to the door and left them to it.

With a little help from Dr K, the four boys took the two unfortunate teenagers off across the atrium having kicked them to their feet. Giving them frequent prods and pokes with their highly prized batons as reminders of their defeat. Taunted and tormented, by the time they arrived at their destination the two youngsters were close to collapse, both beaten and broken.

Dr K opened the door to a small dark, dank room. He peered

inside and felt an uncontrollable urge to chuckle loudly. Crouched on the floor against the far wall were three semi-clothed men. Shaking and shivering either from the cold or in fear of what was about to happen to them. Only one of the three looked up and defiantly directed his gaze at the open doorway. Still a bit of fight left in that one, thought Dr K to himself, that will make it all the more fun later on. He turned and with a big grin on his face, he gestured to the four baton wielding boys to push their quarry into the room.

"Go on, go in and knock them all about a bit. Have a bit of fun with them before I take you off for a well-deserved breakfast. A couple of minutes should do the trick. Give that guy whose eyeballing us an extra whack just for me. Not too rough though, just enough to remind them you're in charge. We do need them to be conscious and able to walk when we come back for them later."

When they shut the door behind them, all five occupants were left battered, bloodied, and bruised on the cold, hard floor.

"Let's get some breakfast, eh boys. Then we'll go and get you kitted out with your new suits. After that you can sort the other boys out and put them to work."

Dr K took them off to the food hall. Their mouths watered as the smell of sausages and bacon wafted around the hall. The four boys sat and talked as they ate their way through a hearty full English breakfast. Dr K watched them with interest. It was plain to see they considered themselves top dogs and they were reveling in it.

*

In a room not so far away, the CCTV footage from the dimly lit room was being watched and recorded. A slim figure stood smiling with satisfaction at what she saw. Another successful outcome. Excellent progress, even better than expected. Just the girls to go now, she thought, then probably only a day or two more before we can really up the ante. It was then that her phone pinged and vibrated in her pocket. Her eyes lit up as she read the message.

'Can confirm protests going ahead today at 11.00am. List of locations attached.'

She opened the attachment and viewed the details of the twelve locations. Then sent a short reply.

'Necessary action will result. Keep away if possible. Stay in the shadows.'

Next, she sent a group message to her recently appointed regional Security Commanders. This would test their loyalty. She had overseen each appointment personally. They had been handpicked by her for their special qualities. She was confident they would carry out her orders to the letter.

'Move to full alert. Action instructions at 11.00am this morning. Details of venues attached. Authorization confirmed.'

Her final message was sent to the Head of the Media Service.

'Prepare peaceful protest footage. Release on all network media platforms at exactly 11.30am this morning together with attached statement.'

She clicked send for the third time in quick succession. Put her phone back into her pocket, turned and walked to the door. She was off now to tend to the girls. There was an air about her as she left the room. A radiance that portrayed the belief that all was fine and dandy in her world. The Mandate for Salvation was well underway.

Chapter 21

The girls had spent the night together in one of the rooms on the other side of the atrium. They had been given blankets and had a slightly more comfortable night than the boys.

Jessie had found a spot in a corner of the room to settle down in and had laid out their blankets on the floor. She had sat with Katie until her younger sister had dropped off into a light sleep. Then she quietly got up and went on a quick walk around the room to help clear her mind of scary thoughts and the frightening images of what happened earlier.

As she walked, she went over all that had happened since their arrival at the holiday camp. Had she really seen those poor men being led away yesterday? She pictured the scene. Yes, she had locked eyes with one of them and the look he gave her somehow made her feel all was not lost. How strange that one glance from a complete stranger could give her hope.

Dragging her thoughts back to the present, she focused on her surroundings. The room was fronted by large glass windows and glass double doors. There was another single door on the right-hand side wall with a small circular window in the centre of the top half. Jessie recognized it as the sort of door that would normally connect a restaurant area to a kitchen.

On the far left of the wall was another door marked 'Toilets'. This must have been a small food outlet she thought. Thankfully, Katie was still sleeping when she had finished her walkabout. She sat down and curled up beside her in the hope that she herself would eventually drop off to sleep. It wasn't long before tiredness crept up on her and carried her off to a land of strange dreams and disturbed sleep.

It was early morning when she awoke to the sound of a loud horn followed by a deep male voice shouting for them to wake up and pay attention.

"Good morning girls." Jessie recognized the softer tones of a woman's voice. It was Kelly.

"Please could you all come forward and sit down here in front of me. Let's see if we can begin a new day with a smile, shall we?" Kelly beamed.

The girls got up and moved slowly forward. Jessie shook Katie very gently and whispered softly to her that they needed to join the others. Holding hands, they sat cross-legged towards the back of the group who had formed into a semi-circle in front of Kelly.

Kelly surveyed the wide-eyed children sitting in front of her as if she were scanning them for information. Some were visibly shaking and looking at her waiting hesitantly for her next instruction. She could see their young faces looking up at her. Anxious eyes looking out over sad smiles. She counted them in her head. Twenty-eight, a good number, about average for a primary school class, she thought.

"Girls. Pay attention please. We are now going to split you

into two groups. One will stay here with me, the other will join Sam over there near the front windows. When I point to you, please stand up quietly and walk over to Sam. Put your hands up to show me you understand what I want you to do."

Slowly and tentatively, the girls raised their hands. A real sense of panic swept over Jessie. What if she and Katie were put into different groups. Katie just wouldn't go without her and that could only mean trouble for them both. She squeezed Katie's hand so hard Katie winced. Please don't point at us, please don't, she pleaded to herself. She looked up at Kelly and muttered the words in the hope somehow Kelly would hear and understand how important it was that she and Katie stayed together. Kelly's eyes rested on the pair of them for a brief moment and then moved on. It looked like Jessie's prayer had been answered.

At the end of the separation process Sam had a group of twelve which left sixteen girls sitting in front of Kelly including Jessie and Katie. Sam was talking to his group and directing them to line-up facing the glass window. Jessie could hear him telling them to stand up straight and to smile. Kelly spoke and Jessie switched her attention back to her main concern which was what was going to happen to them now.

"Please stay where you are for a little longer. Very shortly Sam's group will go off and then we will get you all sorted. I know you must be quite hungry but just be patient and very soon we will take you off for some breakfast. Just sit quietly for me. If any of you need to go to the toilet, please put your hands up so we can send you in a nice orderly fashion."

The fearful expressions on some of the older girls' faces

seemed to lift a little at the sight and sound of Kelly's seemingly caring demeanor. Perhaps there wasn't so much to worry about after all, thought Jessie. She turned towards Katie and gave her a warm reassuring smile and a quick hug.

Things seemed to happen quite quickly after that. Jessie watched as a group of adults appeared outside and peered in at the twelve girls standing on the other side of the glass. Jessie counted four men and four women. She felt sure she recognized the woman in the smart blue suit who was clearly directing the others as if they were on a sight-seeing tour. They were chatting and pointing at the young girls. She could see one of the men dressed in a now familiar blue suit was moving amongst the six men and women chatting, pointing, and taking notes.

The woman in the suit opened the door, stepped in, followed closely by the note taker, and beckoned Sam to join her at the end of the line of girls. Jessie watched the one-way whispered conversation take place with Sam's only contribution appearing to be a few nods in the right places.

Sam, under the direction of the notetaker, proceeded to pair off the twelve girls. He positioned each pair in an order clearly dictated by the notetaker's occasional glance down at his clip board. The correct positions were confirmed by the adults nodding their approval from the other side of the glass.

The woman joined the group outside and gave them a wide grin. It was evident the men and women were more than satisfied by whatever had just taken place. Minutes later, they were ushered across to the other side of the atrium to be shown the small group of twelve young boys Mandy had lined up for them.

Chapter 22

Back at Obi's house, the real seriousness of their predicament was beginning to take hold. They were four young friends who had been drawn close together by circumstances well beyond their control. Circumstances that threatened them, their families, and from what they had discovered and experienced, the very fabric of a free society. Three of them were engrossed in their tasks, happy to have a new focus in their lives despite the obvious and perhaps unavoidable danger their actions would put them in.

JJ on the other hand had little to occupy him once he finished making them lunch. He had been pacing up and down the room and was starting to drive Sally to distraction. Danny was too absorbed in interrogating the screens in front of him and anyway was deaf to the world around him as he had his earbuds in.

Obi was sitting quietly next to Sally watching closely how she was using his phone and her computer to track numbers in an attempt to find the exact location of his family. She was not having much luck. Verging on the point of complete exasperation Sally turned to JJ and watched him complete one more circuit of the room. She took a long, deep breath and sighed.

"Is walking up and down making you feel any better?" she asked rhetorically.

"Because it certainly isn't helping us. Look, whatever we do next is likely to involve travelling somewhere incognito. Why don't you do something useful and pop back home to get a change of clothes and anything else we would find useful. I'm sure no-one will be watching your house now so you should be able to get in and out safely. Take your phone and let me know when you have arrived and when you leave so I know you're ok and when to expect you back here."

The concerned look Sally gave him spoke volumes. For a split second he was about to argue with her but then thought better of it. He knew what she said made sense. He needed to do something and anyway it would be good to pop home as he could check the house was okay. He thought for a moment about Billy and their mum. They should be safe at Grandad's however mum would be worrying about him. He could text them once he had visited the house to let them know all was as well as could be expected.

"I guess it makes sense to pop back home and collect some more gear." he said with an air of resignation. His mood lifted almost immediately when he saw the smile Sally gave him.

"You're right Sally. I should only be gone for a short while, and I can't see why anyone would still be watching the house. Even the nosey neighbours should have found something better to do by now. If I get in and out really quick, I doubt anyone will even notice I was there. Also, I've got some extra cash stashed in my room which we're probably going to need at some point."

Throughout the short exchange between the two Obi had been a silent observer watching the interaction with keen interest. He had seen the expression on Sally's face from close up and it had confirmed what he had already suspected.

"Do you want some company?" From his tone this was clearly intended more as a statement than a question.

"To be honest. I don't feel like I'm really helping much sitting here. The thought of a drive out into the countryside, a daring trip into the unknown sounds pretty good to me." He smiled at Sally and then gave JJ a challenging look that said he was going with him regardless of any objections. Sally nodded her approval and JJ shrugged his acceptance. Underneath, he was pleased to have Obi along for company.

It was decided. The two adventurers would set off in JJ's car, take a roundabout route out of town to the house and a different route back.

Hooded and masked they left Obi's house two minutes apart and went different ways to the car. They were pretty confident no one was actively looking for them but thought it was better to be safe than sorry.

Having been the first to leave and taken the shortest route, JJ was already sitting behind the wheel when Obi arrived at the car. They exchanged a nod as JJ started the engine, put the car in gear and pulled away from the curb. There were a few cars out and about on the road out of town but nothing to make them feel concerned. JJ frequently checked the rear-view mirror until he was satisfied no-one was following them and then relaxed a little.

Once out of town and onto the country roads they both felt

more at ease with what they were doing and where they were going. The familiar sights of the countryside lifted their spirits to the point where they started up a bit of banter. JJ said he thought they were a bit like Butch Cassidy and the Sundance Kid although he had both the brains and the lightning quick draw. Obi's reply was that they were probably more like Thelma and Louise, only better looking. The banter continued until they arrived at JJ's and turned into the drive.

They hopped out of the car and walked calmly to the door as if to give anyone watching the impression everything was above board and no cause for concern. Once inside they adopted a much greater sense of urgency. The least time spent there the safer they thought they would be.

JJ directed Obi to the front room to keep a lookout from the window and then dashed upstairs to his bedroom. He grabbed his empty rugby kit bag, sorted out a few clothes and some toiletries and stuffed them in the bag. He collected the rainy-day cash and went back out onto the landing. He called down to Obi to ask him if it was still all quiet outside but got no response. He called out again from halfway down the stairs. Still no reply. What's he doing down there, he thought.

A sense of foreboding took hold of him. What if someone had been watching or even worse had been waiting in the house. Don't panic, hold it together, he told himself.

He ran back upstairs into his brother's room and grabbed the old cricket bat they used to play with in the garden. Stealthily, he descended the stairs and tiptoed along the hallway. The front room door was half open and he peered in. He could see a figure sitting with arms folded and legs crossed in front of the settee. It was Obi.

Until you're faced with a certain situation you never really know how you will react. JJ had already taken on a couple of burly intruders with the help of his brother but that was face-to-face against a visible opponent. This was different. He couldn't be sure who was threatening Obi nor how many there were in the room with him. His flight or fight response was arguing it out in his head, but he knew in his heart he had no choice but to enter the room and help his friend.

Pushing the door slightly with the end of the cricket bat, JJ crept cautiously forward. He assumed whoever was there was most likely to be positioned behind the door. He was wrong. He moved forward and into the room holding the bat high in front of him in both hands in anticipation of the confrontation he knew was coming.

In the movement of an eye, a huge hand darted out from his right perpendicular to the open door on his left, grabbed the middle of the bat and with the combined element of surprise and the force of a grizzly bear yanked him forward. JJ spun into the room, lost his grip, and crashed into and over one of the arm-chairs and onto the floor.

By the time he had steadied himself he was looking up at the end of the bat positioned just inches from his face. His eyes walked the length of the bat up to the huge forearm now attached to it. He knew instantly any resistance would be futile. His first reaction was to momentarily close his eyes in anticipation of the blow about to be rained down on his head.

A second later when the blow didn't come, his instinct for survival took over. He made a grab for the bat at the same time as he tried to twist his body in a concerted attempt to make his head less of a target. It was all to no avail.

He felt the sudden impact of a size fourteen boot as it stomped down on his chest and pinned him to the floor. He thought for a moment that his chest was going to cave in. Struggling to breathe and faced with a distinct weight and strength disadvantage, he relaxed his body and looked up at the figure towering over him.

The size fourteen foot belonged to a huge mountain of a man. A solid block of muscle that he doubted even he and Obi together would be able to lift off the floor, let alone take down in hand-to-hand combat. From JJ's current perspective the man looked almost as wide as he was tall. A kind of superman that had somehow even managed to develop muscles on his muscles. The expression on the big man's face was a mix of anger and in some strange way relief. Then he spoke.

"Just calm down and stop squirming around. Please, don't make me hurt you."

The soft low tone of his voice took JJ completely by surprise. He was expecting to hear a much deeper, threatening sound coming from the massive bulk now moving back away from him.

"As I told your friend already" he swung the bat in Obi's direction, "I'm not going to hurt you, I'm on your side. I'm here because I'm a friend of your father's, who right now needs my help. Come to that, frankly, so do you JJ."

The use of his name made an instant impact by reducing the

tension in the room. Obi regained his composure and asked if he could sit up on the settee as his legs were starting to cramp. The grizzly bear nodded and beckoned JJ to do the same. That way he could talk to both of them from the centre of the room and at the same time keep an eye on the road outside.

"I'm Marty." he said softly with a smile. "Your dad and I have been in contact for a while. Two days ago, he sent me a message to say if anything happened to him, he would leave a package for me here at his house. Then I got a short message to say it had started early and to come here asap. I arrived yesterday, collected the package, and hung around in the hope you or your brother would return so I could check you and your mother were ok. I was just about to move off when I saw the two of you arrive."

Suddenly conscious that he was waving the cricket bat around in front of their faces as he spoke, he casually tossed it to one side.

"In a minute I'll explain a bit more to you about how I know your dad and what's in the package. But first, tell me what's happened to your mum and Billy and why you and your friend here came back and seem to be in such a rush."

Neither of the two young men were in any doubt that the figure towering over them was telling them the truth. In no doubt that had he wanted to, he could easily have dealt with both of them without breaking a sweat. This is definitely someone we need to have on our side, thought Obi, especially when we find my family. All JJ could think of was how did this man-mountain know so much about his family and yet his dad had never mentioned him. How could he not have told him about a man such as this?

Trust established, JJ recounted a short version of the events beginning with the knock on the door to what happened at the protest and ending with why he had come back home. When JJ had finished his brief account, he asked Obi to fill in the part about what had happened to his family. JJ finished off by telling his dad's friend about what Sally and Danny were doing and where they were based. Their story was met with the a few nods, a few grunts, and a few slow shakes of the head. A worried look spread across the big man's face when JJ talked about what his two friends were doing back at Obi's house. These kids have no idea what they're getting themselves into, he thought. As clever and as gutsy as they are, should the bad guys come looking for them they'll stand no chance, like lambs to slaughter, that's what they'd be.

"Right. Have you got what you need?" JJ nodded in confirmation. "Then let's get out of here and back to your friends. We'll leave your car here as they may be on the lookout for it. Here's the keys to the black saloon parked just around the corner. You two leave first. Get in the back and wait for me. I'll follow once I know no-one has been watching you."

The two boys left. Followed a few minutes later by the man-mountain called Marty once he was sure the coast was clear.

A quick three-point turn out of the cul-de-sac, and they were on their way back to Obi's. Obi gave directions from the back seat for the first twenty minutes just in case they were being followed.

Satisfied they were in the clear, Marty pulled up in a country gateway, leaped out and moved swiftly round the car and got into the passenger seat. Obi hopped out and back in to drive the rest of the way. This guy's very agile for someone so big, thought JJ, so glad he's on our side.

Obi took a winding route through the side streets and parked up in the still empty space from where, less than two hours ago, they had set off for JJ's. They had brought back with them much more than just some cash and a few clothes. Now their number had grown to five.

Chapter 23

Jessie never saw the group of twelve girls again. She never gave them a second thought. They were gone, that's all there was to it. Out of sight and out of mind. Jessie had more important things to worry about. It had been over a day now since she and her sister had been separated from their mum and the responsibility weighed heavily on her shoulders.

Jessie had so many questions and no answers. She felt a sudden urge to do something, to stand up and demand to know what was going on. To ask why they couldn't be with their mum. What was the reason for keeping them apart? Then she felt Katie squeeze her hand a little. Jessie looked across at her young sister sitting quietly next to her. Waiting patiently, looking out at the world around her through the eyes of an innocent. Now was not the time.

The girls sat and waited. Hunger was starting to bite and stomachs to rumble. Jessie adjusted her position on the floor and looked up to see four boys in blue suits and the nasty man in the white coat walk in. Kelly and the man had a quick conversation then he left with two of the boys in tow. Kelly moved forward with the boys he left behind and positioned one on each side of her. The trio stopped in front of the seated audience and Kelly clapped loudly to get their attention.

"I am pleased to tell you we are all going off to get some breakfast and then to get you a change of clothes." she said with a warm smile. "We will do so in a quiet, orderly fashion. No pushing or shoving and no talking."

Now they were closer, Jessie could see the two boys were holding batons just like the ones the men had used yesterday. They were grinning like Cheshire cats and looked every bit as though they were enjoying their status just like Cheshire cats that had licked the cream.

"These two young men will be looking after you from now on. Please do as they tell you otherwise you might upset them. Trust me when I say, that would not be a good idea. I will of course be around to make sure everything happens as it should. Ok then, please stand and line up behind one another in pairs and we'll go off to eat."

Katie smiled at Jessie. She was hungry and so the mere mention of food was enough to get her up and ready to go. They stood side by side about a third of the way down the line. Kelly and one of the boys were at the front whilst the other boy walked down the line and stopped at the back. The two men who had been standing watch over them stood together and nodded to Kelly in an acknowledgement that their role in this current parade was over for the moment.

The march to the food hall took just a few minutes and went without incident. The girls were lined up in front of a self-service counter and hurried along by four women supervising and serving them from behind the counter.

Some of the girls recognized the women and vice-versa. Smiles and nods were exchanged which transformed into quick hugs and whispered encouragements. Jessie could see the tears of relief making their way down the flushed cheeks of the women. Tears flowing from tired eyes constantly darting around the room in fear that too much contact would spark swift retribution. None came.

The girls were ushered to a group of tables and told to sit and eat. Jessie watched as the women were herded together and told to stand still behind the counter. Their faces showed all the emotions of mothers desperate to rush forward and cast a protective ring of love and tenderness around their children. They clearly knew better than to try.

As the girls were eating the man in the white coat appeared with a line of young boys following on behind him. The four women moved back into position. The line was being moved along by the two boys in blue suits who seemed to be taking great pleasure in giving the odd whack to a few of the boys in the line. The victims looked like they were being selected at random but as Jessie watched she realized most were being targeted deliberately.

One of the mums suddenly broke rank and moved forward having spotted her young son in the line. Any mother would consider it a totally understandable reaction but under these circumstances it was only ever going to end up as a really big mistake.

Surprisingly, the first to react was one of the boys who had been put in charge of Jessie and the girls. He had been watching his two comrades with envy as they tormented their charges. He was standing just a few metres away from the food counter and was the first action, moving forward to intercept the woman before his two tardy comrades had time for cogs to whirr and to assess what was happening. He seemed to have anticipated what she was going to do. Or maybe he was just waiting, already on his toes, hoping for an opportunity just like this to present itself.

A few seconds later no one in the hall was in any doubt that he was by far the most vicious of the four boys. He came at the woman side on and hit her once on the side of her head. The blow sent her sprawling on the floor, arms and legs flailing wildly as she fell. As she tried to get up, he planted one foot firmly down next to her and then kicked her hard in the ribs with the other. She rolled sideways clutching her side and gasping for air. She saw what was coming next and reached up in a vain attempt to prevent the obvious. She screamed as loud as she could. Just one word, loud and long.

"No!"

On seeing his mother knocked over onto the floor her young son launched himself forward in an attempt to defend her. His fists raised, he charged at the bigger boy just as he followed through with the kick. The bully boy saw it coming in time to avoid being knocked off his feet but not quick enough to escape a fist to the side of the face. Boiling with anger at being hit he turned on the boy with just one intent. He was going to make him pay for that. He was going to hurt him big time.

The younger boy swung round determined to land another punch only to come face to face with an enraged psychopath. He saw the baton coming down and managed to get his arm up just in time to protect his head. His forearm took the full force of the blow.

The boy's young bones were no match for the hard wood of the baton. He screamed as the bones in his arm splintered and broke. The next blow was to his other arm, high up above the elbow, leaving him helpless to defend himself against further strikes from his merciless attacker.

His mother made a grab at the bully boy's leg to try to divert his attention back to her, but he just kicked her hand away, hitting her son hard on the side of his thigh. No-one intervened. Her son went down on one knee and was grabbed by the throat.

"I'm going to kill you, you little shit. But first I'm going to make you suffer."

He put the baton down, put his hand in his pocket and pulled out a flick knife. He let go of the boy's throat and grabbed his right ear with his left hand. In a single swift movement of his right hand, he pressed the sharp blade against the boy's head, sliced downwards and cut off his ear.

The boy gave out a gurgled scream. He could only look on in pain and horror as his tormentor skewered the ear with his knife and waved it in front of his agonized face.

There was an audible gasp from around the room. The colour had drained from Kelly's face. She waved frantically at the two guards mouthing for them to put a stop to the barbarous spectacle.

"Move, now." she shouted. "Get him away from the boy."

The two men walked quickly forward. Still holding the knife

with the ear attached, the young thug was too wrapped up in the violence, too deep in red mist to notice them coming towards him. Before he knew it one of the men had grabbed his arm twisting it hard behind his back and forcing him to drop the knife. The other grabbed him by his shirt and together they pushed and pulled him back and away from his victims. Kelly moved forward and picked up the knife. She turned to the man in the white coat who had sidled up next to her.

"Did you know he had this?" she snarled at him. "We need compliance and obedience. We don't need any gratuitous violence just for the sake of it. Go calm him down and explain the rules to him. He steps out of line again and he'll join the other unfortunates. Make sure he gets it. Tell those two to organize another clean-up crew and get the other ladies back into the kitchen. I'll get everyone away, get them kitted out and off to work. The three boys should provide enough threat to keep the other boys and the girls in order. You know she'll hit the roof when she hears about this."

The shocked children were ushered out of the hall in silence. They were taken to what seemed to be an old dance studio that looked like it had been converted into a makeshift clothing outlet. Kelly and the three youths lined up the girls and boys in the corridor telling them to stand still and wait until they were told to go in.

If this wasn't so scary it would be funny, thought Jessie, as she pictured them waiting to go into their primary school classroom. That seemed so long ago now, a dim and distant memory of time spent with her friends. How she wished she could travel back to the time when she skipped home from school looking forward to tea with her family and a night curled up in front of the tele.

The line in front of her started to move and she took firm hold of Katie's hand, determined to keep them together.

Once inside, a woman directed them to a table upon which were spread out bright yellow coveralls stacked in piles of different sizes. Two more women were sizing up each girl and handing them what they judged to be the right size. A fourth woman then directed them through another door where they were instructed to put them on over their clothes. Jessie looked at the women's faces, etched with pain and anguish. Mothers desperate to be reunited with their children. Jessie's eyes darted around the room in the hope her own mother was amongst them. Disappointed, she followed Katie through the door.

When the turn came for the boys, they were directed to a different table and handed drab grey coveralls.

By the time they were all changed the man in the white coat had returned with the fourth youth in tow red faced and clearly not as cocky as before. After a short conversation with Kelly, they took charge of the boys and marched them off in the direction of a large flat roofed building. Kelly organized the girls and they set off in slow pursuit.

Once inside the building, Jessie realized why they had been given coveralls to wear. They were going to be put to work. There were two distinct production lines with work laid out ready for them. Jessie strained to see what the work was. One line had what looked like sets of sewing machines laid out in rows. The other looked like some sort of packaging process. Jessie wondered if there was any real purpose to the work or whether this was some sort of test, an experiment they were all a part of. Either way Jessie knew they had to comply.

Some women dressed in similar fashion to the girls emerged from a side door and were directed into specific positions on both lines. Jessie looked down at Katie who was studying the women's faces. Katie's looking for mum, she thought. The forlorn look on Katie's face told her all she needed to know. None of the women was their mum. Her attention was drawn away from Katie's despair by the sound of Kelly's voice.

"Ok girls. In a minute you'll be taken over there and shown what we want you to do. Follow the instructions very carefully and make sure you understand. If you work hard today, you'll get more to eat and somewhere better to sleep. If not, well, let's not think about that, eh?" Kelly shrugged her shoulders as if dismissing that as an option.

"Right, let's get to work, shall we?"

Worrying thoughts went through Jessie's young head. This isn't going to end well, she thought. None of us will know what to do and some, like Katie, are far too young to cope. Anxious and afraid, Katie looked up at her big sister for reassurance. Jessie looked down, fighting to hide her worries behind a smile.

Chapter 24

Battered and bruised, he pushed himself up and off the floor. He flinched with pain as he twisted around into a sitting position, his back pressed against the wall. He ran his hand down the left side of his chest feeling each rib in turn and wincing when he pressed the last two. That had been some vicious kick, aimed and executed with just one intention. To inflict as much damage as possible. As much lasting pain as possible.

He stared into the gloom at the figures lying in front of him. To his right lay the two young boys. What on earth have they done to deserve this, he thought. As he looked at them, beaten and unconscious, one face-up, one face-down, he had to stop himself from imagining that a similar fate had befallen his own two sons.

The boy on his back was breathing heavily and making a disturbing gurgling sound. Dark red bubbles were growing and shrinking around his mouth with each completed breath. The boy was hurt and hurt badly. Calling on all his strength and overcoming the intense pain in his side he edged over to the boy. If nothing else, he should be able to make him a bit more comfortable. As gently as he could he rolled the boy over and into the recovery position. How ironic, he thought, recovery will have little to do with the position I've put him in. He shifted his attention to the other three.

The nearest of the two men was curled up on the floor in the fetal position. He was sobbing softly to himself whilst rocking back and forth in a slow, rhythmic movement. The other man was sitting himself up. He could see through the gloom that the man was rubbing the top of his thigh.

"How badly are you hurt?" he said in a dry rasping voice.

"My thigh hurts. Feels like someone gave me a dead leg." He would have laughed at his choice of words but there was no funny side to their situation. He continued his reply.

"The lad that came over to us was nowhere near as vicious as the other three. He seemed almost reluctant to beat us. He spent most of the time staring at what the others were doing to those two." He pointed to the two boys lying motionless on the floor.

"How are they?" he asked.

Inching his way past the boy he had already assessed he moved closer to the other one. He knew immediately there was nothing he could do for him. Even in the half-light he could see the sheen reflected off the pool of dark liquid beside the boy's head. His head was twisted to the left making the right side visible. He could see that the boy had suffered a severe blow. He had felt the full force of the baton as it fractured his skull. His right eye was open and staring blankly at the ceiling. The boy was dead.

A wave of sheer anger came over him and he banged a clenched fist against the floor. They were just kids. Not much younger than his own two sons. He had seen what was coming but never once imagined it would be like this. Maybe, just maybe if he had acted sooner then he could have stopped them. He had known they were growing stronger by the day. He had made the decision to let them show their hand first. Had that been a big mistake? This was no time for hindsight or regret. This was just the beginning, just the tip of the iceberg. Moving against them early may have won the first battle but it would not have won the war. He knew they were preparing to unleash horrors on a far greater scale than this.

He peered across at the two men. Even through the gloom he could see they were broken. He calmed himself down. He must keep it together. He had sent word. He needed faith. He needed to believe that his friends would find him. Until then he would have to play along. There was only one plan. Survive at all costs. Then when the opportunity presented itself, he would act. Even if it cost him his life, at the very least he would go knowing he had done all he could. He looked back at the two boys. He swore an oath to himself. Someone was going to pay dearly for this.

Not too far away eight women were being crammed into a tiny room. It was the size of a small storeroom and without light. The women were stood together packed in like sardines in a can. The air was hot and stuffy making it hard for them to breathe. One of them had fainted but was being held upright by the tight-knit group around her. Jessie's mum was one of them. It was difficult for her to tell how long they were locked in and by the time the door opened they were in a desperate condition. Whoever was in control knew exactly how long to leave them in there.

The familiar man in the white coat was standing outside waiting patiently as the women were pulled out of the tiny space. Jessie's mum was the third one out. She stood shakily next to the other two. All three were gasping down deep breaths of the cooler fresher air. They were joined by three more hot and dehydrated companions. A deep matter-of-fact voice spoke from inside the room.

"Two of them have collapsed on the floor. What do you want me to do with them?"

The man in the white coat smiled at the other six. Close-up he had a wide toothy grin. Jessie's mum found herself thinking it was nothing to smirk at. She had an overwhelming urge to step forward and slap him hard in the face. She squashed it. Her mind was willing, but she knew full well her body was now far too weak and the consequences far too great.

"Take them to the Treatment Room. We'll deal with them once we have entertained our friends here."

Those still standing were led away. They were lined up against the wall and told to wait. The man in the white coat disappeared inside only to appear a minute or two later. He nodded to the blue-suited Cleo watching over them who then rather surprisingly asked them very politely to move on inside. In the middle of the room stood the white-coated and smiling figure of Dr Caroline Bramney.

"Welcome ladies." The enthusiasm in her voice made it sound like she was welcoming them to a meeting of the Women's Institute."

"Please take a seat. I'm sure you need to sit down after that awful and unnecessary ordeal. Please accept my humble apologies and let me make it up to you."

In front of her were six well-spaced chairs. Two more Cleos moved them forward and strapped the ladies in one at a time.

"Are you sitting comfortably?" chuckled Dr Bramney. "Then let's begin."

Today was a busy day for Dr Bramney. She had a full schedule planned but still had plenty of time in this session to enjoy herself. An hour later when the screams had subsided and she had had her fun, Dr Bramney left for her next appointment. Delighted with her latest work.

A short while later the door to the large, refrigerated unit was pulled open. Four more bodies were laid out beside the other frozen residents. As the door closed on the neat line of bodies now numbering eleven the two Cleos nodded to each other.

"We've reached double figures. Soon be time to fire up the new system." he said gleefully. "If it all works, we should soon get some new guests to take good care of."

"That's shocked me that has." came the serious sounding reply. "I didn't know you could count beyond ten!"

They laughed loudly together and slapped each other on the back. Pleased at the thought that soon it would all be operating at full swing.

PART 4

Lessons from the Past

Chapter 25

Obi parked up the car, turned to the big guy sitting next to him and gave him simple directions to get from where they were back to his house. As he was talking, Obi realized he was probably being a bit stereotypical. Just because Marty was big it didn't follow automatically that his monosyllabic responses meant he wasn't taking it in and so needed everything spelt out through slow, laborious repetition. When Obi finished giving directions Marty turned to face JJ sitting in the back seat and winked at him.

"Ok sonny Jim, you go first and me and satnav Suzy here will follow on." He pointed at Obi, gave him a broad grin, and turned his attention back to JJ. "Best you give your friends the heads up before I barge in on them. Yes?"

JJ nodded, got out of the car, and headed off down the first side street on the left. A couple of minutes later Marty went next, turned in the opposite direction to JJ and disappeared down an alley between two shops. Obi locked the car and took the same route as JJ. The chance was he would get back before Marty which would be good. He wanted to be there when Marty arrived if only to see the faces of the other two when they opened the door to the big man and then to hear JJ's explanation for bringing him back.

It went as Obi had hoped it would. JJ was in the hallway talking to Sally when he opened the front door and stepped inside. Marty was still on his way.

"You told him where we are?" he heard Sally ask incredulously.

Before he could stop himself, Obi replied on JJ's behalf.

"Worse than that. We brought him back with us and he's on his way here right now."

The conversation was cut short before Sally could express herself fully. There was a soft knock at the door. Three times in quick succession. Being the nearest Obi opened the door and stepped back. He knew the visitor would need a sizeable space to step into. The look on Sally's face was a real picture. At five foot two, the man in looming large front of her was nothing less than a giant.

"Sal, meet Marty." JJ wanted to reach across and gently push up her lower jaw. Her chin had dropped almost to the floor. He looked across at Obi and the pair of them couldn't help themselves. They sniggered at each other like a pair of silly adolescent schoolboys. Sally was not amused. Swiftly regaining her self-control, she glared at the two of them then turned to welcome their guest.

"Pleased to meet you, Marty. I'm Sally. Ignore these two infants and come and meet Danny."

"Pleased to meet you too Sally." His voice soft, his countenance showing he felt genuine pleasure at making her acquaintance.

All four went into the dining room. Danny swiveled round on his chair to welcome back his friends. He had overheard the conversation in the hallway and so seeing Marty walk in came as no surprise to him.

"Danny, Marty, Marty, Danny." The two nodded in acknowledgement of each other.

"Right." said Sally, taking control of the situation as usual.

"Sit down Marty and tell us why you're here. First though, would you like a drink and something to eat?"

"A cup of tea would be good."

Sally looked across at JJ and afforded herself a little smirk.

"Make yourself useful and go make us all a drink. Be quick about it too."

Marty saw the twinkle in her eye and heard the mischief in her voice as she gave the order to JJ. The big softy smiled to himself. Such innocence. Oh, to be young and in love, he thought. A memory returned and a sadness touched his heart for a fleeting moment. He gently caressed it and then let it go.

Sally smiled and sat Marty down at the table so she could at least look him in the eye as they waited until JJ returned with the drinks. Marty took a sip of his tea and launched into his story.

"Back in the late nineties and early noughties me and your dad were part of a special covert operations team. There were four of us. Our job was to carry out, how should I say it, difficult and dangerous tasks in countries considered dangerous or hostile at the time. Thinking about it now, I guess some of the things we were ordered to do weren't very nice but at the time we believed what we were doing was helping to keep the world a safer place.

Each one of us was hand-picked because we had special skills and because we had responded so well during the special training. As you can tell by just looking at me, I provided the brawn rather than the brains." Marty paused and smiled at the four of them. They didn't laugh. They just looked at him totally awestruck by everything about him.

"I was also a small arms specialist. Guns and bullets basically. Your dad was our engineering and comms expert. He had a dual role. His first was to gather all the details about the upcoming operation, analyze the situation and come up with the modus operandi. He also developed a knack for uncovering all sorts of secrets, both theirs and ours. His other role was as a hands-on fixer during the mission. We liked to use nicknames and it sounds pretty lame now, but we called your dad Brains after the Thunderbirds character."

Marty took another sip of his tea and looked around the table. He could tell by their faces they were hanging on his every word. He sensed from JJ's expression that this part of his father's past was all new to him.

"Jake was a Sergeant in the Royal Engineers. We called him the Joker. Jake the Joker. Always messing about and doing stupid things. He liked to make loud noises, big bangs. He was our explosives expert. We always thought that one day he would blow his own head off but Joker or not, he was, he still is, one of the best at his job. If not the best." The emphasis of the word 'the' and the warm tone of his voice made no secret of the strong bond of friendship between him and Jake.

"Finally, there was our intrepid team leader Johnny-Boy

Brown. He was our senior officer and held the rank of Lieutenant Commander RN. I guess it would be fair to say Johnny-Boy was the most mature of the four of us. He was our tactician and linguistic expert. Wherever we went he always seemed to be able to speak the lingo."

"During our time together, we did some good things, and I have to admit we did some pretty bad things too. I guess looking back on it now, we did what we did because it was our job. It was what we were trained for. Eventually of course our time together came to an end. We had one last night out on the town and then went our separate ways with a vow to always keep in touch. Brains, sorry your dad, being the man he was, set up a special system for us. Whilst he hoped we'd keep in touch through the usual channels, Christmas cards and the like, he knew that was never going to happen, so your dad set up a way for us to communicate under the radar just in case something, or someone, ever came back to haunt us."

"It wasn't long after the team split up that me and Jake left the service. I got a job as a bouncer before setting up my own business as a personal trainer. Got some pretty high-profile clients too. Jake became a special effects technician working in the TV and film industry. He developed quite a reputation for his creative art of whizzes and bangs. I think he's still much in demand throughout the industry. Or at least he was until all this kicked off."

"Johnny stayed on and went to work for the Home Office. He was promoted into some sort of security role. Your dad stayed on for a while and worked for the Ministry of Defence. Then he met your mum and I assume you know the rest from there. Johnny and your dad were better at keeping in touch than Jake and me. We had all moved on with our lives or so Jake and I thought, until about six months ago."

"Your dad sent us a message via the emergency channel. Every year the cheeky so and so paid an annual subscription to RAF News for all four of us. We had agreed that should any one of us need to make covert contact with the others they would put a special ad in the paper. Two months ago, that's what your dad did."

"Shortly after that I got a preprogrammed pay-as-you-go phone through the post with some simple instructions. To stay alert, switch on the phone, and wait. I assumed Jake had got a similar delivery. Within minutes I got a text to say the phone was safe and encrypted. Then very soon after that I got sent more details about what was going on."

"Apparently good old JB, bless him, had stumbled on to something strange linked to one of our missions from years earlier. During that particular mission, your dad uncovered links to some sort of secret society that was sponsoring unrest around the world. It wasn't part of our brief, so we didn't pursue it at the time. Six months ago, Johnny sent Brains some information and files and asked him to see what he could find out. The two of them stayed in almost constant communication after that until things suddenly went quiet at Johnny's end. It turned out that late one night he had been run down and killed in a hit and run accident at a zebra crossing. However not before he sent your dad one last coded message." Marty stopped again. He looked at his cold cup of tea. From the look on his face, it was clear he could do with a sip of something much stronger. He continued.

"Your dad told us Johnny's message had read: Take extra care. They know about us. They know we're looking into what they're doing. Brains said he couldn't find any CCTV footage of the hit and run. Your dad knew for sure that it was no accident that killed our Johnny-Boy. He also knew that whatever had happened Johnny would have given nothing away. Nothing at all. He was one of the two hardest men I've ever known." Marty looked straight at JJ. "Your dad is the other."

A strange sense of pride swelled up in JJ's chest although somehow this came as no real surprise to him as deep down, he always knew there was much more to his dad than met the eye. His first thought was to wonder how much his mother knew about his dad's past life. He pictured them together and instantly he answered his own question.

Sally and Danny were already joining up the dots in their heads, expecting what was coming next. Obi on the other hand, had gone into a complete state of unconditional hero worship of the big man. Marty continued his story.

"Everything went quiet for a while. Then a couple of days ago I got another message. I knew your dad wouldn't let it go so it was no surprise to hear he thought they would be coming for him soon. He was sure the secret society was behind Johnny's death. He believed something big and bad was going to kick off within the next few days. He said he didn't know what exactly, but he was getting prepared for the worst. He left us in no doubt that we needed to be on our guard."

"Your dad said that if and when they came for him, he would buy enough time to send me a very short code red. Being taken seemed to be part of his plan. He asked me when the time came to make sure you, your brother and your mother were safe. He also told me to collect a package hidden at his house. The package he said was the key. He made it clear I had to collect it and pass it on as it would help to explain everything he knew and how he might be found. Early the next morning he sent us the short, coded message. That was the last we heard from him but he's as tough as old boots, so I know he is still very much alive and kicking. I just don't know where. That's why I was waiting at your house JJ. That's why I'm here now."

The four youngsters had listened, transfixed by Marty's story. Sally had watched the expression on JJ's face as the story about his dad had unfolded. It was obvious there was much if not all of it that was new to JJ. Once again it was Sally, as composed as ever, who got straight down to the nitty gritty.

"I guess we can assume you found the package and you've got it with you?" she asked looking across the table at the huge man with the gentle manner sitting opposite her and in no doubt that there would have been no stopping him from carrying out his friend's request.

Marty nodded and pulled out a padded A5 envelope from the inside pocket of his jacket. Obi's eyes widened as he caught a glimpse of the gun holstered under Marty's jacket. There was no doubt left in his mind. This guy was definitely a real force to be reckoned with.

"Let's see what's inside?" continued Sally, pointing at the envelope.

Marty opened it and emptied the contents onto the table.

They could see by his lack of reaction that he had already looked at the contents and had read the note now lying on the table in front of them.

"The note is from your dad telling me to find you JJ and give you the USB thingy. I'm guessing the information from Johnny and stuff your dad found out is in it. At the end of the note there's two words above a six-digit code and what looks like a website address."

JJ picked up the note and scanned down it to the two words. The message was simple. Find me. He looked up to see Sally and Danny were already busy uploading the information from the USB flash drive to Danny's computer. As the two set to work, Marty directed his attention towards JJ.

"I know your dad must be very proud of you. He asked me to find you because he knew I would need some help from someone. Someone he trusted and believed in. That's you JJ. He told me you were more than just a chip off the old block. He told me you and your brother Billy would prove to be much better than he was. I always trusted your dad's judgement so let's prove your dad is right. We need to work together as a team if we're going to get your dad back. I won't lie to you though. I think you already know this is going to get very dangerous very quickly but at this point you still have a choice. If you and your friends tell me to leave, I'll go once I know where to find your dad."

JJ looked at Sally and Danny swarming over their computer like bees over a honeypot. Then he looked sideways at Obi shaking his head from side to side as an indication that he wanted Marty to stay. Obi had already planned on getting Marty to help find his family too.

"Look around Marty. Does it look like we want you to go?"

Marty smiled. Brains was right again. Not just about his son but about his son's friends as well.

"That's great, but if we're going to do this then we're still going to need help from a friend. Best I get him here asap."

Marty pulled out the pay-as-you-go phone. JJ watched as Marty let his sausage-like fingers do the talking. It was agonizing to watch the big man struggle with the technology. Both JJ and Obi let out a sigh of relief when Marty finally hit send.

Chapter 26

Sally and Danny had been pouring over the contents of the uploaded folders from the USB flash drive JJ's dad had left for Marty to collect. With each file they opened they became more and more animated. A story was unfolding before their very eyes. The story of the emergence of a secret society that appeared to have been in existence for decades. A powerful society with ambition to bring their own particular order and salvation to the world. The pair now understood the full meaning of the strange briefing Danny had web-crashed nearly two days ago.

There was an audible gasp when the two of them opened the file marked 'Donations'. The document consisted of four columns. In the first was a list of the names of prominent national and international figures. Certain well-known names sprang out at them. The second column contained the details of the person's role and the organisation they worked for. Sally and Danny followed across the row of a very famous and very wealthy individual to the third column which contained a number with a lot of zeros.

A look of intrigue crossed Danny's face when he got to the

final detail in the fourth column. It contained a short descriptor made up of two letters, instantly recognizable as the person's initials, and a single number. There were three descriptors for this individual. The third was marked with an asterisk.

Sensing the excitement emanating from the document Marty and JJ were peering over the shoulders of the two whizz kids. Sally turned her head to the side and looked up at JJ.

"This looks like all these people have a connection to some weird society dad refers to as SPAWN. If you run your eye down the money column that's an awful lot of donations. It must be a very wealthy and therefore presumably an extremely powerful organisation. Certainly not short of cash or influence."

As Danny scrolled back up to the top of the document, he noticed something he had missed the first time. He almost poked the screen as he pointed to a handwritten comment in the margin.

"Look, it's a website address." The excitement in his voice was clear for them all to hear.

An instant response came from the other side of the room in the best Scouse accent Obi could muster.

"Calm down, calm down." He said in a Geordie accent and knew at least Danny would get the joke as they had watched the re-runs of the Harry Enfield show together on TV. Marty smiled. He'd seen the shows first time around. It was good that even under these circumstances there was still room for a little humour, a bit of banter, he thought. Danny was especially pleased that Obi was able to share a laugh despite the worry about his family.

Sally looked at the figure sitting across the room, grinning broadly back at her.

"Thanks, Obi, for your words of wisdom. You're absolutely right. We need to slow down and go through everything first before we go off on any tangents."

She looked towards Marty. He was still smiling and unsure whether Sally had got the joke until he saw the sparkle in her eye as she continued on regardless.

"Do you think it would be safe for us to print some of this off so we can study it better?"

"It should be fine. Look at it this way. If anyone finds the hard copies, then they will have found us and the disc anyway. It will help us, well me, because I prefer to look at bits of paper rather than squinting at a screen."

Danny looked a little annoyed and clearly angry with himself.

"I didn't bring my encrypted printer. Couldn't carry it. Before you say anything Obi, not because it was too heavy but because I couldn't get it in my bag. I'll need to go home to get it."

"I'll go with you. I could do with a bit of exercise and some fresh air."

Danny welcomed the idea of a walk with his friend. He also felt he needed to pop home. He could let his mum know he was ok. Like Sally, he had sent a text to his mum to say he was staying over at a friend's house, but it would be good to see her in person if she was home.

As impatient as ever, Obi was keen to get going and already reaching for his coat.

"Come on slow coach. Get your shoes on and let's get the

show on the road."

Now it was Danny's turn to put on a Scouse accent as he repeated the two-word phrase back to his friend.

"More haste, less speed." he added, knowing full well this was an old adage his impatient friend was almost certainly incapable of following. Five minutes later the two companions set off on the short journey to Danny's strolling side-by-side, eyes alert to their surroundings. Danny felt safe with Obi at his side and Obi pleased to act as Danny's minder once again.

Whilst they were gone things progressed at pace. Marty received a reply from Jake to say he was on his way. Sally, with JJ sitting close beside her, had been busy working on the nine-digit code and the website in his dad's note to Marty. The website appeared to have been created by JJ's dad and required the code to enter the site. From the name and the sparse front page, it was unlikely anyone would come across it by accident during a normal search. Even if they did it looked innocuous and would most likely warrant a swift glance at best before they moved on.

On entering the code, a download screen appeared. The instructions were simple and straightforward. Run the download then enter the code again. JJ sat watching Sally as she confidently followed the process. He looked at the split screen in front of him and marveled at how she switched effortlessly between the download on one side and the security scan running on the other. He didn't quite understand exactly what she was doing but knew she was making sure everything was safe. No hidden malware surprises.

A click of the mouse and they were looking at a satellite picture on the full screen. Sally turned and looked at JJ with eyes that were shining so brightly that he was almost blinded by her beauty.

"Look. Just look at that. This is amazing." Turning in her seat she waved at Marty to get his attention. Sally clicked on the satellite picture and zoomed in.

"Marty. I don't think JJ's dad has lost his touch. I can see why you called him Brains. That's us. That's Obi's house."

Marty walked across to see what all the fuss was about. Computers and associated technology really weren't his thing. His forte was more hands-on. Simple things like guns and knives. The things he could control. The things that kill your enemies. As quietly and efficiently as possible.

"This is a very sophisticated track and trace program. I'm betting that if I type in the nine-digit code in that box there," she pointed at the screen for Marty's benefit, "somethings going to flash back at us."

JJ read out the code and Sally typed it in. The screen went blank for a second. Then as Sally had predicted a different satellite picture appeared. It was from a coastal area and sure enough there was a red dot flashing at them from the centre of the screen. Zooming in showed it to be a camp of some sort with a red dot blinking at them from one of the larger buildings.

"JJ that's got to be where your dad is. We've found him. Or rather he's found himself for us." Sally sounded in awe of the man.

"I think he must have injected himself with some sort of microchip device. A bit like microchipping your cat but this one transmits a location signal. Like your phone does when it's switched on. Genius."

Sally paused. Another thought had just struck her. If any of Obi's family still had their phones with them and switched on, they could probably find them too. Chances were that JJ's dad had designed the software to track phones as well. She turned and instinctively gave JJ a big hug. Marty smiled as he watched JJ's face flush bright red. These two need to get a room he smiled to himself.

Sally took a screenshot of the picture in front of her, zoomed out and repeated the process twice more. There was enough in the pictures to identify the exact location of the tracker signal.

"Do you think your dad might have designed this for mobiles as well? I'm wondering about that because he sent Marty and Jake phones and that may have got him thinking about it. Shall we give it a try before Obi gets back. I don't want to give him false hope about finding his family."

JJ and Marty looked at each other. They weren't quite sure which one of them Sally was expecting to answer. Or even if her questions were to them or to herself. A conversation going on in her head but being expressed out loud. It was JJ who answered.

"Give it a try Sal. Whose number should we use?"

Before he even got to the last word of his answer Sally was typing numbers. It was her own number. She clicked on the screen and waited. It didn't work. She tried it a second time without the zero in front. It didn't work. Then she had yet another thought. The original code was nine digits long. Third time lucky, she muttered out load. It worked. A new satellite picture appeared with the flashing red dot blinking at them from the screen.

"Sal you're a genius." JJ wanted to reach across and kiss her but saw she was in a different moment altogether.

"How did you do that?" asked Marty.

"I thought as your dad used a nine-digit code maybe the input had to be nine numbers. Every mobile number starts with zero seven and is eleven numbers long. I just put my number in without the zero and the seven. That flashing dot is us."

Sally looked at JJ. Her moment had changed. She turned, bent forward, and kissed him. It took him by complete surprise.

"Don't you get carried away, young man. That was for your dad. He's not here so I thought you would have to do." she said teasingly.

JJ blushed a little. Marty laughed.

"What are you two like?"

Before either of the love birds could reply, Marty's phone bleeped. It was a message from Jake. He was just about to set off with an ETA of about an hour and a half.

"Jake's on his way. Prepare yourselves. He can seem a bit odd when you first meet him. Too many loud bangs." Marty put his hands to either side of his head and made a gesture like his head was exploding. He was pleased with himself. He had made them both laughed.

Chapter 27

When Danny and Obi struggled through the door with the printer and other assorted items, they found the other three huddled around Sally's computer. Obi made a comment about bringing everything back except the kitchen sink, but the others were too preoccupied to acknowledge his remark. Sally had opened a few more of the documents from the flash drive and now they were focused on one in particular.

"Hey, look, we're back safely. Did you miss us?" Obi was determined to get them to register his and Danny's safe return.

Sally glanced up.

"Danny, get in here and get your printer installed. We need to print some stuff off. Quickly, both of you, we've got some good news to tell you too. Obi, stop faffing about and let Danny get in here with the printer."

Obi let out a disgruntled snort as he moved out of the way to let Danny and his printer pass. JJ sniggered to himself. He had the suspicion that Sally was deliberately toying with Obi so that when she gave him the news about the phone tracking and the possibility of locating his family, they would be able to see his mood change in an instant.

Sally left Danny to work with the printer and joined Obi, Marty, and JJ at the table. She knew Danny could multitask with ease. Working with his beloved IT and listening to Sally at the same time would be no problem for him.

"The first bit of good news is we know where JJ's dad is. Or at least his tracking device which we have to assume is still on his person. The second is, using the program, we can track and trace mobile phones. Obi that means if any of your family have their phone switched on, we can find out where they are."

Sally was right about his reaction. Obi punched the air narrowly missing Marty's left shoulder. His excitement had definitely got the better of him.

"Let's do it. Let's find them."

The look on Marty's face was noticed by the two sitting opposite him. Solemn and thoughtful would be the best way to describe it. Finding them was one thing, getting all of them back here safely would be something else. They would have to have a good plan and planning was not his strong point. He saw the other two were watching him and his expression changed. He smiled. Maybe he should stop worrying. There were two people in the room he could trust to come up with a plan and he was looking directly at them.

"Printer's ready." called Danny rather triumphantly.

Sally almost broke into a run as she dashed back to her computer. Within seconds the printer hummed into action. Sally opened and closed a few more of the uploaded files from the flash drive, lingering a little longer on some than others. She used her own judgement to select which would be most useful in hard copy. Enough to give everyone something to read and discuss. It took a few minutes before the printer went silent. Danny had collated each document and took them across to the table. Sally followed him across the room.

"I've printed off a few things for us to look at. I think they'll give us an insight into what's going on. I suggest we divide our resources and then come back together to discuss what we've found and what we might do next."

Sally paused and waited for any objections. It was no real surprise to her when none came.

"Danny, this is the list of names with the codes and website on. Your mission is to find the website, hack into it if you can, and see what the codes are for."

There was no need to ask twice. Danny was on to his task in a flash. Sheet of paper in his hand he was pressing keys on his laptop almost before Sally had finished speaking to him.

"Marty and JJ, you two have some background reading to do. For you JJ, this is a paper of sorts that looks like your dad was compiling about the origins of this SPAWN titled 'From Lecture to Law'. I think that will go some way to explaining the who and the why, generically at least. There are other documents on the flash drive that might help if need be. Your dad must have done some research on the net and copied any useful information he discovered. Use my other computer if you need to."

"For you Marty a more technical job. There was a folder marked 'New Project' which contained some technical designs and drawings. Are you ok to look at them and see what you think the project is all about? Please."

As Sally had only just met Marty and judging by his size compared to hers, she thought it best to ask him very politely. She saw from the nod and the smile he gave her she needn't have worried about it.

"What about me?"

Obi being Obi was as impatient as ever.

"Saved the best until last." came Sally's enthused reply.

"We're going back over there to find where your family are. That ok with you Mr. Impatient?"

JJ and Marty looked down at the papers in front of them and fought back a giggle. Obi hmphed then smiled, stood up, and followed Sally to her computer.

They all proceeded to set about their tasks with great gusto. The first to have some success was Sally and Obi. They had inputted Jessie's nine-digit phone number and were looking intently at another flashing red dot. However, there was no punching of the air, no celebration. The expression on Sally's face suggested something was wrong.

"Let's run it again." she said to Obi, trying to keep the mood positive.

The flashing red dot reappeared in the same location.

"Surely that can't be right? Can it?"

Marty looked up and across at them.

"What can't be right?"

Sally swung around on her chair to face the two still sitting at the table.

"It's the same place. The dot is flashing in almost exactly the same place as it did when we put in JJ's dad's code. According to this they can only be a few metres apart. That seems too much of a coincidence to be right. But why would it be wrong?" Sally looked puzzled. Obi looked like he wanted to hit something.

"I've seen and done a lot of things where what you might call luck or coincidence played a big part. In my experience it's something more than that. You have to believe in what you see. Blow up the area and print it off so we can see what's on the ground. My guess is what you're seeing is right. Brains is too clever for it to be wrong. If the dots are flashing, then that's where they are. If they're flashing in the same place, then that's where they are. In the same place. Somehow it makes sense to me that would be the case. Think about it. They, whoever they are, are doing things they want kept secret. Why not do them in the same place? Somewhere no-one would think to look."

Sally swung back into action. Seconds later the printer came alive again. Two satellite pictures popped into its' tray. Screenshots of each of the red dots. The locations of the members of the two different families were just metres apart. Families connected by two friends, miles away from them and sitting just a few metres apart. This was something else for Marty to look at.

Chapter 28

A positive mood swept across the room. Danny and Sally were engrossed in their work. Muttering and nodding to each other and peering occasionally at each other's screen. Marty and Obi were studying the satellite pictures and comparing them with the road map Marty had fetched from his car. They had identified the exact location of the red dots. Obi was a bit confused by it as it appeared that his family were actually staying at a holiday camp on the coast after all. A state of mind that swiftly passed when he pictured Jessie texting him. His sister, levelheaded and never one to panic, would not have got it wrong.

Marty, sensing Obi's disquiet, asked Sally if she could find any further details that might be useful to them. In particular he wanted the physical layout of the camp site. Sally obliged. The printer came to life interrupting the studious silence for a few seconds. Obi collected the printouts and laid them in front of Marty on the table.

The pair now had a colour version of the layout and other general information about the holiday camp. Their next job was to put the satellite picture together with the old layout merging the two to give an updated plan of the camp itself and the surrounding area. They could already see from the satellite picture there had been some significant changes.

In particular, the satellite pictures showed that a large building had been constructed on the north edge of the camp site. It was impossible to tell how recently it had been constructed but it certainly looked very new from the picture they had. On a comparative scale to the buildings, they could identify they were able to make a good guess at its dimensions. It was big. Marty shuffled the sheets of paper and pulled out the technical drawings for the construction project. He turned to Danny.

"Fancy a flutter. If I was a betting man, I'd put money on these details being a perfect match for that building and what's inside it. My young friend, this is good, we are making progress."

He gave Obi what he thought was a light tap on the shoulder with his fist. The playful punch almost knocked Obi off his chair. Obi shoved Marty with both hands to no effect, like a resistible force meeting an immovable object. The second time around Marty pushed him off his chair, wagged a finger at him and as Obi rolled onto the floor the pair burst into laughter.

Up until then JJ had been immersed in his father's research into this mysterious Society. Hearing Marty's positive comment and the laughing as Obi was knocked off his chair by the big man made him look up and shoot a discernable glare in their direction. He huffed at them for breaking his concentration.

"Sorry." whispered Marty with placatory sarcasm. He looked sideways at Obi sitting next to him and raised an eyebrow. The pair chortled like they were naughty schoolboys whispering in the school library.

It was enough to win JJ around. Not enough to stop him from exacting punishment for their crime.

"For that you can go and make me a cup of tea. Sal, Danny, what about you?"

Nods from across the room indicated that was an affirmative.

"Three cups of tea it is then. Obi, if you would do the honours, please. Oh, and make one for yourself and your comedian friend there if you feel the need."

"Why of course your Lordship. How about some cucumber sandwiches while I'm at it?" Obi turned immediately to Marty.

"Cup of tea, Marty?"

Marty gave him a thumbs up and Obi went off with a grin to make the tea.

JJ returned to his studies. He decided the best approach was to make a few notes as he went along. He had read some of the historic background research from the websites and turned his attention to his dad's summary paper. It was in three parts. What he discovered both fascinated him and frightened him in equal measure. He now fully understood his father's choice of title. He double-checked his notes as he went along to make sure he had the full story. They too were in three sections.

The first section told the story of SPAWNs origins. The journey from the Lecture to the Second World War. Whilst the philosophy behind the Society could be traced back as far as Plato it was Sir Francis Galton, the half-cousin of Charles Darwin, who began the journey when he pioneered the philosophy of eugenics.

Scholar that Galton was, he took the name from the Greek

term 'eugenes' which meant 'good in stock, hereditary endowed with noble qualities', put simply 'well-born'. Building upon his cousin's ideas of natural selection, Galton wrote a series of books and articles in the 1860s and 1870s before introducing the term 'eugenics' in a work entitled Inquiries into Human Faculty and Its Development in 1883. His philosophy was based on a strong statistical approach and his ideas grew in popularity. Based on a study of upper-class Britain, his belief was that selective breeding could guide the future of humanity.

To re-launch his vision Galton gave the Huxley Lecture at the Royal Anthropological Institute in October 1901. It was at London University on May 16th, 1904, that he presented a paper for debate to the Sociological Society. A paper presented to a very large audience of eminent physicians and scientists.

JJ had read through the transcript of the paper and the critiques. Prominent figures including George Bernard Shaw, Benjamin Kidd and H.G. Wells had all entered into the debate.

More widely JJ found that there were other leading figures of the time that had given their support to his ideas. He looked at the list with some degree of astonishment.

One on the list, John Maynard Keynes, became the Director of the British Eugenics Society. At the time he considered eugenics to be the most important and significant branch of sociology.

There were many other names most of which JJ had never heard of. One such was that of a Sir Albert Bartholomew Bramney. Great, great grandfather of someone very much in the present-day public eye. Someone he had heard of. He didn't register the connection. At the time there was no reason why he should.

His interest in the history of eugenics growing, JJ made notes on the movement in the USA which had developed in a similar fashion.

The first name on JJ's list was Charles Davenport. Born in Stamford Connecticut in 1866, educated at Harvard University, scientist Charles Davenport has been considered to be one of history's leading eugenicists. He became acquainted with Galton and his work in 1897 and developed eugenics from a scientific notion to a worldwide movement implemented in many countries. In 1925 Davenport became the first President of the International Federation of Eugenics Organisations.

During the early decades of the twentieth century there was widespread acceptance and support for the eugenics movement across the USA.

History, JJ continued after a short shake of his wrist, records that the popularity of the eugenics movement peaked during the 1930s and was starting to wane at the start of the Second World War. The use of eugenic principles to justify the atrocities of Nazi Germany all but put an end to its credibility as a field of study and eugenics became almost universally condemned.

Almost but not quite. Some eugenics programs continued quietly for decades after the war had ended. Pre-war eugenicists went underground taking their beliefs with them. Many of them to emerge in the post-war era reborn as well-respected biologists, anthropologists, and geneticists. As JJ wrote that last sentence, he felt a cold shiver go down his spine. Where were these people now and what had they been working towards.

A sip of lukewarm tea and a rub of his eyes later he moved on to part two of his father's paper.

Chapter 29

There was no comfort to be found in the thought that forces unseen had been at work since the end of the Second World War. JJ was struggling with the list of an assortment of post-war activities contained in his father's research paper. He could not believe the number of countries reportedly to have continued with some form of eugenic practice through the latter decades of the twentieth century. Some, he thought, were to be expected, others came as quite a shock to him. He searched again on his phone to confirm his father's information was accurate. He sighed. There was no doubting its legitimacy.

The information in part two that interested him most covered the first two decades of the twenty-first century. It was the thought that this was during his own lifetime that disturbed him the most. He decided to keep his own notes brief as he read through the more detailed account in his father's paper. He would then go back and check he had captured the main points.

JJ focused on four individuals and what they had to say as he thought this might help him understand better what was happening now. There was no evidence to suggest any of the four had ever been involved or connected with SPAWN in any way. Critically, their analysis and comment simply provided a backdrop to the frightening content in part three of his father's paper.

The first individual was the American evolutionary psychologist, Geoffrey Miller. JJ had made particular note of an article Miller wrote in 2013 titled 'What should we be worried about?'. He had found and read through the short article. It was focused on how over the past thirty years the Chinese had been running the largest and most successful eugenics program. JJ's notes were succinct. He had written down that the article claimed that the program might allow the Chinese to increase the IQ of each subsequent generation and if this were to happen, Miller suggested that soon Western global competitiveness could be over.

JJ then made a particular abbreviated note on two of Miller's statements. The first was concerned with the closeness of the relationship, the cooperation, between the Chinese Government and the various key elements of its society to promote the idea of a utopian state. JJ continued and underlined part of the next sentence in his notes. He had heard people repeating that it was all for the safety and welfare of the people so many times recently. He looked down at the page in front of him and at what he had just written and wondered what it meant for the world and all their futures.

This, he thought, led nicely on to the next comments. His dad had included details of two articles in his paper written by an American science journalist, John Entine. The first from 2012 and the second titled 'Let's (Cautiously) Celebrate the New Eugenics' published in 2017.

JJ mused over the use of the word cautiously.

His dad had made only a short note that both articles contained reference to an American historian, associate professor at the Institute of the History of Medicine at Johns Hopkins University, Nathanial C. Comfort. It was the associate professor that caught JJs interest. To keep his notes brief JJ only included a popular quote from Comfort's 2012 book, 'The Science of Human Perfection: How Genes Became the Heart of American Medicine'. He read the quote again. Wrote it out and underlined the key words as a note to himself for when he talked to the others.

Underneath it he scribbled a few of the words in his own handwriting for further emphasis and as another reminder to himself as to the nature of the quote.

The final figure he decided to make a note of was Richard Dawkins. A British ethologist, evolutionary biologist, and author. JJ noted that he was an interesting figure who from 1995 to 2008 was the University of Oxford's Professor for Public Understanding of Science. It was Dawkins' concern about overpopulation that JJ referenced.

Dawkins, JJ noted, first expressed his concern about population growth in 'The Selfish Gene' published in 1976 and then again in 'The Selfish Green' at the opening event of the 2004 Wildscreen Festival in a landmark debate on the future of conservation.

With all that he had read, he wondered why no-one with the power to act had listened, had understood, had seen what was coming and had cared enough to do something about it. Maybe someone was.

Looking around at his friends hard at work on their individual tasks, JJ considered asking Obi to make another cup of tea. He could see they were all deeply engrossed, and he presumed making good progress, so he thought better of it and moved on to part three.

What he read next took him a little by surprise. The final part began with what could only be a direct message to him from his father. How could his dad possibly know he would be sitting here reading it?

JJ's hands were shaking slightly as he read on.

'Hi JJ. I'm guessing right at this moment you're wondering why and how my note is here and to you personally. I'll do the how first. I knew there was a strong chance they would come for me, so I left the package for Marty to collect. If you're reading this then you have already met the marvelous Marty, so no explanations are needed on that count. I had every faith in him to get this to you just as I have every faith in you to help him find me. I know you're asking why this was not at the beginning of my notes. The answer's simple. Because you're my son. Because I know how thorough you are and how putting in a little bit of history at the start would whet your appetite and there would be no way you could resist reading to the end. Bet you did some more research too. The history lesson of parts one and two was one thing, the information contained in part three is another. How's the saying go? Leave the best 'til last. Well, the last part isn't exactly the best, but it is the most important. It's the information you need to share with Marty and Jake, he will arrive if he's not there already, and of course your very clever young friends. This is what they all need to know about. This is the part that will help you decide what to do next. I put my trust in you and my old friends to come up with a plan.'

JJ stopped and ran his hands through his hair. Marty was watching him from across the table. Studying his reaction in anticipation of the questions he knew would be asked of him. Marty got in first and fired the first question at JJ.

"How are you getting on?"

"How good was my dad, Marty? He knew we'd meet up and you'd get this to me. He knew you'd get Jake to join us. He wants me to read through and share the information with you. He wants us to come up with a plan."

From the tone of JJ's statement Marty could tell he was feeling a little emotional. Can't be easy finding out your dad's a fortune-teller, thought Marty. Even harder when he puts all his faith in you.

"Best I can offer is, that's your dad for you. If Brains put his faith in us, in you, then that's good enough for me. Read the stuff and then we can put all our heads together using what we know to plan our next move. Obi, go put the kettle on. Brains Junior, you get reading."

Sally had been listening to every word. She saw that Marty was trying to bring a little bit of light relief to the situation by asking Obi to make the tea. Sally joined in the fun.

"Two teas over here. Milk no sugar. Thanks Obi." She and Danny laughed.

"Who do you lot think I am? The general dogs body?" moaned Obi, refusing to see a funny side to his situation.

"If the cap fits." responded Danny with a grin that broke Obi's feeble resistance. With a shrug and a smile Obi went off to make the tea.

By the time he returned with a tray loaded with steaming mugs JJ was already reading on. Unsure of what he would find out, he had picked up his pencil, put his head down and began again from where he had left off.

Chapter 30

'The information that follows is about a group known simply as SPAWN, the Society for the Protection, Advancement and Welfare of the Nation. I first suspected such a group existed about thirty years ago. At the time, they didn't seem to be a great threat, so I didn't report my suspicions and we moved on to a new job. From what I know now, this group grew out of the remnants of the old eugenics movement and morphed into an organisation with much more sinister aims. At the end of these notes is a list of names of people passed to me who are reportedly members of this Society and who like to refer to themselves as Spawners. As you will see, their tentacles reach far and wide across the globe.

It was an old friend who got me back on the case when he sent me new information about a secretive organisation that had an ambition to rule the country according to its own philosophy. Johnny had found evidence that SPAWN did exist. He sent me a lot of information which you now have access to. I asked him how reliable it all was. He explained that he had been contacted by a fairly senior civil servant, a Doctor I believe. Someone he had befriended some years earlier who was clearly spooked and in need of his help. His friend knew of Johnny's past history. He knew about me, Marty, and Jake too. Johnny set up a rendezvous and they met up just once. He told Johnny he was actually a member of SPAWN himself and had been for a long time. He said when he had joined, he truly believed their aim was to improve the welfare of all people. Now he doubted that was ever the case. When the new Society President was elected, he said the real agenda became very clear. He told Johnny what they had planned was the free world's worst nightmare.'

'Johnny told me he had never seen his friend in such a state before. Absolutely terrified of being found out but determined to do something about it was how Johnny described him. Apparently as soon as he handed Johnny all the information, he left. Johnny said he literally ran away but not before he made Johnny promise to keep his involvement hidden. The odd contradiction, Johnny said, was that he ended by saying if Johnny ever needed his help, he would try to find the courage to stand up and be counted. Johnny said it felt like his friend hoped we could stop them somehow. So that's what he set out to do. Good old Johnny-Boy was always up for a challenge. The greater the odds the greater the satisfaction is what he always used to say.

I started looking into the information and at a few of the names on the list. Johnny did the same. He poked his nose around the Home Office whilst I called up some favours from some old friends at the MoD. We were both met with some very stony silences. Then came one of the saddest days. Johnny had been killed. I knew it was no accident. He sent me a last message telling me he knew they were on to him and probably me too, but he knew even knowing the danger he had placed me in I would carry on regardless. His message ended with just three words. Be very careful. Tell Marty and Jake no matter the odds we will get our satisfaction, but you must all be very, very, careful.'

JJ shot a glance across at Marty. He wondered how on earth the big man and four inexperienced friends would ever be able to bring down an organisation as powerful and connected as this. What on earth was his dad thinking? Was he mad?

As he put his teacup to his lips, he realized he was shaking a little. He drank down his tea hoping it would calm his nerves. It didn't. He read on anyway.

'I'm guessing you and your friends have looked at some of the information already. I'll keep this as short as I can. Try not to be too shocked by what this Society intends to do. Think about your current circumstances and then decide what you need to do. Take the fight to them, don't let them bring the fight to you. Come for me only if it's the right thing to do. I'll understand. You need to understand you're my son and I'll always be very proud of you. Tell Billy the same if he's there with you or when you see him next.

What's quite clear is that this so-called SPAWN has been waiting for the opportunity to rally its troops and take control of the country. It's unlikely they will stop there. I suspect they have their eyes on ruling the world. Events of the last few years have given them the perfect conditions to conduct their social experiments and to gradually erode the freedom of the people.

It could not have been any better for them as they could pronounce that all their actions were to ensure the health, safety, and welfare of the people. They could have no better alibi than that. Once taken, they have no intention of giving freedom back. Ever.

They have set out to purge society by stealth. SPAWN plans to carry out a systematic cull of the population under the banner of ensuring the salvation of all humanity. The planned removal of the underprivileged and the weak. Those that the eugenicists of old would term defective stock.

However, SPAWN turned eugenics on its head. Rather than nature, they consider nurture as far more contributory in shaping humanity. Nurture of the ideology that their truth and wisdom will bring salvation to the world. Nurture of the strong so that they become even stronger.

Their murderous intent is terrifying. Their actions are cold, calculated, and callous. Having infiltrated all walks of life it will be difficult to know who to trust. They are very powerful people with very powerful friends. These people plan to build a series of what they refer to as 'Recycling Plants' and 'Holiday Camps'. They have already constructed a pilot site and in all likelihood, this will be where they will take me. From the drawings given to us they would appear to be constructing the method and means to process those they identify as undesirable. To put no finer point on it, they're intending to build death camps.

How our inside informant got hold of the data I don't know but he provided details of the target groups. The old and infirm. The millions of people on waiting lists, people who cannot afford private treatment, people who would have to wait years to be treated. Then there are the millions of unemployed. The shifting economic sands and changes in consumer habits give little optimism for a swift revival of their fortunes. Our insider names the uneducated masses as another unfortunate group. The children who are so far behind that no amount of extra schooling will ever be enough to help them catch up. Millions of men, women and children chosen on the basis of economic worth. Chosen to serve SPAWNs purpose.

I think the thought of the consequences of SPAWNs vision must have horrified him. There was one final group that would certainly have given him the jitters. Those that challenge or threaten SPAWNs Mandate. He would have considered himself included in it if he were ever to be found out. It's the group Johnny was in and now I have fallen into it too.

SPAWN has created their opportunity by fanning the flames of fear about the future of the world. Expressing their concern for the welfare of humanity and the need to address the global crises.

Contrary to what they claim, they have been systematically destroying the health and well-being of humanity. With the power they now possess they intend to begin reducing the population by removing those they deem to be economically worthless together with anyone who they believe challenges them.

From what the insider gave Johnny, it looks like they plan to begin what he described as their Mandate for Salvation very soon. Numbers will start small and grow to many thousands being processed each week in the first year. How many after that he couldn't predict. Possibly over a million a year and no-one would really know so no-one would really care. Even if anyone did, their voice would be silenced, snuffed out like a candle in the rain. By then the Spawners would be too powerful to stop but for now we must believe it is still possible.'

JJ knew he would have to brief the others on what his father had found out about the Spawners. He knew he would have to précis his notes. No way would they sit still and listen to him for more than fifteen minutes. Anyway, the most important part was about what was happening now. Part three. This was the really scary part. The rest, of course, was history.

He read the final paragraph. Another personal message from his dad to him.

'Whatever you do next be very careful. Trust in Marty and Jake. Listen to what they say but decide for yourself. Be prepared that it may be too late to save me but not too late to be able to save many others. Do what you can, but please, for me and your mum, be careful, stay safe and stay alive.'

JJ stared down at the table. He had gone pale, almost white in the face. Sally was first to notice his obvious distress. She walked across and squeezed herself next to him, sharing his chair.

"Everything ok JJ? Why don't you take a break and finish the rest in a bit? In fact, I think we could all do with a break. Let's me and you go and make a few sarnies and cold drinks for everyone."

Sally took hold of his hand and gave it a gentle squeeze. Simultaneously she bent forward so she could look him in the eye and gave him a reassuring smile. It had the desired effect. The colour returned to JJ's face. He nodded in the affirmative and smiled back at her. She took him off to the kitchen still holding hands. Marty smiled at them for a second time. That's what life should be about, he thought, being young and in love.

There was a sudden loud knock at the front door. Marty's

expression changed in an instant. He got to his feet primed for action. Coiled and ready. Stay calm, he said to himself it's probably Jake arriving, and about time too.

Chapter 31

When the Cleos-cum-porters arrived with two more casualties there were only two patients still occupying beds in the Treatment Room. They were welcomed by an enthusiastic Dr Sterbenson.

"What have we got here then?" he asked more of himself than to the two make-shift porters.

He cast a cursory glance over the two battered bodies cramped together on the trolley in front of him. Both of them looked to be in a very bad way. He laid his fingers onto the neck of the one nearest to him and felt for a pulse.

"Ah, no pulse. This one can be moved on."

He walked around the trolley to look at the second of the two. Eyes wide open, his body limp and lifeless. No need to check this one, thought the good doctor.

"This one's definitely a goner too. Take both of them off to the Recycling Plant. Put them in the fridge next to our friend the eunuch."

"Yes sir." came a very respectful reply.

They knew full well when the doctor said jump, you jumped.

This was one place you wouldn't want to visit as a patient. If you did, you had bought a one-way ticket for a journey to oblivion.

Henry was the first to take the journey. He had died in absolute agony whilst Dr Sterbenson watched on making notes in his little blue book.

The woman and the young boy were still undergoing treatment. Both were on their third dose, and both were in excruciating agony. He didn't expect the young boy to survive the fourth injection. The woman on the other hand he hoped would last for a few more yet. It was all neatly recorded in his precious little book. Disappointingly Henry had lasted for just two jabs. The serum was working but it needed a bit of tweaking.

This was the culmination of years of collaborative endeavor. For many years his mentor had been working with the USA on the development of suitable drugs and the appropriate dosage for use in the legal process of death by lethal injection. When Dr Sterbenson joined as his protégé the Professor had been working with sodium thiopental alternately known by its trade name, sodium pentothal.

As Master and Apprentice, during the first decade of the twenty-first century they began working with pentobarbital as a possible alternative. The two men worked on the hypothesis that the most efficient process would be a single injection to induce the required states of unconsciousness, paralysis of the respiratory muscles and ultimately cardiac arrest.

They felt the method of using three separate intravenous injections, pentobarbital, pancuronium bromide and potassium chloride, was cumbersome and inefficient. They had noted the development of the Ohio Protocol which eliminated the use of the latter two drugs but replaced them with the use of an intra-muscular injection of midazolam and hydromorphone.

Another reason, although of less real concern to the two scientists, was that there was evidence from the USA of executions resulting in the condemned suffering pain, convulsions, and other issues, in some cases for over forty minutes. They had no concern over the suffering inflicted they simply thought it should be quicker. They needed it to be quicker and less messy.

For the past ten years Dr Sterbenson had worked long and hard in his quest to develop a fast-acting single jab that would result in death within a maximum two-minute period. He had religiously recorded every detail of his work in his little blue book together with the company names and contacts of those that had, and still were, supplying him with the various drugs. Now he was on the verge of a ground-breaking success.

By the morning of the second day both the young boy and the woman had been moved to the Recycling Plant. Preparation was now being made for the expected new arrivals.

Dr Sterbenson and his small team were busy in the laboratory checking the vials and their contents. They arranged them on the bench in order of concentration, starting with the strongest on the left and ranging to the weakest concentration on the right. The team had worked well into the evening of the night before preparing the doses in accordance with the Doctor's instructions. The young nurse who had fetched the glass jar placed a large box of syringes beside the vial furthest on her right. Everything was ready, all they needed now was some more patients.

At about eight thirty that morning their first visitor of the day breezed in. Caroline thought she would spare a few minutes to catch up with Dr Sterbenson, Needles as she liked to call him, and to make sure he and his team were ready for the day ahead. His eyes lit up the moment he saw her enter the room and he rushed out to greet her.

"Hello Needles. You're looking fine and dandy this morning."

He gave her a beaming smile. He loved it that she had a pet name for him that only she used. The flame in his heart still burned strong. He hadn't given up on winning her over and probably never would.

"My dearest Caroline I was hoping you'd pop in today. I have a small gift for you. Nothing special, just something I put together as a little memento for you. Close your eyes and just wait there for a second."

She smiled at him as he scurried away. Just like a little pet dormouse she thought to herself, her smile turning into a little chuckle. Surprisingly, even to herself, she did have a soft spot for him, and she liked it when he did silly little things for her. Everyone feels good when they know someone really cares about them and Caroline was no exception to that particular rule. She closed her eyes and waited patiently for him to return bearing his gift.

"Hold out your hands." his voice gatecrashed the darkness in her mind.

He placed the jar carefully into her cupped hands and she caressed the cold glass jar with her fingers.

"What on earth can this be?" she asked in a quizzical, playful tone.

She cocked her head a little to her left, eyes still closed, teasing him with her act of shy anticipation.

"Open your eyes and see."

She could hear the expectation and excitement in his voice as he spoke. Caroline looked down at the jar and then up to him. She could see he was fit to burst and that he was just dying to tell her what it was.

"They're his. I preserved them especially for you. I knew you'd want to have them as a keepsake. Was I right, was I?"

She smiled, an involuntary action to a moment of pleasure.

"Absolutely. What a wonderful gift. You really are too good to me. You know me all too well. Every time I look at these, I'll be reminded of what Julia will never experience again. Poor old Henry. I assume the rest of him is at the plant keeping cool. I hope you treated him as a special case."

"Absolutely." came the nuanced reply.

Caroline laughed. She had thought of something else she found funny.

"Of course, we know someone else who could do with these. Have you got another pair for the Prime Minister? He lost his ages ago!"

The two of them burst out into side-splitting laughter. By the time Caroline left tears were running down her cheeks. Sometimes it's good to laugh, she thought as she glanced back and gave him a quick wave. Now she was off to have some more fun.

It was very soon after Caroline had left that they had an influx of new patients. The first to be welcomed into the Treatment Room were a young boy and a woman. This time they were mother and son. Both were badly beaten. The boy, Dr Sterbenson decided, was of little use to him as he had also been stabbed and was very close to death. He selected a vial from the left of the row and gave the boy a single injection. Within half an hour the boy was being taken away to be put on ice with the other five frozen corpses.

There seemed to be a trend beginning as another two young teenagers arrived. Their stay was very short lived as they were DOA.

Bodies were starting to pile up in the Recycling Plant and they were expecting a delivery after lunch that would almost certainly overwhelm both the Treatment Room and the Recycling Plant. Time to crack on he thought, no rest for the wicked.

Things slowed for a while and allowed the team to focus on treating the woman. Picking up where they left off the night before they began her treatment with the equivalent third dose they had administered to the previous incumbent of the bed. All useful data in the calculation of the dosage for the perfect single jab for women in the thirty to sixty age group. In due course there would be enough data to model the dosage and the time it took to complete the treatment.

By the end of the week, they were expecting to have processed many more of the holiday campers, twelve at a time, in readiness for a new intake.

Dr Sterbenson was looking forward to treating the younger age groups as he expected a much faster throughput once he had established the ideal dosage. A ten-minute assessment, one jab, a ten-minute observation and then discharged to the plant room.

In, out and no fuss. He liked the efficiency of it all.

When the two quite healthy women arrived to take up occupancy there were smiles all round.

"What happened to these two?" he asked, making an entry into his blue book.

"These are two of the dissenters. After spending time together in the small waiting room with the others they fainted. As there are only six chairs in the Therapy Room, we were told to bring these two straight to you. Sir."

The Cleo added the 'sir' not necessarily out of respect for rank but more out of the fear of the man.

"Excellent. Put them on the beds over there next to the other woman. Strap them in nice and tight for me please."

The Doctor and his team worked on the three women throughout the afternoon. Their efforts resulted in another page of notes in his book and a significant amount of pain and suffering for the patients. One of which got discharged to the plant room midway through the session.

When word came that there would be another nine, three men and six women, on their way later in the evening Dr Sterbenson sent two of his minions off to get coffee and sandwiches for everyone. As it turned out Caroline had sent four of the women straight to the Recycling Plant. That left five, three men and two women, which pleased him. That meant he could accommodate seven wounded protestors when they arrived. He envisaged a very satisfying and productive night ahead.

Chapter 32

Marty arrived at the door just as the second knock echoed in the hallway. He braced himself just in case, always expect the unexpected was one of his many mottos. He stretched out his hand and opened the door. He was right, the person standing on the other side of the door wasn't Jake. This was definitely an unexpected visitor. Marty recognized who it was not because they had met before but from a strange familiarity and a description he had been given by a loving father. The tall, broad-shouldered figure standing in front of him wearing a big grin was Brains' younger son, Billy.

"Hi I'm Billy. I've been told my brother is here with you. You're Marty aren't you."

With a rather puzzled look on his face Marty invited Billy in and called out to the others.

"Folks it's not Jake. JJ, I think you should come and say hello. It's someone you know well."

The two brothers bumped fists in the hallway. It was the nearest either would get to showing affection to the other. Billy put his bag down on the floor and followed JJ and Marty into the room with the others. Marty was eager to know how Billy knew who he was. JJ was just as eager to know how Billy had found them and how their mum was. Sally was just pleased to see him. The other two seemed non-plussed by it all. They were waiting for Jake and from how Marty described him the goodies he would be bringing with him.

Sally could see Billy was about to get bombarded with questions so moved swiftly forward, gave him a sisterly hug, and sat him down at the table.

"To save asking a thousand and one questions, why don't you tell us how you found us and how you know who Marty is. I suspect the two might be connected."

JJ and Marty nodded their approval. Billy looked at the three of them and then spoke directly to JJ.

"You know what mums like. It didn't take long before she was itching to come back home. She was driving herself and us crazy because she was worrying about you, dad, the house, and because she wanted to be doing something. You can imagine how irritable mum was just waiting around with nothing to do. In the end we gave in and agreed that me and mum would drive back to our house but at the slightest sign of trouble would head back to Grandad's. We decided not to text you until we got home. We thought that was best for a number of reasons."

JJ smiled at his younger brother. A sympathetic smile mixed with a great degree of empathy. He could imagine exactly what their mum would have been like and why she would not have wanted him to know what they were about to do.

"When we got back home it was clear someone had visited the

house in our absence. Mum had a feeling you'd been back but there were also signs someone else had been ferreting around. It didn't take long for us to find out who it was. We'd only been in the house a few minutes when we heard someone coming in through the back door. Before we could decide what to do next, he called out to mum, shouted that everything was cool, and that he was coming through to join us. Mum knew who he was as soon as she saw him."

Billy paused and changed the focus of his attention. Typical thought JJ, my brothers going for the dramatic effect as usual.

"Marty, it was your friend Jake."

"Let me guess. Brains sent him a message telling him where some of our old gear was stashed and that was somewhere in or near your house. He saw you arrive, thought he'd go say hello, and then you persuaded him to let you come with him. I doubt that took much. Jake always wants to chatter on to somebody about something. Usually complete gibberish. So where is the loony tune?"

Billy laughed. Marty certainly knew his friend very well. Jake had hardly stopped talking during the entire journey. Billy wondered if that was another reason why their mum had insisted on staying behind at the house.

"He's parking the car. Should be here in a few minutes. He did give my eardrums a bit of a bash on the way here. Made me laugh though. Told me a few stories about the things he and dad got into when they were younger. Told me a bit about you too Marty."

"Yeh I'll bet he did. I wouldn't believe everything that headcase tells you. One thing for sure though, he's a genius at what he does and if he's brought with him what I think he has then everything will go with a bang whatever plan we come up with."

As Marty uttered the last word the doorbell rang three times. Trust Jake to ring loudly rather than knock quietly, thought Marty. Thinks he's using some spy signal like ring three times and wait for the password the idiot.

Marty went and let him in. He had with him a big old dusty black suitcase and on his back an old-style military rucksack. Not the most inconspicuous figure to come knocking on the front door at a time when drawing attention was the last thing they wanted. Jake's boundless enthusiasm and his delight at seeing Marty prevented any rebuke. Jake was Jake and that was all there was to it.

Now they were seven.

They exchanged pleasantries and short introductions. A rather disgruntled Obi was dispatched to make the teas and coffees again but lightened up when Danny said he'd do it as it had to be his turn. Danny knew full well that Obi wanted to be there when Jake opened up his bags hoping to see guns and explosives by the bucket load pop out. Obi wasn't disappointed at all by what emerged.

Jake had collected the suitcase from under the garden shed floor at the back of Brains' house. When the team disbanded, they had entrusted their dad with keeping a special collection of items in a safe place just in case they were ever called into action again. They were items with a very long shelf life. Jake laid them out very carefully on the table.

Two SA80's, four Browning 9mm pistols, four silencers, extra magazines, and plenty of ammunition for all six guns. It looked like they were prepared for quite a battle should the need ever arise. Next came eight oblong blocks about six inches long double wrapped in brown greaseproof paper together with a rectangular cardboard box slightly longer and wider than a school lunchbox.

Jake carefully lifted up the lid of the box and peered inside. His expression suggested the contents had lasted the test of time and were in good condition. He picked the top one out, slowly unwrapped the paper surrounding it and unwound it from the piece of card. He placed the two wires carefully between his fingers keeping the ends separated and wrapped them a few times around his index finger leaving the attached thin silver cylinder perpendicular to the back of his hand and suspended about an inch away from it. He lifted it up and gave it a quick kiss.

"Hello my little beauty. Long time no see."

Marty looked at the others.

"It's ok you'll get used to it. He thinks they're all his old friends. Then he gets upset when he blows them up. Daft as a brush he may be, but he knows exactly what he's doing and what the effect will be. He can blow up anything. From a hundred and ten floor building to the head of a pin."

After carefully packing the detonator away Jake moved on to emptying the top of his rucksack ignoring Marty completely. He piled various bits of electronic equipment and a small tool kit next to the cardboard box and then pulled out a brand-new box putting it down with a huge grin. Inside the box was a complete long range communication set comprising of four earpieces and a central hub.

"As most of our stuff was old and ancient like you Marty, I thought I'd bring us into the twenty-first century. I use this kit to communicate with my special effects team when we're on location. It works a treat. Keeps us all on the same page. It's for people like me who just love to talk, even has a range of over two hundred miles so we can talk more often! I knew you'd like the thought of that."

Marty feigned a wince, grabbed Jake, encircled him in his huge arms and gave him a big bear hug.

"I'd squeeze the breath out of you if I didn't like you so much, you fool."

He let Jake go and they laughed together.

Now all they needed was a plan.

Chapter 33

The body count was mounting up. There were nine in the fridge, two waiting to be discharged from the Treatment Room and very soon a delivery from the morning protests. A few from the delivery would possibly go to the Treatment Room first but that would still leave too many bodies to put on ice in the refrigeration area. It was time to start up the plant and do a test run.

The building had been constructed to house both the refrigeration room and a series of multi-chamber incinerators built and designed by a reputable crematorium company. The company was owned and run by SPAWN.

Construction at the holiday camp had taken place shortly after the building of the much-publicized emergency hospitals. It had never been seen as an issue that the emergency hospitals were never occupied by patients. That was never the purpose SPAWN had planned for them anyway. They were destined to become bigger and more efficient versions of the Treatment Room in turn feeding bigger versions of the Recycling Plant. One of which Obi's dad was about to begin work on.

The task of managing the test run had fallen on to the shoulders of Dr K. The company had supplied a supervisor and two technicians to run and maintain the plant, all three indoctrinated into SPAWN. Loyal Spawners. For the test run, the heavy lifting was to be done by four hand-picked Cleos. It was expected that in future at the larger plants the manual labour would be done by selected workers who would be given a simple choice. Work at the plant or join your family for a single jab and come back as a welcomed visitor.

The data collected from the test run was to be used by SPAWNs mathematical modelers to calculate the likely number of bodies that could be processed on a larger scale. The current assumptions feeding the model were first of all that there would be six hospitals each with a capacity of five hundred beds. It was assumed a patient's waiting time would be up to one hour. The invited patients would arrive at a rate of fifty per hour and the hospitals would work an eight-hour day. Based on the work of Dr Sterbenson the second assumption was that patients would be undergoing treatment with a single jab followed by a thirty-to-forty-five-minute wait before being discharged to the plant. This data would be updated following the Doctor's latest trials and most certainly looked to be an over-estimate.

The test Recycling Plant had been designed with a large refrigeration room and a single bank of four incinerators, each capable of processing three bodies at a time. Until the test run data was available the modelers had used the company's data sheets which suggested a time of between twenty to thirty minutes to complete the incineration process. Allowing for loading and cleaning a time of fifty minutes had been inputted into the model.

There would be an individual plant for each of the hospitals and each plant would be constructed to house ten banks of four incinerators. The Recycling Plants would operate on a twelve-hour shift basis. The final assumption was that the hospitals and the plant would operate the whole year round on a 24/7 program.

The results of running the model showed that hospital capacity and transportation were the limiting factors as the plants could process almost seven times more units in a single day.

The current advice was that there may be no immediate need to run the plants for more than a single twelve-hour shift. Further data and analysis were needed on hospital throughput, which would only be possible once the system was up and running.

The modelers reported to SPAWNs President that they predicted that the best available data indicated that the system would be capable of processing just under one million people per year. On that basis the program would have to run for between six to ten years to sweep the country clean. The model did not account for any increase in particular populations as this was the responsibility of the social scientists and their own modelers to predict.

The President was not best pleased with the numbers. It did not fit with SPAWNs five-year plan. This was just not good enough.

The President knew and trusted that Dr Sterbenson would ensure the procurement of sufficient doses of his drug via SPAWNs own giant pharmaceutical company. That was not going to be an issue. The drug would be legitimately supplied under a registered tradename. The Director General would be tasked with ensuring the Government initially funded the production of the first five million doses. The added bonus was that SPAWN would make a tidy profit from the order to add to its' swelling coffers.

The main issue was with the efficiency of the hospitals. Running the programme for twenty-four hours a day would triple the throughput but would require considerable staffing levels. A number of suitable candidates for directly administering the jab had already been identified from the medical and scientific communities. Menial workers would not be hard to find. Especially once the workers realized it meant safety and security for them and their families and with an alternative too terrible to contemplate. Besides, experiments at the Holiday Camp had shown that with the right incentive even mothers could be turned into frenzied killers.

In a personal message to both Dr Sterbenson and Dr K the President had made the importance of the data from the trials and test runs abundantly clear. Both men were under extreme pressure to deliver results. The former was unconcerned. He was relaxed and enjoying his work. The latter was a nervous wreck and feeling the pressure. This was very evident from his manner and tone as he barked the order to fire up the incinerators.

Twelve of the thirteen bodies were loaded into the incinerators as Dr K watched anxiously on making copious notes about the process. He knew he couldn't afford to miss a single detail which just piled on the pressure and added to his already nervous condition. His biggest concern was the one he viewed as the closest to home. He knew he would have to report chapter and verse to Caroline then answer any questions she may have. He wasn't a brave man. Always happy to act tough but that was what it was, an act. He was at his best when ordering others to inflict the pain and suffering whilst he stood and watched with a twisted sense of enjoyment.

Caroline scared him. Really scared him. The very thought of the psychotic doctor and what she could have others do to him terrified him. What she might do to him personally, hands on so to speak, terrified him even more. No, he really wasn't a brave man. Not brave at all and as for briefing the President, well that was her job not his. That was definitely above his pay grade and way, way beyond the limit of his nervous disposition. He comforted himself with the thought that she would be the one doing that job.

Thirty minutes and pages of notes later Dr K was standing in his shirt sleeves with his blue jacket and white coat draped over his left arm. Gets very, very hot after 20 mins was the latest addition to his notes. He had assumed the supervisor was recording the actual figures and he would be able to collect them off him at the end of the test.

A moment of sheer panic passed over him. What if the supervisor wasn't doing his job properly? They would both be for it, but he'd be treated the worst because he was in overall charge. He rushed over to the control panel to be met with a malevolent glare from the supervisor and a cursory glance from one of the technicians.

"Got a problem?" rasped the supervisor, throat dry from the

heat and low humidity.

"No, no problem. Just wanted to record the temperature in my book. I know you're recording all the numbers, but I wanted to know exactly how hot it was in here now. That's all."

"31 degrees." came the gruff response with an unmistakable message of go away. "Centigrade." He added in a derogatory tone.

As someone who had spent a lifetime recognizing even the slightest nuance in a situation, especially if it threatened his well-being, Dr K retreated back to his original observation post. The Cleos had watched the proceedings, jackets off and sleeves rolled up. The sight of the scrawny man scurrying across the floor like a frightened rabbit brought some amusement to their tiny minds. They were not at all amused by the heat.

"It's going to get a lot bloody worse once the next lot arrive. I've heard from my mate he loaded over fifty of them protestors onto his truck and is heading here to dump them with us. Probably more like twenty I'll bet. Old Petey's always been a bit prone to exaggerate." A hot Cleo muttered as he wiped the sweat off his forehead and from the back of his tree-trunk thick neck.

The other three shook their heads in some sort of yes and no agreement.

"We need to ask for a supply of cold drinks if we're expected to do this all day long."

"Your idea so you go ask. The little weasel over there doesn't look very happy."

All four looked across at Dr K in unison. It didn't take much of an IQ to see he was hot, bothered, and in such an agitated state that any request put to him would go exactly nowhere. Nowhere perhaps other than a leap out of the job and into the fire.

Best I bring drinks for myself next time, thought the nominated Cleo, don't think I'll stick my neck out for those three losers today. Or any day for that matter.

"No," he replied. "I don't think I will."

PART 5

The Good, the Bad, and the Plan

Chapter 34

By mid-afternoon on the second day Jessie and Katie were working side-by-side on the production line. Most of the younger girls had struggled a bit to start with but the mothers had moved among them to help them along. Kelly had stayed with them and was now acting as the line supervisor.

The two bully boys lurked in the background occasionally giving their black batons a swing just to show they were ready, extremely willing, and very able to inflict a beating on anyone who stepped out of line. A Cleo stood by the door, presumably as back-up, with the changing of the guard every hour.

Jessie's prime objective was to keep Katie well out of harm's way. So far so good, she thought.

From a glance across at the boys' production line Jessie could see the situation was pretty much the same as theirs. The man in the white coat had left a few hours ago leaving Sam in charge. The younger boys were being helped by the older ones and they seemed to be getting on with the work. There had been a slight ruckus a while earlier when one of the younger boys started crying and had a tantrum, but it was quickly sorted out by one of the mothers. Jessie wondered if it was the boy's own mother, not that it really mattered. All now seemed calm.

At five o'clock they were told to stop working. Kelly assisted by the two youths lined the girls up in twos. Sam and his two sidekicks did the same with the boys. Orders were barked at them, and they obediently marched back to the food hall for their evening meal.

Jessie studied the women's faces for the second time that day still hoping she would see her mother smiling back at her. They were the same faces. Her mother still wasn't there. Try as hard as she could, she couldn't stop the wave of panic coming over her. Jessie had seen what these people were capable of and now she sensed something bad had happened to her mum. Without realizing it she squeezed Katie's hand so hard it made her young sister cry out in pain. Jessie scanned the room in an instant to check no-one had paid any notice to her sister's yelp. Thankfully there was too much background noise for anyone to hear.

"Sorry Katie." she whispered. "I didn't mean to squeeze so hard. Grab a tray and follow me. Ok?"

Katie smiled up at her big sister and nodded. She trusted in Jessie to look after her and keep her safe from the nasty people. Katie still looked at the world through the innocent eyes of the young child she still was. In contrast Jessie had grown up faster than she would have liked during the last twenty-four hours. She felt for the phone in her pocket. Jessie trusted in her big brother in the same way Katie trusted in her. Obi will come for us. I don't know how, she thought, but he will find a way. Jessie clung to that hope. It was all she had left.

Jessie didn't know that her mother was only a short distance away from her. There were only two of the six women left after the Therapy Room session with the dark-haired woman in the white coat. Her mother and one other woman of about the same age. The six women had been subjected to different degrees of treatment as part of Caroline's physical and psychological experiment to make them 'better' citizens, citizens of her own Oceania.

In her early teens Caroline had read George Orwell's 1984 many times. The book enthralled her. She especially enjoyed reading about Winston's visit to Room 101.

In Caroline's Therapy Room Jessie's mother had watched as four of her companions had succumbed to the pain. She had fought to the bitter end to stay alive. Fought to hold on to her own thoughts and beliefs but it had been hard. Her mind was in a state of utter befuddlement. She knew she was still in the land of the living and that was about it. She had no idea why two of them had been spared. Caroline knew. Caroline admired strong women and these two were definitely that. They deserved to spend a little bit longer on this earth, Caroline had thought. These two deserved to be allowed to die with a little dignity. Swift and relatively painless deaths. She could rely on Needles to see to that later.

There were now five in the small cell a short stroll from the Therapy Room. The two women had been put in with the last three of the men. None were in particularly good shape.

When the door had opened, he was expecting another dosing with the cold-water jet. His initial surprise at seeing two women being hauled in was quickly replaced by a feeling of rage and frustration. Two young boys and now two innocent women. He was keeping score in his head for when the time came for retribution as he was sure it would. He could sense that time was drawing ever closer. He had a feeling, his sixth sense was tingling, a telepathic intuition that help was coming soon.

The two women were dazed and confused about where they were and, in some sense even who they were. With the help of one of his fellow survivors he eased each of them into a more comfortable position sitting with their backs supported by the damp wall. He wished he had some water he could offer them, but he knew any call to the guards would not end well. The only water they would get would be from the end of a pressurized hosepipe. At least they were still alive. He expected that when they were ready to talk the women would tell a sad story about some that had not survived the treatment. He remembered the young girl and her friends he had seen. No doubt these women were connected to those children in some way. Most likely their mothers. His line of thought made his blood boil. He punched the wall in sheer anger.

"Steady on friend." came the whisper. "Save your strength. Maybe we'll get one chance to have a go back. Likely just the two of us. I guess neither of us is in the best of health, but he looks hurt pretty bad over there, too bad to fight back I think."

He appreciated the sentiment. It brought him back from the brink, back to his training. Back to the knowledge that the key to winning the fight was to stay calm, stay in control. Succumb to anger and rage and you create a greater enemy within. He remembered now, feed your enemies fury, provoke an uncontrolled attack and the advantage will always be yours. Dead men's fury the team had called it. Their enemies last futile act before they sent them on a one-way trip into the valley of death, no bugle charge, no galloping horses, no heroes.

"Sorry I lost it there for a minute.' He paused. "I agree. They give us any chance to hit back, we take it, but let me take the lead. Believe me when I say I'm no stranger to violence but let's stay alive a little longer eh. Let's try and keep them alive a little longer too."

"I knew you were here for a different reason to the rest of us. You're some sort of trained soldier or spy, aren't you? I watched you earlier when those boys were brought in and it all fits together now. You're more than just an unfortunate whose here because he spoke out. Just be sure I'll do the best I can when you give me the nod. It doesn't take much to work out if we do nothing were dead anyway."

The exchange followed by a glance at the women was sufficient acknowledgement and a signal to end the conversation. He wasn't sure what, if anything, the two of them could do in reality but at least it had given the other guy hope. A brave guy who deserved at least that.

Chapter 35

The grumbling Cleo had been right about Old Petey. Nonetheless it had been hard work unloading the refrigerated lorry and moving the twenty-six bodies into the Recycling Plant.

Across the country other dead protesters were being taken to a chain of local undertakers, another enterprise controlled by SPAWN, for disposal locally. A fact of little interest to the four grunts on their journey between the lorry and the plant.

Dr K had instructed them to put the bodies into the cold storage room alongside Henry who had pride of place and was waiting as patiently as a dead man could to go on his final excursion. The temperature in the main room was too high to leave bodies lying about for a couple of hours he had told them.

They were not best pleased with the idea of moving them in only to have to move them all out again a short while later. Reluctantly they complied having contemplated the result of the alternative option. Even with their limited intellect they decided they didn't fancy moving hot dead flesh about after it had sat for hours in thirty-degree heat. Especially as it looked like they were all going to be stuck there together for a good many more hours.

"Sir. Can we go get something to eat and drink now? We'll only be a few minutes. With this heat and all."

Finally, the heat, their thirst, and their hunger had won over the lack of courage from before.

Dr K looked at his watch. Five thirty-seven. He was expecting a visit but not until after six. The thought of a cool drink and the mention of food suddenly made him feel parched and hungry himself. His heightened state of anxiety and insecurity had masked his physical needs until now. No harm in taking a short break. Give the techies time to get everything ready for the next batch. Dr Bramney would understand he muttered to himself rather unconvincingly.

"Okay. Fifteen minutes and be back here prompt. Be late and you'll end up in there."

He pointed towards the incinerators.

"Bring some food and drink back for those three. Understand."

He put full emphasis on the last word, mustering as much authority and veiled threat into his tone as he could. The four men nodded in unison for a second time. However, their compliance had nothing to do with any fear of him or his implied consequence.

They knew if they just went without his permission, he couldn't stop them and it was highly unlikely he would want to make enemies of them, they were Cleos after all. He wasn't that stupid. Anyway, it was much more likely they would cook him long before one of their own. Dr K knew they knew he was all mouth and no trousers.

The Cleos ambled off and Dr K followed, relieved to get a breath of cool fresh air. Make a note the heat may present a real problem flashed into his mind, adding to his disquiet with the situation he now found himself in. He didn't feel confident highlighting possible problems. He was well aware it wasn't going to be the best approach to tell her things she wouldn't want to hear. Better to let someone else be the bearer of bad tidings. Perhaps he could prime the technical supervisor to tell her, yes, that would be the way to do it. He smiled to himself and went off to enjoy the respite.

Thirty minutes later they had all returned and the incinerators were being fired up for the next twelve customers. Henry's patient wait was about to be over.

Dr K was going into overload and was flapping about in anticipation of the expected visitor. He didn't want to keep everything on hold for too long for fear of mutiny in the ranks. A mixed expression of relief and panic swept across his face as Caroline entered the hot, sweat-infused plant room. She had come to say one last farewell to Henry. Not a fond or sentimental farewell. Caroline just wanted to feel good as she watched him burn.

"Sign this."

She handed Dr K a death certificate to sign. A little present to send to Julia. Maybe when they meet up next Julia can hear the whole story chapter and verse. Caroline laughed.

Dr K almost fainted from the shock of the mere sight of her laughing and from the fear of whatever she was going to do next. She scared him right down to the marrow. He signed the certificate and barked orders to the others to get started. His fear of her made him determined to show her he was in full command of the situation. Show her how they all jumped to his command.

Caroline was too absorbed to notice, watching gleefully as Henry disappeared out of her life forever. Even more satisfying was the thought he had left Julia's life too. It was a hollow victory. Caroline knew only too well he would never be gone from Julia's heart.

Bringing her focus back to the things at hand, she told Dr K to make sure he had collected any personal effects from the protestors so that they could be identified. Each would need to have a death certificate raised and for these they would show a virus infection as the cause of their demise. If we already have total control of the people, do we really need to do this now, wondered Dr K. No way was he brave enough to ask her that.

"What about the others." he asked instead and instantly regretted his own stupidity.

"They're not a problem you idiot. The holidaymakers were all sent a personal invitation, so we know exactly who they are. Their certificates are already in the system. As for my special guests, they were hand-picked and collected straight from their homes. You just focus on your job and leave the thinking to me. Got it."

"Got it." he concurred meekly.

With a sigh of relief, Dr K watched as Caroline left him to get on with his task. He had given her a short update on the process and the timings he had recorded so far. She seemed pleased with his results but then it was always difficult to read her mood.

The bodies of two more women had arrived just before she had left. Two more of Dr Sterbenson's test subjects thought Dr

K. He was envious of him for two reasons. His closeness to Dr Bramney and his high-profile research that was seen as so important to the cause. There was no love lost between the two of them. They were colleagues at best, friends they would never be.

Caroline had one more stop to make before she returned to her apartment in the accommodation block specially selected for her arrival at the Holiday Camp. Her condo as she called it. She just wanted to pop in to check Needles and his team were coping with the new influx of patients. She knew a second lorry had arrived with some wounded protestors who had been sent directly to the Treatment Room. She was also aware she had instructed the Cleos to take the remaining three men and two women across to him. They had served their purpose and provided her with some useful data. She intended to continue her experimental therapy with some new volunteers.

When she waltzed in Needles was busy talking to his young female assistant. The young woman was clearly his new protégé. He turned and greeted her with a gleam in his eye.

"Everything ok?" she asked with a warm smile.

"As you can see," he replied waving his arm in an arc towards the occupied beds. "Were now at full capacity and I've got another eight waiting in the room opposite. I hope you don't mind but I sent a message to your Cleos to keep the five you were working on in their room for the time being. I said I would ask for them to be brought across later this evening. We just need to do some work with these patients first. Should get some useful results as they are from younger age groups across both sexes. Just twelve would have sufficed but we'll manage the twenty. Will old

Dr Anxiety be able to cope when I send this lot down to him?"

Caroline shrugged.

"Well, he better. I see your training up your young assistant. Do you think she'll be able to take on the running of one of the new hospitals when the time comes? I'd like you to run the first and her the second, then each of you take on an apprentice. That way we could then open up the next two for business. A repeat would then give us a competent person in all six. Would that work?"

"Absolutely." Came the instant reply. "Young Alice is probably ready now and certainly more than capable of overseeing operations at a hospital."

"Good, that's settled then. I'll let you carry on in peace. Thanks once again for my special present. You know me too well you do."

Caroline smiled and a hint of playful wickedness flickered in her eyes. Dr Sterbenson blushed. If only there could be something more between them. He stopped himself just in time from saying something really stupid and embarrassing himself in front of her and his team. He did his best to stutter a short reply.

"I do, don't I." was all he could muster.

Things were going well for Caroline. All the pieces were starting to come together, the finishing touches to SPAWNs grand design. She strode off as happy as Larry back to her condo. She checked the time. Just coming up to six forty. Enough time for a bite to eat and to prepare the presentation for her briefing later in the evening.

The meeting at eight needed no pre-planning but the briefing at ten needed a bit more thought. Relaxed and smiling to herself she skipped into her small kitchen to make some dinner. Yes, so far, so good, she thought to herself. Nothing and no-one left to stop us now. It's downhill all the way to the finish line.

Chapter 36

Having admired all the hardware, the old and the new that Jake had brought with him, Marty was busy checking over the guns and ammunition. All looked to be in good working order. Obi watched on with wide eyed anticipation.

"Will they all work?" he asked, hoping for an affirmative and the offer of a closer look at one of the handguns.

"Won't know for sure until we fire them but there should be no reason why not. You look keen to get your hands on one. Watched a lot of blood and guts thrillers, have we? This isn't a movie my young friend this is real life. If we have cause to find out if these all work, then someone won't be walking away. It'll be no picnic, no gung-ho John Wayne movie, no A-Team shootout where no-one ever dies. Kill or be killed. Two simple choices, live or die. Take one of these and that's where you'll be at. Understand?"

Obi nodded. He had watched a lot of violent movies but that was nothing compared to the time he had spent playing video games in what he now considered his younger days.

"I understand. It is my family as well as JJ's dad were planning to rescue remember. My family and I want the chance to do whatever I can. I know you're one of the best and I'm a quick learner so just show me what I need to do. You know you'll need a good wingman and that'll be me."

Marty sighed. This kid's determined to get himself shot, brave but naive.

"Ok. On one condition. You always do exactly what I tell you. Got it?"

"Got it." Obi said with a huge grin on his face. He'd follow his newfound hero into a fight with anyone, anywhere, anytime. That was a no-brainer. But they still needed a plan.

With the table cleared Sally and JJ laid out the drinks and the plates of sandwiches. Food for thought. Together with Danny, these two were definitely the brains of the operation. Danny had been talking to Jake about the comms system and how they could combine it with JJ's dad's tracking system to give on the ground intel. Jake as always had become quite animated, the complete foil for Danny and his quiet, careful, methodical manner. They made a successful complimentary couple.

Billy was the first to grab a can and a plateful of sandwiches.

"Got enough there, Billy?" Sally was back in playful mode.

"He's a still a growing boy who needs his grub. Look at me, I should know. I'm still a growing boy myself."

Marty puffed out his massive chest and flexed his biceps.

"Shame you can't grow your brain a bit bigger. You big muscle-bound lummox." Jake laughed.

The others looked at Marty waiting for his reaction before they dared show any sign of laughing at him.

"Don't push it you scraggy bag of bones. I'll turn you upside down and bounce your crazy head up and down on the floor if you don't pipe down."

Marty glared at Jake. Jake waved his arms about in mock fear. Then they both burst out laughing. Sally smiled. This was clearly their little routine. An act they played out time and time again. She could see they were the very best of friends, comfortable in each other's company with a bond of trust and respect that could never be broken. She wondered what they had seen and done together to make them so close. She cleared her head of such ponderings. It was what they all needed to do now that really mattered.

"Stop messing about. Sit down, have something to eat and drink and then we need to put our heads together to come up with a plan. Time is ticking by, and we need to get going."

"Yes ma'am."

"Certainly ma'am."

Sally put on her best schoolteacher expression and frowned at Marty and Jake. JJ sat down with the glint of love and admiration in his eyes. Sally instinctively glanced across at him and he could have sworn he saw the same look mirrored back at him. A reflection of his own hope or feelings reciprocated, he asked himself. Sooner or later, he would have to find out.

Putting down his half-eaten sandwich, JJ picked up his notes. Time to brief the others on what SPAWN had planned. He took a sip of his drink and cleared his throat.

"I'll start by telling you what my dad found out." He saw Jake fidget. "Don't worry, I'll keep it short. Then I think we need to work out how we're going to get in and out of the camp they're in. I don't think we can go much beyond that to start with. How or what we can do to address the bigger schemes of this Society, SPAWN, will have to wait."

JJ talked through the key points of his notes whilst the others listened quietly. By the time he had finished they all understood the situation. Seven of them against an organized and very powerful Society didn't make good odds by anyone's reasoning.

Odds didn't matter. They were all up for a rescue mission.

Marty and Jake warmed to the idea almost immediately. This was their forte. Both were men of action not words and they could see the group of young friends in front of them were ready for action too. Ready to grow up fast. They had been locked down and couped up for far too long. Together they were prepared to fight for freedom. Together they were a team.

They all had a job to do, and they all seemed to know what that was without having to be told. Danny resumed his seat in front of his screens. He was busy linking the intercom set with the satellite tracing program. He could follow each earpiece on a split screen so whichever four wore them they would be in contact with him and each other. Danny would be able to coordinate their movements and direct them to where they needed to go. His other screen showed the red dot location of JJ's father and Obi's sister. The former appeared not to have moved. He watched as the latter appeared to be on the move.

"The tracker's working. The only problem is if your sister's phone cuts out. I guess we would go on her last location with every chance she would still be there or at least close by."

Obi followed Danny's eyes to the clock on the mantlepiece. It had just gone seven o'clock.

"Sorry but I'll have to coordinate you from here. No way we can set all this up at a remote location. I'll plug all your mobile numbers into my phone as a back-up comms system. Sally, I assume you'll stay here with me?"

"Too right. Sally stays with you Danny." JJ answered without hesitation or forethought.

"No. I'm going with the rest of you. Danny can cope fine on his own. You'll need some eyes and ears on the ground and that'll be me. I can call up the satellite picture and watch everyone's movement including the bad guys. I can also be a getaway driver if need be. No. You're not leaving me behind."

That was that as far as Sally was concerned. No further discussion required. She turned to the four still at the table.

"We'll need a way in and out. Probably a diversion of some kind too. Especially on the way out. Just like in the movies but I'm assuming like real life for you two."

Sally looked to Marty and Jake for reassurance.

"We're already on it." came the assured reply.

Chapter 37

Jake had been studying the layout of the camp as Sally was talking and was busy marking one of the two maps Danny had printed off for them with a series of big red crosses. Billy wondered what to make of a man that carries a pack of Sharpie pens around in his rucksack. Watching him in action answered the question.

"Me and Billy will go in first and set up a few surprises that'll draw attention away from the two locations. That's where I'll blow holes in the fence with the last two. I'll set them all off five seconds apart when you give me the signal Marty. I'm assuming you'll make your own way in as always. Where have you got in mind?" Jake handed his comrade-in-arms a green marker pen.

"I reckon here." Marty pointed to a position on the perimeter fence some distance from Jake's two crosses.

"That would put us between our two rescue targets. Once we have the birds in our hands, I'll give you the nod to light up the sky. You and Billy will need to position yourself here if you can and then follow us out. JJ, you, me, and my sidekick here will go first for Brains and then for Obi's sisters. Then we'll all head back out to Sally who'll be waiting for us at the cars. Experience says it will be a darn site easier getting in than getting out."

"What about my mum? She's in there somewhere. How do we find her?"

"Chances are she'll be with your sisters." Danny piped up trying to bring some optimism into the conversation.

"And if not?"

"Sorry son."

Marty's other motto was you do what you can and accept sometimes that isn't always enough. False hope does no-one any good.

"If she's there we'll bring her out. If not, we won't. The place is too big to go looking for her. They'll be on us before we know it and then no-one gets out. Remember Obi, just the two choices. We live, we go on to fight another day. We die, it all ends there."

Blunt and to the point thought Jake. He'll never change. They shouldn't be coming with us, brave hearts or not, that's really the bottom line.

"Timings. Let's talk timings." Jake thought it best to get back to the detail they controlled.

"It'll take me a good half hour to set up the firework show under the cover of darkness. The plan was to go in after dark anyway I assume. I can use two different frequencies for the charges inside the camp and those by the fence. That way they won't all go off together. Will we be able to get there by ten?"

JJ turned to Sally. She shot him a cold frosty glare for his earlier lack of support before she responded to Jake's question.

"I'll do a couple of routes and see what the timings would be.

I think we should be able to get there by then. Are you going to give the boys guns? Scares me to think about you boys with your toys."

Jake shook his head. Obi gave a knowing smile. JJ and Billy replied like they were telepathically linked.

"We can shoot."

"Jinks you owe me a soda." shouted Billy.

"This is no game you two. Shoot what? BB guns? Airsofts? What would your dad say if he were here now? From how proud he is of the two of you I think I know although I suspect that might be overridden by the desire to keep you safe." Marty saw the look of disappointment on each of their faces and watched as it changed to one of impending defiance.

"Yes, you can each have a gun. Just remember all three of you" he moved his gaze from Billy to JJ to Obi. "don't shoot us because remember, Jake and me, we're on your side."

Sally didn't laugh. Danny was shaking his head at the very idea of giving them guns and pitting them against armed Cleos. His expression said it all. A recipe for disaster if ever there was one. He stayed quiet. He had nothing to say. He could see there was no way they would listen to his voice of reason. No way they'd listen to common sense.

Marty got out the handguns, fitted one with a silencer, and handed the other three to the eager young men. He gave them a short demonstration on how to fit the silencer, load and eject the magazines, how to cock the gun and how to release the safety catch.

"When the time comes, I'll load and cock them for you so all you'll have to do is release the safety catch, point at your target and pull the trigger." He said as he took the guns back off them. "I'll give you each a spare mag but if all goes well you won't need it. I'm hoping you won't even need to shoot at anyone. Me and Jake will do that if and when the time comes. Jake, you'll have one of the SA80's and I'll have the other. I'll give my Browning to Brains when we get to him. That'll give us extra fire power on the way out should we need it. You know it never sounded that easy when Johnny-Boy told us the plan. Must be the way I tell it."

No-one laughed. The seriousness of what they were proposing to do had just hit home.

"10.15." Sally's voice broke the silence. "10.15. That's when we should plan to be there and in position. Jake, you said you needed thirty minutes to set up so the show would start at about 10.45. It would be dark enough by then too. Will we need to do that synchronizing watches thing?"

Her last comment broke the mood. Marty couldn't help but laugh. He wasn't a spy and Jake most definitely wasn't James Bond. One glance at him told you that.

"No, I don't think we'll need to be so precise. This isn't a movie. It starts for real when we go in and gets lively when I tell Jake to hit the button. After that, we won't be worrying what time it is as we'll have other things on our minds. What is important is what time do we have to leave here. We'll need to take two cars. Me and my two buddies in one, Jake, Billy, and you Sally in the other."

There was a short conversation between Sally and Danny and then the printer kick started into action.

"Two route maps and the rendezvous postcode. One for you and one for us. We'll leave at 8.30 and you, Marty, at 8.40. Either of us hits a problem, we let Danny and the other car know. I think we have a plan."

They spent the rest of the time preparing for the mission. Jake had the most to do as he needed to carefully prepare his special effects. Danny checked the earbuds and phones were fully charged and tested everything for a third time. They were ready to go a good twenty minutes early.

JJ had one last thing he had to do. He waited until Sally wandered into the kitchen and followed her in with two crumb covered plates. She turned and he saw she knew what he was going to do. She held out her hand. He took it and gently pulled her to him. They kissed for the very first time.

"Be careful." she whispered.

"I love you." he said, looking deep into Sally's eyes.

Sally hugged him and then softly pushed him away.

"I know. Now get back in there before anyone notices were both missing, you silly lovelorn puppy dog."

She laughed with a tear in her eye. She loved him too.

A nod and a wink when he walked in to join the others told him it was too late. They were all wearing the same knowing smile. They had all noticed. About time too, thought Danny. Get a room, thought Marty.

Chapter 38

The eight o'clock video conference went very well. The international attendees had listened to her opening address and then contributed to the discussion. Caroline had shared the details of the progress made over the previous days and stressed that everything was proceeding according to plan. It was important that her foreign counterparts understood that they were integral in ensuring the fear factor remained high overseas which in turn made it easier for her and SPAWN here at home. Footage of their overwhelmed hospitals and makeshift morgues had proved to be very effective additions to the news bulletins as had footage of towns and cities devastated by floods, tornadoes, and the inevitable food shortages.

The most powerful nations were all represented by having one or more senior figures at the video conference. It was their individual responsibility to keep the global situation running according to the broader plan. Some of the countries represented already had well-established political regimes that would allow them to move through the stages at greater speed. Others would make slower progress. It was unlikely that there would ever be unified global domination, there were always going to be a few rogue nations, however it remained a serious aspiration.

Caroline signed off and closed the conference satisfied that it had gone as well as she had expected. A full-on focus on the international agenda would follow soon. The immediate priority was to put her home nation on an irreversible roadmap to deliver her Mandate for Salvation. Already some way down the road, the data from the last two days would move things on at pace. Very pleased with herself, Caroline trotted off to make coffee as if she didn't have a care in the world.

Just over an hour later she was once again sitting in front of her screen. This time it was for a national presentation at 10.30 pm. No debate, no questions to be asked of her. She would speak and the rest would listen. She knew one of her ardent devoted followers would be busy elsewhere and he already knew and understood her message. Sound and true. Dedicated and reliable. Needles would forever be her loyal assistant, maybe even the closest thing to a friend she was ever likely to have. The rest she treated with dispassionate indifference. They were her sheep, there to be sheared if they ever let her down.

The screen in front of her was in a state of flux as groups and individuals joined the meeting. Caroline ticked them off mentally as each signed in. Behind her hung the familiar banner that read 'Truth. Wisdom. Salvation'. On the shelf to her left stood a glass jar. She adjusted her robe, pulled down the front of her hood and began her address.

"My loyal servants, in the two days since I last spoke to you, we have moved ever closer to our vision of the future. It is time now for me to expand the Inner Council as the need for very specific action is upon us. A chosen few will be invited to join me very soon. To the rest of you I say do not be disappointed. You will still have a key role to play as much will need to be organized and managed. I will lead the Inner Council and we will in due course present to you our five-year plan. Together we will make it happen. Together we will bring Truth, Wisdom, and Salvation."

Caroline paused to allow the echo of her words to subside. Although she could not hear the response of her loyal followers, she basked in the moment for a few seconds more. Under her hood her face shone like a beacon of light. She was the President. She was Caroline Bramney, the most powerful person in the country, if not soon to be in the world.

A sudden impulse overtook her. It was time. Some already knew, some would be shocked, some would be frightened. Relationships and hierarchies would change. It no longer mattered. It was time. Caroline lifted her head and threw back her hood.

"Behold. I am your President. I am your truth. I am your wisdom. I am your Salvation. Together we will save humanity. Tonight, you pledge your allegiance to me personally. Tomorrow, we build our future."

The silence in the oak paneled room was so pronounced they could have heard a spider's footsteps as it ran across the wooden floor. In front of the occupied semi-circle of chairs stood the tall, hooded figure in his blue robe, edged in gold silk and white fur, his eyes wide and jaw dropped. The Director General stood there stunned by what he had just witnessed. He stared first at the screen then at the faces looking up at him, some with broad smiles, some with puzzled brows, some just shadows in the dim light. He was not one of her Inner Council, not one of the privileged few that had known she was the President.

Believing himself to be a very senior Spawner, he had often wondered who the President was and why they had never met in person. He had never raised the courage to ask the question. Now he knew the answer. He was no fool. He saw immediately that had he known about her position their working relationship would have been completely compromised. She was very good, even better than he had believed. She had worked for him but all along he was really working for her and not once did she let it show.

He calmed his thoughts and emotions. He was thinking rationally once again. Thinking how he could make this work for him. Now he could foster his ambition. President of the Society was a position he had envisaged would one day be his. His first thought was that Caroline coming out had closed the door to his aspiration. He smiled to himself as he pictured his new situation in a different light. Opportunity knocks he thought, the glass is half full after all. The sound of Caroline's voice brought him back from his reverie.

"Together we are taking great strides towards our goal. Much progress has been made in the last two days."

Caroline continued by laying out the key points from the recent events. An explanation followed of the significance of this to SPAWNs objectives. Tempted as she was, Caroline refrained from giving them any detail of her own personal involvement at the Holiday Camp. This she felt came under the remit of her day job not something for the President to discuss with her subordinates.

An elite hierarchy had started to manifest itself in her thoughts. Moving forward she had recognized the need to create a strong team around her to see it through to the end. Together they would create and govern the new mandated state.

She was smiling as she spoke into her webcam. Happy, confident, and assured. To be forever remembered as the woman who saved humanity and created a new world order. What greater accolade could history bestow on her.

In his usual seat at the end of the back row he sat staring at the screen. Quiet and innocuous. No-one paid much attention to him at the best of times. A cursory glance or the occasional nod from some of his peers was about the best he expected. Once it had bothered him. Now it suited him to remain plain and ordinary, an unremarkable and unobtrusive figure, a humble man who had always considered his job was to save lives not to destroy them. When he had joined, he had believed SPAWN to be a force for good. How wrong he had been. He despaired. He was angry with himself. How could he have been so naïve?

He had left it too late to contact his old friend and now his friend was dead. What had he expected of him anyway.

He surveyed the room. A few against so many. There was nothing he could do but accept the inevitability of the final outcome. The face on the screen and the baying jackals in the room told the whole story. This was the future. Cautiously, he wiped away another tear.

The President's address was coming to an end. Caroline had

been talking for almost forty minutes, pausing at the right moments for effect and to take a breath. All was going swimmingly.

She was about to give her grand finale when her dialogue was interrupted by a series of very loud bangs. The video onlookers gasped as they heard the noise, as the vision of their beloved president shook and then froze before their very eyes. Bewilderment and disbelief spread across the faces of all but one. His eyes lit up with a new hope. Maybe, just maybe, this wasn't all over yet.

Chapter 39

The six of them had set off for the camp leaving Danny with some spare time to kill. He had everything set up to track the two cars and to chat to them if the need arose. He was hoping beyond hope that wouldn't be the case. Having listened intently to JJ's vivid description of this SPAWN and its evil intent, he decided to see if he could do more to track the identity and whereabouts of the hooded figure who he had recorded two nights ago. He pulled up the video on screen and then went to the original link he had used to hack the site.

There it was. An IPS address. It took Danny just a few seconds to access the address, only to face a mixture of pain and pleasure. Whoever it was had been wise enough to use either a proxy server or VPN which would mean it would be harder for him to trace them. Harder, he thought, but not impossible. Maybe the person had taken the quick route and used their mobile phone's data.

Whether it was good luck, coincidence, or fate he wasn't sure, but he was doing the right thing at exactly the right time. There on the screen in front of him was his alter ego's invite to another live video conference. He signed in, making sure his addition to the group went undetected. As he expected it was the eerie hooded figure in a meeting with what he only just managed to identify as a worldwide audience after some careful wizardry. He recorded the presentation and looked to see how many of the attendees he could identify. All were too astute and tech-savvy for Danny to have any success in the short time he had available, so he diverted his attention back to his friends.

A glance at his other screen showed all seemed well with the car journeys. He wished he could be there with them, but he knew in his heart he would be able to do much more to help them by staying where he was. He was their eyes in the sky, their ears on the ground, their centre of communication.

With the worries of the world weighing heavily on his shoulders he wandered into the kitchen to clear his head. Sipping from a steaming cup of hot coffee he stood at the door staring across at the four flashing dots on his computer screen. Two were his friends in their cars and two were their family. He was going to do all he could to make sure he would see them all again. All he could to guide them safely home.

Marty had told them to keep radio silence unless there was a real emergency. Danny had thought Marty was showing his age as they were using modern technology with encrypted earpieces with in-built microphones not some handheld radio wave transmitters. Still, he understood Marty's logic. No news was good news as far as it went. Any unnecessary chatter would only intrude on their thoughts and their concentration. Danny looked across at the clock. It was just coming up to 10 o'clock.

Jake's ensemble was the first to arrive and park up in a quiet side street perpendicular to the camp fence.

"We've made it in good time. All we can do now is wait for Marty and the boys to arrive." Boys, he thought, boys about to come of age. About to grow up real fast.

"Once I get the signal, you and me Billy will grab the bags and head for the fence. Sally, you need to sit here and be ready for when we get back. You've probably got the hardest job. All you can do is sit and wait. But keep alert and ready to go. If things go well, you should be able to drive us away nice and sensible like without drawing any attention to us. You've got an earpiece so you can listen in but stay off the airway unless absolutely necessary. I'll make sure I let you know when we start to head back. Trust me, we'll all get back safe. I can feel it in my fingers." He tried to shake out the song he had just put in his own head. Damn he thought, I'll be singing that all night now. Still, not a bad requiem for the evening. The irony of it appealed to him as he sang it to himself. He turned and glanced up at Sally's reflection in the rear-view mirror.

Sitting in the shadow of the back seat Sally gave the best smile she could muster under the circumstances. Then Billy chimed in with his usual blunt words of wisdom.

"Yeah, you don't have to worry. We'll make sure we keep my big bro safe and in one piece for you. Wouldn't want anything to get in the way of a good romance, would we Jake."

The two in the front seats guffawed at their childish innuendo. At least they're on the same wavelength and getting on well together Sally thought, even if it is at my expense. This time her smile was genuine. She was fond of them all but only one had captured her heart, and too right, they had better bring him back safely to her and all in one piece.

At the same time as Marty was telling Jake that they had parked up further down the street. Danny's ears were multi-tasking. He was listening-in to them through the hub next to his computer and to the on-screen video that had just become live. Same place, same dark figure, same rhetoric.

Danny was peering at the background to see if he could see anything that would help in his quest to identify who the self-proclaimed President was. There were no photos, no books, no chance. He switched back to the satellite maps where his attention was best placed. He could study the recorded video later.

Jake had agreed with Marty that he and Billy would wait in the car until they had watched the other three go past. Sally watched on as Marty strolled by as if he were on an afternoon walk in the countryside. A short hunting trip perhaps with his rifle slung over his left shoulder. She looked around fearfully but there was no-one around to notice, no-one around to care. JJ and Obi walked with a stiffness that showed the tension in their minds and bodies. Unlike Marty, this was a completely new experience for them and a very scary one at that.

"Let's go folks." Jake's calm tone soothed her own heightened sense of anxiety.

"We don't want them hanging around too long at the fence waiting for us."

He hopped out, opened the car boot, and passed one of the rucksacks to Billy.

"Be careful with that Billy-boy. Should be safe enough but we don't want to lose our heads unnecessarily, do we?"

As Sally stood on her self-appointed look-out Jake handed her the spare set of keys he always kept with him in his rucksack. Brains had sometimes referred to him as Just-in-Case Jake. Marty preferred to call him Head-Case Jake.

"Remember, stay alert and be patient. We'll be back sooner than you know."

He handed Billy one of the pistols, tucked the other in his belt and picked up the SA80.

"You hold on to this for me. You can ride shotgun until we've put on our special display."

Billy beamed like a Cheshire cat that had just eaten all the cream. He had one thing on his mind. To make his dad proud. He knew full well the dangers they faced but he was prepared to do his bit. He remembered his dad telling him and his brother that the biggest fear, the greatest enemy, is fear itself. Everyone experiences fear, those that survive are the ones that never let it take them over. Billy was ready.

They met up at the fence as planned. Marty snipped the fence and pulled it open enough for them to pass through.

"Danny, we're in. Stay alert and stay on air as you're going to have to guide us to where we need to go. Jake will let us know when he's ready then it's over to you."

"Roger that." His response was instinctive. What an idiot, he thought, why on earth did I say that.

Marty looked at Jake and they both laughed. They bumped fists in a ritual that looked like second nature to the two of them and the two parties split off. The rescue was underway.

PART 6

The Incursion

Chapter 40

Jake and Billy were moving in a clockwise direction around the camp dodging between buildings to stay hidden from view. The paths around the camp were well lit and from what Jake had seen so far, the only Cleos on duty were those at the entrance.

They reached the first location without a problem. Billy looked on and marveled at the dexterity of his comrade-in-arms. It took Jake just a few seconds to lay the first charge from Billy's rucksack.

"One down five to go." said Jake as he passed the rucksack back to Billy. "Then we wake up the neighbours. Boom-bing-a-bang, Billy-Boy, boom-bing-a-bang and then we're out of here."

Once all were in position, each charge would be activated by a signal from Jake's hand-held transmitter and would detonate with a five second delay between each. The show would last just twenty seconds but cause enough panic and confusion that should last long enough for them to make their escape. The first two laid at the fence would be the last to go up.

Whilst Jake and Billy got to work, Marty was having a continual dialogue with Danny back at the house.

"We're moving forward and to the right. There looks to be a series of older buildings in front of us converging to a larger multi-complex. Are we getting close to the first signal?"

Marty's voice was low and calm. He remembered from the map that the large complex consisted of an atrium with a series of corridors branching off in numerous directions. The rooms facing into the atrium were mainly the old glass-fronted shops or restaurants. The rooms down the corridors were an eclectic mix of shop fronts, workshops, and function rooms.

"The signal from JJ's dad is coming from inside the large complex, the Pavilion. The dot moved about a hundred yards a short while ago but is stationary right now. The satellite picture can't see inside the place but I've overlayed it on the old campsite layout. The signal's coming from the northernmost branch about midway down. The map shows it as a large function room, but it may not be the same now. I've been scanning the rest of the camp for signs of movement, but it all seems fairly quiet at the moment. There has been some toing and froing going on around the large hangar at the far north of the camp. Looked like some sort of changing of the guard. Over."

"For heaven's sake quit with the Rogers and Overs Danny." Marty said, trying unsuccessfully to hide his irritation. "Just say what is necessary and then wait for an answer ok. We're going to try to enter through the main door at the end of that corridor. We'll work our way around and then I need you to tell me when we get right on top of the signal from Brains. Got it Danny."

"Yes sir. Will do."

Marty signaled to JJ and Obi that it was time to move. JJ had been scanning the surrounding buildings taking note of those with the lights on and assumed they must be occupied. By whom and for what purpose he couldn't see.

The main door to the corridor proved to be a good choice to access the complex. It was open and completely unguarded. The whole place oozed over-confidence and complacency. JJ and Obi nodded to each other. Acknowledgement that they were both thinking this might be easier than they had imagined.

"You're right by the signal."

"Thanks Danny. Now stay quiet until I ask you for the next location."

Danny was so nervous and tense he knew he needed a short distraction, so he turned his attention to his other screen. There was another speech going on by the hooded figure. It was being recorded but what he saw immediately focused his attention. The hooded figure was in the process of disclosure. He drew a sharp breath. The President was a woman. A woman he recognized from the broadcasts. He racked his brain for a name. That was it, she was Dr Bramney, Dr Caroline Bramney. He inched up the volume to hear what she was saying. He glanced back at the other screen. The two of the dots were merging together.

The sign on the door read Treatment Room 1. Marty pulled out his silenced Browning and put his hand on the round silver door handle.

"Stay behind me. Take your guns out if you want but don't shoot anyone ok. We have no idea what we're walking into so let me do the talking and any shooting if I need to. Just try to look as menacing as possible. Ready."

Obi reached for his gun, caressed it, and nodded. JJ just nodded. They were ready.

Marty slowly turned the handle, pushed open the door, and barged in. Obi and JJ followed and flanked him on either side. It must have taken Marty an instant to scan the room and assess the situation.

"Stop what you're doing right now."

What faced the incoming trio was a series of beds each occupied by patients that looked to be in varying degrees of pain. Hovering over the bed at the far end of the room was a small man in a white coat holding a hypodermic syringe in his left hand. Two beds away from him was young woman, similarly dressed, and similarly armed with a syringe. Two more white coated figures were busying themselves behind a glass window.

Stunned by the sudden and totally unforeseen intrusion, all four stood staring at Marty. JJ blinked and took a mental picture of a scene frozen in time.

"Who the hell are you?"

Dr Sterbenson had regained his composure and was now confident he could assert his own authority over the situation. His assumption was that they were stupid Cleos who had been sent there to help move his patients but had somehow misunderstood the order.

"We're your worst nightmare pal. Put the needles down and back away from the beds. You two get out here now." Marty pointed his gun at the glass window and beckoned to the two behind it to come out and join them.

Marty switched his attention back to the end bed. The person in it was speaking to him in a low, hoarse, and barely audible whisper.

"About bloody time too. You always did go for the dramatic late entrance."

"Well, my old friend, we're here now so just you be thankful for that for the time being. Let's save the hugs and kisses for later."

Their sentimental reunion was interrupted as Obi took a step forward and shouted at the young woman to back away. Alice looked back at him as cool as you like.

"Now why should I listen to you?"

"Because that's my mum and I'm holding a gun, and if you don't, I will kill you."

Alice smiled and slowly lowered the syringe. At the same time Dr Sterbenson moved forward in an attempt to inject the content of the syringe into Brains' arm whilst holding his other hand up in a gesture of surrender. Marty didn't hesitate and shot him twice in the chest. Needles, syringe still in his hand, was dead long before he hit the tiled floor.

As Alice made her move Marty shot her in the shoulder. At such close range the momentum of the bullet knocked her sideways and onto the floor. Marty shook his head.

"Some people just don't listen, do they."

Obi rushed forward and looked at his mum, her eyes closed and near death. Overtaken by rage he grabbed the syringe off the bed and bent over Alice.

"What have you done to my mum. What the hell is this stuff? How about I give it to you. How does that sound?"

Alice looked up at him in sheer terror. She struggled to hold him off.

"Please no. Please. No."

Obi knocked away her outstretched hand, pushed her head sideways and stabbed her in the neck with the syringe. He slowly pushed down on the top of the plunger and emptied the contents into Alice's vein.

"I hope you take a long time to die." he said with no emotion and no remorse.

From the look on his face and the tone of his voice there was no doubting he meant it.

Alice's eyes rolled up into her head and she started to convulse on the floor. She'd been injected with the final dose meant for Obi's mum. It would take many agonizing minutes before she gasped her last breath. Obi turned his attention to the occupant of the bed and his whole bearing changed in an instant.

"Mum, it's Obi." he said as he took her hand in his and gave it a very gentle squeeze. Her hand was cold to the touch and her breathing was slow and laboured.

"Mum, can you hear me?" he whispered softly bending close to her ear.

Her eyes opened and she struggled to turn her head. A faint smile of recognition flickered for a moment and Obi felt her finger stroke the back of his hand. He lent forward and kissed her gently on the forehead before turning to face the two lab technicians in their white coats now standing in front of the glass window.

"What have you done to her?"

The reply came from the hoarse voice in the end bed.

"They've been injecting everyone with some kind of lethal drug. Different doses, I think. You're mum's a real fighter. She even helped me and the guy next to me attempt an escape. They left me 'til last because they wanted me to see everyone else's pain."

Whilst he was talking JJ moved across to his dad's bedside and undid the restraining straps. He could see his dad had suffered quite a beating and was struggling to overcome the effects of the injections.

Then one of the white coats made a huge error of judgement. He spoke up.

"There's nothing we can do."

He pointed at the body on the floor at JJ's feet.

"He was the one who told us what to do. We just followed his orders. I think once they've had two doses their done for."

Marty saw that Obi was shaking with a mixture of rage and utter despair. He stepped in front of the two technicians and turned his back on them to face Obi.

"See to your mum, son. They're not worth having on your conscience."

Marty swiveled around to face the two minions. The one that had spoken smiled at him as if they were old friends. Marty was smiling back as he shot him right between the eyes. Judge, jury, and executioner all rolled into one. Guilty of crimes against humanity. A heartbeat later he shot the other one. Justice dispensed, punishment administered, swift and sweet.

"No loose ends as Johnny used to say."

Brains smiled at his friend.

"No loose ends and no-one to raise the alarm once we're gone, eh Marty. Besides, these people got away lightly. They didn't deserve to die so quickly and painlessly after what they have been doing."

He looked across at his brave companion in the bed next to him. At least he died knowing they gave it one last go. A hero if ever there was one. He sat up slowly and fought the pain as he moved his legs over the side of the bed. JJ held him by the shoulder to support him in his effort to re-join the living. His dad looked up at him, pleased to see his son, strong and brave, standing there in front of him.

"Good lad. There's a book in one of his pockets. I watched him and he treated it like it was his precious. His One Ring. Everything they did he wrote down in the book. He recorded everything. Get the book JJ and let's take a good look at it."

JJ could see exactly where the book was. The dead man's hand was clasped around it in one final attempt to protect it. Or maybe to take it with him so together he and his precious book would burn in hell. JJ pulled the grasping hand away, slid the book out of the white coat pocket and passed it to his dad.

"I can see why he kept it so close. It's got just about every detail of his work in it. Even lists of names and companies. JJ, you take it and keep a good hold of it. With him gone, and us with the book, that ought to slow them down a bit. I think it will keep some good people alive a bit longer too. Feels good to throw a few spanners in the works, doesn't it?"

He passed the book to his son and lent on him for support as he forced himself up and onto his feet. He winced as he tried to walk and clutched his side. He knew he was in a bad way, but he was determined to make no show of it.

Marty didn't notice his friend's pain as he was busy sizing up the two bodies in front of him. He bent over one, pulled off the dead man's shoes and then his white coat.

"Best I can do." Marty passed them across to Brains. "We're not going to a pyjama party so get those on. Do you want his socks?"

The shooting and the talking seemed to have raised Obi's mum's level of consciousness. She squeezed his hand and used every ounce of her strength to caress his face with her other hand. She could see the distressed look on her son's face and the tears welling up in his eyes.

"Obi my darling, be strong now. Your sisters need you. Go find them and make sure you keep them safe for me. Promise me you'll keep them safe."

"No Mum, you're coming with us. We'll go get them together. We'll keep them safe together." His voice was frantic, the tears were rolling down his cheeks as he pleaded with his mum not to let go.

"Obi, you have to go, for me, you have to go. Jessie and Katie need you. You're the son every mother wants hers to be, and you're mine which makes me so proud. Please, promise me, then go. Tell them I love them as I do you and your dad. Always and forever. Tell them and remember, always and forever."

The tears were streaming down Obi's face. Marty walked across and his mum looked up at the big man. She smiled at him, and he nodded back.

“Look after my family for me. Please.”

Marty nodded for a second time and put his hand on Obi’s shoulder. She squeezed her son’s hand for one last time, closed her eyes, and smiled peacefully as she slipped away.

Chapter 41

"Danny, are you listening? We're on the move to go and find Obi's sisters. Tell us the way to go."

There was an urgency in the tone of Marty's request. Danny sensed something was not quite right.

"Everyone ok?" he asked, hoping for a positive response.

"Sort of. There's four of us now and you need to guide us to Obi's sisters and fast, so stop asking fool questions and tell me where to go ok."

Danny relayed directions that took them to the room where the girls were being held. It took them longer than Obi wanted as Brains was struggling to walk and was having to be supported by JJ.

Marty read the look on Obi's face and knew he might not be able to save his conscience a second time. He stopped his team at the edge of the window.

"Brains, take this just in case you see someone I don't."

Marty handed across his Browning together with the spare magazine. Brains took the gun in one hand and dropped the magazine in his coat pocket with the other. Brains saw his son feel for the gun in his belt and put his hand over his arm as a signal to leave it there for now. JJ responded. He stood beside his dad, cool, calm, and collected. They looked every bit the proud father and his clever, courageous son.

Peering into the room Marty could see a group of girls sitting at the back along the length of the far wall. It looked like it was a makeshift dormitory. Two youths in blue suits were standing chatting together with their backs to the window. Marty surmised that they were discussing their interest in one or two of the older girls.

Against the far wall he could see two big blue suited figures dozing on chairs. Chairs that looked too flimsy to support the men for very long before they legs would collapse under the weight. He couldn't see if there were more men against his wall. Those he could see didn't pose too much of a problem but another two hidden from view could prove difficult if they were armed and alert. Even so, not very good odds he thought, for them.

This play would be all about making an entrance. Surprise followed by calm appraisal, followed by swift and decisive action. The surprise double act would have to be him and Obi. The strong supporting cast Brains and JJ. Quick, quick, slow, and enjoy the show.

"Me and Obi will walk in cool as you like and you two follow on in your own time. We'll take the big guys out first. Are we ready?"

"As we'll ever be." JJ, his mind free from pain and despair, said what the other two were thinking.

Marty pulled the door slowly towards him and as he had expected it opened. They had made it all too easy, which was understandable because they perceived there was no threat to them here. Holding the SA80 in front of him he walked in followed by Obi who had positioned himself on Marty's right so that Marty had a clear view of the two bums on seats.

"Everyone stays calm, and no-one gets hurt. You two stand up real slow like and step back up against the wall. Keep your hands where I can see them."

The two youths turned around, each holding a baton and looking like they wanted to rumble. They still had the scent of blood in their nostrils. The sight of a giant holding an assault rifle made them think again. How they looked and what they were holding made no difference to Obi. He strode towards the pair of them intent on putting them down. He didn't need to know whether they had hurt his sisters or not. He didn't need them to give him a reason, he already had one.

One of the youths made towards him swinging his baton in the air thinking he would be quick enough to knock the gun out of the hand dangling casually at Obi's side. He got almost within reach when Obi raised it through forty-five degrees and put a bullet into the youth's left leg shattering his knee cap. The youth screamed in pain and fell to the floor. The second youth dropped his baton and raised his hands. Obi was in no mood to accept his surrender. The gun continued its upward arc and the youth twisted backwards as a 9mm bullet passed through his right shoulder and out the other side.

One of the Cleos took advantage of the noisy distraction and went for the gun nestling under his jacket. There was a small pop and a louder thud as he crashed to the floor. There was a second pop as the scene repeated itself.

"Got your back Marty, as usual."

Brains and JJ had joined the fray virtually unnoticed and with a watchful eye. Brains stood smiling as he lowered his gun. He had recognized the two Cleos from earlier in the day and had just passed from judge and jury to executioner in an instant. They were the first to have their account settled. Rest assured, you won't be the last, he thought to himself.

"Saw it coming but knew you were there. Didn't want to spoil your fun. Besides, you always were one to make the hero's big entrance. Likes to have the last word does your dad, JJ."

Slightly taken aback by his dad's action, JJ nodded towards the back of the room. A small family reunion was taking place. Obi and his sisters were in a group hug. Jessie and Katie were crying with relief and Obi was trying hard to fight back the tears.

"I knew you'd find us. I just knew it." Jessie mumbled into her big brother's chest.

"Enough of the reunion already. Let's get the hell out of here, shall we."

"What about the rest of them? We can't just leave them here."

Marty looked to Brains to answer his son. Then thought better of it.

"We can't take them JJ. There's too many of them. Maybe next time. We've got who we came for, now we have to go. That's got to be how this works."

Brains nodded at his son. He understood how hard-hearted

this looked but if they took all the girls, they'd risk getting some of them, and themselves, killed on the way out.

"I get it dad, but it doesn't seem fair and somehow it doesn't feel right. But ok. Obi, grab your sisters and let's get out of here."

"One last thing before we go."

Marty strolled over to the two youths who were still writhing about on the floor.

"You two going to keep quiet for a while for me?" Marty asked as he towered over them. He paused and looked around at the faces of the terrified group of young girls they had to leave behind.

"Sorry." he mouthed to them before turning his attention back to the two figures writhing around on the floor.

"No, I don't think you will, eh tough guys."

He steadied himself, took aim, and smashed them one after the other in the head with the butt of his rifle. Satisfied, he turned and walked slowly towards the door but not before offering a second apology to the girls, this time for his violent but necessary action.

Now there were six of them. Marty felt pleased the plan was working but now they had a different problem. The six of them were more noticeable, more vulnerable, and it was very likely someone had heard the youth scream.

"Jake, are you all set?"

Jake had been waiting patiently with Billy for the green light from Marty.

"That's an affirmative big buddy."

"Danny, when the fireworks start keep an eye out for us and

let us know if you see anything we need to know about." Marty didn't wait for a reply. He just assumed Danny was tuned in and on the ball.

"Right folks here we go. Jake, once we're out of this building you can do your stuff. Give us two minutes then light up the sky."

Half-time and two nil up. Let's hope it stays that way whispered Marty very quietly to himself.

Chapter 42

Danny was listening and watching at the same time. His focus of attention switched between the progress of his friends and the President's address.

On Marty's confirmation, Jake waited two minutes and set off his charges. Five explosions shook the camp.

At first, Danny was uncertain about what he had heard. In one ear, the sound of the explosions was as expected but he was sure he had heard a slightly delayed echo coming out of his computer. Something unexpected was going on. He turned to see the frozen face of the woman on his screen. It shocked him to see such a familiar face. He wound back his recording and listened again. No mistaking the sound a second time. The broadcast was coming from somewhere in or near the camp. Oh yes, the woman was actually in the camp and why not, thought Danny, where else would she be.

A sense of misgiving swept over him. He'd seen enough to know she was the most important person, the President, and so it was extremely unlikely she would be there alone and unprotected. He switched his attention to the satellite picture of the camp.

The north-east corner was alive with movement. Most appeared to be directed towards a central location and he could see a small number of people heading for one particular small building. His friends were right in the middle of a hornets' nest.

"Marty it's me Danny. There's something you need to know. Can you hear me?"

Marty and his band were making their way slowly around the northern edge of the building. He couldn't see the activity going on, but he could hear the shouts of command and the noise of what he assumed were men running around the accommodation blocks. His ears were well trained to pick-up such sounds, and he was thankful that at the moment the running men were heading away from not towards them. His main worry was he didn't know where Jake and Billy were.

"Keep it short Danny. All hell's breaking loose down here."

"They're all to the north-east of you. It's because she's there. The President's the woman from the briefings. I can't be sure, but it looks like there could be fifty to a hundred guards and they seem to be getting themselves organized. You need to get out of there and quickly." The urgency in his tone was unmistakable.

Marty replied with a single one-word expletive.

Jake cut in before Danny could respond.

"Marty, I can see some of the activity. Me and Billy are at the side of a large hanger that looks very new. I've still got the two spare charges so we're going to blow two large holes in it. That should help to draw the attention away from you. We'll mop up here and then follow you out. See you back at the cars big man."

Marty left his mic switched on as he spoke directly to Brains knowing Jake would be listening in and take it as a reply.

"Jake and your lad Billy have got our backs. We need to keep moving and get back to the cars. You good to go?"

Brains nodded affirmative.

"You take point Marty. Obi, you, and your sisters, will stay in the centre and me and JJ will provide the cover from the rear. Girls, as quiet as mice, ok."

Brains put his finger to his lips and gave the two frightened young girls the best smile of reassurance he could muster. Jessie did her best to smile back, Katie just squeezed her sister's hand even tighter.

Two large bangs had left two gaping holes at the front and side of the Recycling Plant. Jake had told Billy to keep two metres to his left as they ran in through the smoke and rubble strewn beside the hole in the side wall. The first thing that hit the pair of them was the heat. The second thing was the smell. The third and final straw was what they saw.

A small group of men were coughing and spluttering around what was clearly a neatly laid out row of bodies. A man in a white coat was standing petrified in the centre of the room. Jake opened fire on the men, his SA80 spraying a short burst of FYV-six 5.56mm bullets that cut the men down before they even saw him. Billy had stopped and was trying to make sense of it all. Jake threw his SA80 over his shoulder, pulled out his Browning and walked towards the terrified Dr K.

"What the hell are you doing here mister? How do I know any of those dead people over there aren't friends of mine? You the one in charge here?" Jake demanded.

The sight of Jake walking towards him pushed the Doctor deeper into his worst nightmare. He started to stutter and stammer uncontrollably. How was he to know if the people had been this guy's friends? All he knew was that he was a man with a gun who had just shot seven people right in front of his eyes.

"Wrong answer." said Jake.

It came as no surprise to Billy when Jake shot the guy. A case of justifiable homicide if ever there was one. Surrounded by the innocent dead, Billy understood there was no room for sentiment and anyway he was in no mood to start raising any conscientious objections. Leave the sniveling weasel alive and he'd more than happily shove them in the oven that was for sure. Besides Billy had a feeling that they had just declared war on the Spawners and their Cleos and neither side was going to follow the Geneva Convention.

"Billy, watch the doorway. I've still got a few bits and pieces left so let's leave here with a bang."

A minute later they were moving at speed away from the hangar. Jake pressed a little button on the remote with his thumb as he and Billy ducked behind the large pavilion. The hangar erupted in smoke and then flames turning the scene into a blazing inferno that lit up the sky.

Caroline was standing in the middle of the small elite group of her personal military guard when she saw the hangar go up. Her cool controlled façade was replaced immediately by sheer anger. The senior officer present was offering an opinion.

"Ma'am, whoever they are, they're still inside the camp. They will be heading towards the south side where I'm sure they'll have some sort of getaway vehicle parked up and ready to go. I recommend I take my men around the outside of the camp to look for it and to be ready to cut them off. I'll leave four that will stay with you and the Cleos can comb the inside of the camp and funnel them to where we will be waiting for them."

"Do it Major. When you get them, bring any that are still alive straight to me. You understand."

"Yes ma'am."

The Major barked the orders to those around him who then split off to carry them out. This was the action he had been waiting for.

The Major led his hand-picked men out of the camp and down to the few side streets where his experience suggested was the best place to stage a getaway. Finally, some real action to get my teeth into, thought the Major, as he signaled to his men to follow him into battle and what he expected would be a glorious victory.

Chapter 43

It had been a slow and cautious journey back to the hole Marty had cut in the fence. Marty had seen them all through safely to where they were now, crouched down in the long grass waiting for Jake and Billy to arrive.

"Danny, anything we need to know?" whispered Marty.

"I can see some movement in and around the camp. They don't seem to be in any hurry apart from a small group that I think are off to your left. Be careful, it's possible you may run into them at some point. Sorry I can't be more precise because the picture isn't too clear around the built-up areas."

From back in the camp came the sound of three short bursts of gunfire. JJ turned around in time to see the flash of the last burst coming from the edge of the old fairground they had just crossed.

"Marty, we've had a spot of bother. Billy's been shot." Jake voice was calm and matter of fact.

Jake and Billy had been making their way to the fence when they had literally bumped into a small group of Cleos coming down the side of the last building before the fairground. There were six of them, all armed, walking three abreast in two rows about five metres apart. Billy was the first to react taking out two of the first row, one with a straight jab to the nose and the other with a fist to the chest. Jake hit the third in the face with the butt of his rifle. One of the three in the row behind opened fire more in panic than in control resulting in most of the spray of bullets going well wide of the melee in front of him. Most but not all. Billy yelped in pain as he caught a bullet to his right shoulder. Jake returned the fire hitting one of the three Cleos who were frantically running for cover. He grabbed hold of Billy and pulled him behind the corner of the building just as another burst of fire went high and wide.

"I think we may need a bit of help here folks. Billy can move ok, but I reckon we're going to need some covering fire to get across to you."

JJ looked at Marty and then his dad. Marty understood the message. JJ had heard it all and there was no mistaking the look of intent on his face.

"Billy and Jake are in trouble. I'm going back to help."

Before either could reply, JJ was off and running in the direction of the shootout. Marty took one look at Brains, and they exchanged nods.

"Jake don't shoot it's me, JJ." he shouted as he sprinted towards them dodging in and out between the rides.

"Hi bro. Sorry about this. They took us a bit by surprise." Billy said apologetically as JJ slid in next to them.

"No problem. Let's get you to the fence." JJ looked at Jake who responded immediately.

"You go with Billy. I'll keep them busy then follow you across."

Jake crouched at the corner, lent forward, and opened fire sending a cascade of bullets in the general direction of the Cleos. The response was immediate. Shit thought Jake, there's a few more of them now. He fired one more burst, turned and ran to the first ride. Another burst of fire whistled past him and off into the darkness. He tried to return the fire but to no avail. He had fired off all the rounds in the magazine. He pulled the empty magazine out and felt for the full one in his pocket. He looked up to see two Cleos running towards him. He muttered a short prayer to himself as he clipped in the full magazine. His prayer must have worked because he heard the repeated hiss of a silenced Browning. Both of the oncoming Cleos staggered and fell to the ground.

"This is the last time I save your scraggy neck, you idiot. What the hell were you thinking getting one of my boys shot?"

Jake smiled, pleased to hear the welcome sound of his friend chastising him once again.

"Sorry Brains. Can we get out of here and discuss it later?"

"You go, I go, you go, I go. Just like in the old days, ok."

"Ok. But you go first. I've got the bigger gun remember."

Those Cleos close enough heard the sound of laughter and wondered who these maniacs were that found the situation funny as they themselves fired aimlessly at shadows in the darkness.

Watching on, Marty was taking stock in his head. Two young girls and their brother, an injured father and his two sons, one of them wounded, our resident comedian, and me. All of us needing to get to two cars, one with driver waiting and one without, and in between a bunch of armed men trying to stop us. He looked up to the sky. Another fine mess Johnny-Boy, yet another fine mess you've gotten us into.

Billy and JJ were in animated conversion when Brains grimaced his way through the fence. Billy was insisting he was alright as JJ was trying to take a closer look at his shoulder wound.

"Sit still and let me take a good look at it."

"I'm doing ok. Anyway, since when have you been a paramedic? What we need to do first is get everyone away from here. Then you can poke me about a bit more, Doctor Dimwit. Trust me, it'll feel even better once we start moving again."

As Brains listened to his sons' bickering, he found his mind wandering to times gone by. Happy times when life was much simpler. A family of four, holidaying by the seaside, ice cream and candy floss, sunshine and sand. Their mum smothering everyone in factor 50 suntan lotion. Fond memories from a bygone age of innocence.

His half-smile was gone in a moment as he coughed into his hand and felt the warm liquid settle in his palm. The damage done to him was taking its toll and even with his high pain threshold, he had begun to feel pain with every breath. He knew he was on borrowed time.

"Marty, Jake, you need to get these youngsters away from here, now." There was no mistaking the command in his voice. "I'm going to stay here and protect your back. You understand, right."

Marty pointed at JJ and Billy.

"They might not come without you."

How does a proud father say goodbye to his sons? How does he stand and watch them as they head off into an unknown and unforeseeable future? How does a father tell them he's sorry he won't be there to keep them safe? How does he tell them how much he loves them and their mum, when the time for such words has come and gone? Brains didn't really know. What he did know was he had to get them to go on without him and he knew how.

"JJ, you have to get your brother and the girls safely away from here. Then the pair of you need to make sure you look after your mum for me. You have to take very good care of the blue book, it's our one big asset. It may prove to be the key that unlocks the door to a better future. Son, I'm depending on you."

JJ touched the pocket holding the blue book as if he was protecting their most precious heirloom. His dad continued.

"Hidden in the list of names on the USB stick is a doctor who you need to go to for help. He was Johnny's contact. Search down the list until you see a name with my middle initials together with a web address with our surname embedded. Go to the web address, type in his name and his details will come up. Billy, you tell your mother that I love her, always have, always will. You both have to understand that someone has to stay here and I'm the only logical choice, right. Besides, you found me once so you can do it again. But don't take too long next time, the food and the service in this place isn't very good, it's not very good at all." He smiled at his sons, reached out with both hands and a father and his two sons embraced for what he knew was likely to be the very last time.

"Remember, I'm very proud of you both." He released his hold, gently guided them away from him and turned to Marty.

"Now Marty, get going before Jake bursts into tears and embarrasses us all."

Chapter 44

Once again Marty took up his position at the front with JJ and Obi on the flanks and Jake at the rear. Billy and the two girls were at the centre of the diamond. His eyes shooting from side to side, Marty was scanning the horizon looking for any telltale signs of movement. Danny had said he had seen some figures going around the outside of the camp and they must have gone past here by now he thought.

"Sally. We're on our way. Is the coast all clear?"

They had just scampered across the road and were huddled at the corner of the side street. It all seemed a bit too quiet for Marty's liking.

"Sally. Where are you?"

Silence.

"Answer me goddammit."

He immediately regretted letting his frustration get the better of him.

"Danny somethings wrong. Sally's not responding to me. Can you check everything's still working and is there anything from the satellite pictures we might need to know about?"

"I'm on it." came Danny's immediate response.

Marty and Jake exchanged worried glances. They both felt the hairs on the back of their necks rising. Jake was the first to break the tense silence.

"This doesn't smell right to me big buddy. I think we need to ditch the cars and find alternative transport."

"But what about Sally." The concern in JJ's voice was all too apparent.

Marty picked up on the question and continued the conversation with Jake.

"The lads right." replied Marty, "We can't just abandon Sally. She could be sitting there just waiting for us for all we know. Let's settle for a halfway house. We'll get Obi and the girls away from here a different way. I assume you haven't lost your touch and can get us another car, right?"

Jake smiled and nodded.

"Right. Take Billy, Obi, and the girls back down there and get them a car then get back here pronto. Obi, you drive them out of here back to your house and get Danny to get hold of Johnny's contact. JJ text Danny the information your dad gave you."

Jessie and Katie had held hands the whole time since they had hugged their brother. Obi whispered to them to follow him as quietly as mice and took hold of Katie's free hand. He was fighting hard against the fact he had left his mother behind and that he would soon have to explain what had happened to his sisters. What would be even harder would be trying to explain all this to his dad. He put his thoughts aside and followed Jake who had spotted a couple of possible getaway cars back down the road.

Clutching his shoulder with one hand, Billy grabbed his brother's arm and gripped it hard.

"I'll see you back at Obi's later, got it." Billy pulled his brother towards him. "No stupid heroics ok. This is about us all getting away safely. Dad's going to make it out too. I'm sure of it."

"Me too Billy, me too."

JJ reached into his jacket pocket and pulled out the blue book.

"Billy, take this and get it to Danny. I'm not sure what it contains but dad thinks it's really important. Keep it safe and you take care."

JJ watched until they disappeared from view.

Minutes later Jake was back, another job done.

"Still got the touch." He announced proudly. "They're on their way home. Good for us that people haven't used their cars much. Found one plugged in and fully charged, they drove off nice and quiet like. No one's going to notice it's gone until morning. I hung around and no one came out to look and no curtains moved in any of the windows. I think Obi realized keeping his sisters safe was more important than venting his anger on someone right now. I told him there'd be a time for that later. I gave him my earpiece so he could stay in contact with Danny. So, my two amigos, what do we do now?"

"Danny, what have you got for us?"

Marty was hoping for some good news from the young man back at the house. There was a short pause as if Danny was preparing his reply. The silence was making Marty feel anxious and impatient.

On Danny's part there had been what he could only consider

to be a serious error of his judgement although that was a rather harsh verdict under the circumstances. He had only been watching the movement of Marty and Jake because they were the main players. Where they were was where everyone else was, except for Sally, and they were in constant dialogue so he could cross-reference their conversations with satellite maps. Sally, he thought, wasn't going anywhere so he hadn't bothered to track her at all.

"Sorry but I think I screwed up. I only tracked you Marty, and Jake, I didn't worry about JJ 'cos he was with you, and I didn't track Sally as she was supposed to stay put. I've been running a trace on Sally, and it's come up to show she's moving inside the camp. I tried to reach her but there was no answer. From the maps it looks like she's near where JJ's dad was. I've also been trying to look at the streets around you but they're very dark. It looks like there could be some people down the street on the same side as you, but I can't be sure exactly where they are nor how many."

If the light had been good enough Marty and Jake would have seen JJ go white as a sheet and then bright red as the shock of Sally being in real danger turned to outright anger. Anger at himself for ever letting her convince him she should come with them in the first place.

"They've got Sally, haven't they? I knew I should never have let her come. I knew it wasn't a good idea. We've got to go back, back to collect my dad and rescue Sally. We've got to."

Marty grabbed his arm and pulled him back against the wall.

"Steady on son. We go back and do what? They'll be wanting us to do just that, waiting for us. We're good, but we can't take on a whole army much as we want to. We've got the blue book your dad thought was so important. Maybe that's our ace in the hole."

Marty could tell by the wild look in JJ's eyes that he wasn't listening.

"Danny, let me know when Sally's tracker comes to a stop." At least we can find out exactly where she is, he thought.

Marty wasn't good at making plans, he was good at making noise. He was good at wreaking havoc and leaving a trail of death and destruction in his wake. This had worked for him before so why not now. When you're short of a plan just do what you're best at because you're best at it for one reason, because it's tried, it's tested, and it works.

"We're going down the street to our cars taking out anyone trying to stop us on the way. We're going to make a lot of noise and dish out a lot of pain if we have to. It'll be a signal to Sally and Brains that we're still in business, and a signal to their captors that they had better think twice before they hurt our friends. You two cross over to the other side to get their attention and then wait until you hear gunfire. Get to Jake's car and get the hell out. Anyone tries to cross the road to stop you, shoot them. Don't worry about me, I'll be enjoying myself keeping them very busy on the way to my car. You ready?"

PART 7

Winners and Losers

Chapter 45

The Major was feeling rather pleased with himself. He had decided the assailants were too good to make the mistake of parking too close to the camp. He had figured that if it were him, he would have parked down a nearby side street and therefore they would have done the same. If he could somehow identify where they were heading back to, he could easily ambush them where and when they least expected. He had ordered his men to check inside all the parked cars they passed on the main road just in case and then sent them down the first two side streets. He was congratulating himself because the result was much better than he had anticipated.

Sally had been sitting patiently listening to the conversations in her earpiece when she heard the loud bangs coming from the camp in her other ear. Nothing on the street stirred. Either no one was home, or they knew the camp for what it was and felt much safer showing no interest in whatever was going on outside. Marty had been absolutely right, the waiting and the not knowing were almost totally unbearable. She was worried about them all but especially about JJ. She wished she had told him how she felt about him long before now.

Just as she was deciding whether she should get out and go to find them the choice was made for her.

The car door swung open, a strong hand reached in, grabbed her arm, and she was wrenched from her seat and pulled out of the car. Facing her and looking very menacing was another man dressed in Karki pointing a rifle at her. Still gripped by her arm, Sally was spun backwards and thrown hard against the side of the car.

"Looks like we've caught us a little fishy. Go get the Major."

Sally tried to struggle free but the more she twisted the tighter the grip became. She relaxed and decided to try to bluff it out.

"I don't know who you are but you're making a big mistake. I was just bringing my sick granny some food and her medicine. I was worried about her and wouldn't have been able to sleep until I checked she was alright."

"Tell it to the Major girlie."

Sally tried to pull her arm free and swung at him with her free hand. It was a foolhardy act of defiance. He knocked her flailing hand away and gave her a hard slap across the face.

"Be a good girl and wait for the Major, ok."

The one with the rifle came running back accompanied by a second athletic figure Sally assumed was the Major. He looked her up and down and Sally did the same to him. He was tall and ruggedly handsome and looked far too young to be a Major. A privileged background fast-tracked in and out of Sandhurst and moved quickly up through the ranks to Major was her initial thought. It was confirmed when he spoke.

"Who are you and what are you doing here? Don't even think about lying to me. I know you're a part of what's going on. Private, search the car."

The side of her face still stinging, Sally was about to tell him the same story when she watched a broad smile sweep across his face. He reached up towards her ear. She tried to turn away only for the hand that had slapped her to grab her by the neck and hold her head still.

"What have we here?"

The Major gently pulled out Sally's earpiece and dropped it into the palm of his hand.

"I think we've found ourselves a getaway driver, don't you?"

Sally's response was to give him a defiant stare.

"Oh, my boss is going to like you. You two take this and her back through the main gate and then straight to Dr Bramney. If she struggles you know what to do but not too much rough stuff. Dr Bramney won't be best pleased if you deliver her broken goods. Sergeant, on me."

One of the soldiers popped the earpiece into his pocket and the two of them manhandled Sally down the street and off to the main camp entrance. Sally was more cross with herself for getting caught so easily than she was worried about the consequences. She contemplated whether to try to break free and make a run for it in the hope she would bump into Marty and JJ, but it was unlikely she could outrun them even if she did manage to escape their grip. She decided to stay cool and keep her wits about her for when she met Dr Bramney.

Back in the street, the Major was still on a high, convinced he would soon have the rest of the invaders either captured or dead. Despite his orders, dead was his preferred option. Whomever they were these people were armed and extremely dangerous so trying to take them alive posed far too much risk to him and his men.

"Sergeant set up an ambush on the other side of the street with this car at the centre. I've sent two of our squad back with the girl so there's just eight of us now. Let's go for the classic 2-4-2 formation. What do you think?"

"Sounds good Sir. I'll take Allen with me as the first pair. You, Sir, take the middle and I'll pick two to send as the last pair. If we let them wander in and get close to the car they'll be caught like rats in a trap."

"Get to it then Sergeant. We may not have a lot of time before our quarry arrives."

"One last thing Sir. Whomever these people are, they must be pretty good or pretty stupid. I think they're professionals. They won't just give up, so I don't think we'll be able to take them alive. Can I pass down the order no prisoners, Sir?" The Sergeant had just put the Major's own thoughts into words.

"Do it Sergeant. No prisoners."

Smiling at the thought of the impending action, the Sergeant nodded, put his hand on top of his head in a signal to the men to gather round him and seconds later proceeded to brief them on the situation.

"Allen you're with me. You three over there with the Major and you two take up position up there as the book end. You know the drill. Anyone tries to make a break for it you take them out.

Everyone clear?"

"Yes Sergeant."

The unified response was a little too loud for his liking but that was his own fault for asking the question.

The Major joined his three chosen men and settled down to wait for the fun. This was going to be a feather in his cap for sure and maybe soon he'd get to add a pip to the shiny crown on his shoulder.

Chapter 46

Smoke and flames were still rising from what was left of the incinerators as Caroline stared through the jagged hole that was once the doors to the Recycling Plant. The four bodyguards had formed a protective arc around her and were constantly scanning the surrounding area, more for effect than out of any real sense of danger. They could see no reason why the perpetrators of this attack would still be in the vicinity. The damage was done, so why would anyone bother to hang around. They could also see that their boss was shaking, not with fear, but with absolute rage.

"You. Get in there and check it out."

Her order was sharp and blunt. Her cold, clipped tone left her emotional state in no doubt.

"I'll be in the Treatment Room. Report back to me there."

Without hesitation one of the four peeled away and disappeared into the hot, smokey building to be met immediately by the rancid smell of burnt flesh. He wretched and hoped for his own sake his boss hadn't seen.

As Caroline and her entourage entered one end of the pavilion building Sally was being pushed through the doors at the other. The two came together just outside the door to the Treatment Room.

"Ma'am. The Major told us to deliver this straight to you."

Still gripping her arm tight, he shoved Sally forward.

"She had this in her ear Ma'am."

Caroline took the earpiece and smiled at Sally. Her smile did nothing to mask the cruel and murderous expression on her face. It wasn't meant to.

"Well, well, well. Who have we here? What's a nice young girl like you doing out after dark?" Caroline's tone hardened and her smile turned to a snarl. "I know you're mixed up in all this so let's not play silly games just tell me who you are and what is going on. No lies. I'm in no mood to listen to nonsense, so don't even think about trying to be clever with me. There's a whole world of pain just waiting to come crashing down on you. You understand. A whole world of pain."

Sally locked eyes with Caroline, determined to give nothing away.

"I don't know who you are or what you want. As I told them, I was visiting my sick granny. Please let me go. Please. I really have no idea what's going on or what you're talking about."

As Caroline stepped towards her, Sally twisted, kicked out at her captor, and pulled her arm free, only for one of Caroline's bodyguards to step in and hit her hard in the mid-drift. The embarrassed soldier yanked her up off the floor and grabbed her hair, pulling her head backwards so she was looking directly up at Caroline. Sally was struggling to breathe. Caroline was smiling.

"My, my, you are a feisty little one, aren't you? I can see I'm going to have a lot of fun with you."

Caroline moved forward and stroked Sally's hair with her left hand. Sally winced and tried to pull away, but the soldier held her head still. He was not going to let her best him again.

"Pretty too. You'll make an excellent replacement. You see I broke my last little toy only recently. You could say we enjoyed too much of a good thing together and the pretty young thing just couldn't take all the excitement."

She gently ran her finger down Sally's cheek and under her chin.

"Oh, yes. You'll do nicely."

"Hurt me and my friends will come back and kill you."

Sally knew that sounded like some line from a movie. Something the defiant heroine says just before the hero bursts in and saves her. Sally knew full well that wasn't going to happen in the here and now, but under the circumstances, it was the best she could muster.

"Let's find out shall we."

Holding the earpiece to her ear, Caroline switched on the mic and winked at Sally.

"Hello out there. I think we should have a little chat. Don't be shy. I've got some news you might be interested in about your young, and dare I say, very pretty accomplice. Don't make me wait too long to hear from you as I'm a bit short on patience at the moment and heaven knows what I might get up to if it runs out."

She switched off the mic and pointed to one of her bodyguards.

"You. Go in and ask Dr Sterbenson to pop out here for a minute."

They had all heard Caroline's call, and they all knew what it meant. She had Sally in her clutches and this woman wanted to gloat about it. Despite what they had done to her Holiday Camp, she still considered she held all the aces.

Marty was just about to give the signal for Jake and JJ to cross the road when Caroline's dulcet tones hit the airwaves. Marty saw instantly the look in JJ's eyes and grabbed hold of his arm in an attempt to stop him responding in haste.

"Slow down there my young friend. I know what Sally means to you, but now of all times you have to stay calm. We can't change the fact that right now they've got Sally so we have to work around it and think about how we can get her back safely. Diving in at the deep end won't help, if anything it will rile the woman into doing something to Sally just to prove a point. The one advantage we have is that we've got that book. It's our only bargaining chip, and if your dad's right, I'm convinced she'll want it back. As hard to take as it is, we have to get you and the book safely away from here and then hope it's worth more to her than hurting Sally. Let's hope Danny's on the ball and starts talking to her."

"We can't just leave her here. You saw what they do to people. I can't leave her. I just can't."

Watching on, Jake saw the anguish in the young man's face and heard the desperation in his voice. His heart was plainly on his sleeve right now and there was no doubting how much he loved Sally. Jake understood how hard-nosed Marty sounded. The lad had already left his dad behind and now he was being asked to leave his girl behind too. Likewise, Jake knew Marty only too well. He knew that he would be desperate to rescue Sally but not in a gung-ho attempt doomed to failure from the outset. They had to get away and live to fight another day. Regroup, reassess, and stack the odds back in their favour. Marty was simply following their rules of engagement.

Jake was about to give them the benefit of his infinite wisdom when he saw by their faces something was going on.

"Hello. Is that you Dr Bramney?"

It was Danny. Clever boy, thought Marty, throwing that at her in an attempt to put her off her stride.

"Yes, we know who you are, and, of course, exactly where you are. We've got eyes on the ground, eyes that right now are looking at you from down the barrel of a gun. Under the circumstances, I think you'll agree, best I tell you what we want to happen next, and you listen carefully. Got it?"

The ploy only lasted a second or so. Caroline was quick to regain her composure and decided to call the bluff.

"No. You listen to me, and you listen well. I have your friend right here in front of me. You surrender yourselves to me now and in return I'll keep her out of harm's way for you. Attractive young thing, isn't she? It would be such a shame if anything should happen to that pretty face of hers. A real shame."

By this time JJ was visibly shaking with anger, a boiling rage was rising inside him fueled by the feeling of desperation and of his total inability to do anything to help Sally. Marty and Jake exchanged worried glances. Keeping him calm and safe was now an escalating problem.

Marty put a finger to his lips as he listened intently to the voices in his ear. Overlaid on Caroline's threat to Sally, could be heard a breathless male voice making a request-cum-plea to the devil woman.

"Ma'am. I think you'd best come and see this. Ma'am, in the Treatment Room. You need to see."

"Keep her here until I tell you otherwise." she barked.

Whatever Caroline expected to see it could not have been anything as bad as the sight that met her eyes when she walked in and scanned the room. The scene was compounded by the foul aroma that filled her nostrils. The room was full of the sight and smell of death.

"Dr Sterbenson's over there Ma'am. I think he's dead." stuttered the Cleo, worried that as the bringer of such bad news he might be held responsible somehow.

As cold-hearted as she was, seeing her Needles, her loyal friend, lifeless and staring blankly at the ceiling caused an explosive surge of emotion in her. Not grief, not sadness, no sudden sense of loss. She was totally overcome by fury and rage. Someone would pay dearly for this. They would all pay very dearly for this.

She shook as she bent over him and searched each of the pockets of his coat. The book, his precious, it was gone.

Caroline headed back to Sally in no mood to play games. She was way beyond that now.

The faint sound of gunfire could be heard echoing around the high-ceilinged atrium as Caroline, face like thunder, approached Sally and her captors. An evil smile crept across her face. That would be her handsome high-flying Major and his band of soldiers taking care of things for her. Doing his father proud. She would be so very pleased if he had captured at least one of them alive. Her revenge would be slow and sweet, and they, like the young woman standing in front of her, would take a very long time to die.

Caroline's mood lifted a little. This was just a small setback to her Society's plans. She already had Needles replacement in her mind and once she had the book, she would quickly get everything back on track. She switched the mic back on.

"Hello again. If there's any of you left to listen, listen well. I've just seen what you did to my friend, and trust me when I say, when I get you, which I will, you will wish you had never been born. Then, as time passes slowly by, your only wish will be to die."

She looked directly at Sally and grinned. Involuntary shivers sped down Sally's spine. There was no pretense here. This insane woman meant every word she said.

"Very soon I'll have you all, and then the fun will really start."

Caroline's words had barely left her lips when they came back to taunt her.

Sally, in her heightened state of distress, heard a pop and a low hiss just before the bullet hit home. The sound had come from somewhere quite close behind her. In that instant, her hopes were raised. Perhaps this was going to be just like the movies after all she thought as she felt the soldiers grip on her tighten momentarily as his body went into spasm, and then release, as simultaneously his head moved sideways, and tiny droplets of blood sprayed onto Sally's hair and down the side of her face. As his body hit the floor, the others scanned the area searching frantically for any sign of the shooter. Two of them formed a human barricade in front of Caroline.

Sally stood still as if she was rooted to the spot. The other soldier who had brought her here made to grab her and use her as a shield but was too slow off the mark. For his effort, he took a bullet to the chest and collapsed in front of her. Two of the bodyguards moved forward and fired at shadows in the doorways whilst the other two were trying to move Caroline back to the cover of the treatment room, but with no success. Caroline had no intention of running away to hide. She pushed her guard of honour forward until they flanked Sally, grabbed her arm, and spun her around so that she was in front of her facing the direction of the onslaught.

The two mobile guards were running to find cover but were too slow and cumbersome in their movements, presenting the shooter with two large, easy targets. They had taken just a few steps before they were taken down in quick succession. If Caroline could have seen the look in her last two bodyguards' eyes, she would have seen the fear and panic set in. They knew they were out in the open and whoever was out there in front of them was too good a shot not to take advantage of their vulnerability. They knew they were presenting an opportunity that was too good to miss. They were right. We knew it must have been the last thing on their minds as the bullets hit home and their dead weight crashed to the ground.

Caroline's grip on Sally's arms tightened. Sally felt the pain as Caroline's fingernails dug deep into her flesh, bringing her out of her state of shock and back into the reality of the situation. Both women knew it would not take long for more armed guards to arrive having heard the exchange of gunfire and then the advantage, the situation, would swing in Caroline's favour. Sally assumed her rescuers must be aware of that too.

They both must have seen the shooter emerge from shadows at the same time as their heads moved in unison towards the laboured movement. Sally did not recognize him as he walked slowly towards them, gun in hand. Caroline, on the other hand, knew exactly who it was.

Chapter 47

Having said his farewell Brains had moved back inside the camp and positioned himself mid-way between the camp entrance and the exit hole in the fence. From this position he had been able to see the comings and goings into and out of the camp, as well as watch for any discovery of the gaping hole in the fence through which everyone had just passed. It was from this vantage point that he had watched the two soldiers march Sally through the gate and up into the building. He knew instinctively it was Sally they had somehow captured, and he knew her fate would be sealed unless he gathered what strength he had left and mounted a one-man rescue mission. His one advantage would be the surprise. Their disadvantage would be the chaos and confusion surrounding them. He followed the captors and their captive unobserved into the building and watched as they met up with Caroline.

Although he couldn't hear what was being said it didn't take much to see Caroline was being asked to go into the Treatment Room. He watched as she entered and waited in anticipation of her reaction. He was in no doubt she would be absolutely furious at the carnage she would discover. From what he had been able to observe of her behaviour and her actions he feared what she might do next, what she was capable of doing to Sally. He pictured the scene unfold in his mind. She will feel no remorse, only the desire for swift and sickening retaliation. For revenge as vile and odious as she could make it and inflicted on her nearest victim. He looked at Sally standing surrounded by her evil entourage and helpless against the muscles and the guns. Clever as Sally undoubtedly was, words and rhetoric would never be enough to save her now. He moved position to give himself a better line of sight. The movement caused pain to sweep through his body. His mind fought back, winning the battle, for the moment at least.

When Caroline emerged and stomped across to Sally with a face like thunder Brains gathered his thoughts, focused his aim, and did what he was trained to do in such circumstances. He knew he would have to act fast. He also knew that the sound of gunfire would bring unwanted attention to the scene but from whom and how quickly he couldn't second guess. With the shots fired and the men down he stood up and walked out to confront the woman who had become his nemesis. Caroline had one hand holding Sally and in the other she was still holding the earpiece. Despite the carnage around her Caroline seemed as calm and composed as ever.

"Let the girl go. She has nothing to do with all this. Let her come to me, we'll walk away, and you'll live to see another day." Brains lowered the browning to his side in a gesture of conciliation as he spoke.

"Neither of you will leave here alive. You hear me. All your friends are either captured or dead and more of my men are about to arrive at any second. You haven't got a chance, and you know it. If you want to be the hero then shoot the girl and then shoot yourself, because if I take you both alive the rest of your dreary lives will be a long and very painful affair. So why don't you do her and yourself a favour and save me the trouble?"

Brains shook his head slowly and stared into Caroline's cold, blue eyes.

Sally looked down at the soldier lying dead at her feet and shook her arm free of Caroline's grip. She looked towards her rescuer standing there in his white lab coat, pyjama trousers, and boots. Not quite a superheroes outfit but that didn't matter to Sally. He was the answer to her prayer. The man spoke to her but kept his eyes focused on the woman standing behind her.

"You must be Sally, yes? Just step slowly over here to me. I'm JJ's father in case you're wondering." His voice was controlled and his tone reassuring but she could see quite plainly that he was in some considerable pain. Something Caroline had also seen, filling her with confidence that she could keep him occupied long enough for her Cleos to arrive. She turned slightly to face him square on.

"You stay exactly where you are." Brains raised his gun and pointed it directly at Caroline to emphasize his command.

As Sally took her first step towards him one of the Cleos rolled over, raised his gun, and fired. Brains reacted instinctively and fired back. A bullet hit Brains in the shoulder knocking him backwards. The Cleo, shot in the head, died instantly.

Seizing the opportunity Caroline darted forward bending down to her right in an attempt to grab a gun off the floor. Sally reacted immediately. With the speed of a cheetah and the strength of a lion she kicked Caroline hard in the ribs sending her sideways onto the floor and out of reach of the gun. Caroline rolled over gasping for breath as Sally slowly bent down to retrieve the earpiece and to pick up the gun. By this time Brains had steadied himself and was standing holding his left shoulder, his Browning still clasped firmly in his hand.

"Quickly, move back behind me. They'll be others arriving very soon, so we have to move fast and get back into the shadows." Brains wanted to tell Sally how well she had done and that he admired her courage and quick thinking but there were far more pressing matters to deal with. None more so than the red-faced woman lifting herself up off the floor and looking deep into his eyes with a fierce, piercing stare.

"You want to hurt me. You want to kill me. I can see it in your eyes. Well, go ahead if you think killing me will change anything. What has happened tonight is just a small setback. You can't win. Someone will already be waiting to step into my shoes." Caroline was now upright. Standing tall, proud, and defiant, showing no fear only cold composure.

"I suggest you and your young friend run away as fast as you can and just to make it interesting, I'll hold my men back for five minutes to give you a head start." Caroline didn't smile. This was a serious offer and she wanted him to see it as such.

Brains half-turned towards Sally as he spoke.

"Get yourself over there in the shadows and if that thing is still working speak to your friend and ask him to direct you out to join JJ and company. Trust me, they're still waiting for us. I know Marty and Jake too well. They'll have sorted things out by now and be waiting for your call. Go, go, and don't worry, I'll be fine. I'll be right behind you all the way." He had every intention of following on but there was something he had to attend to first, something he didn't want Sally to see. Besides, he knew he would have to slow down their pursuers once they arrived.

Sally understood. There was no other choice than for her to follow his instructions. She realized she was still holding the gun she had picked off the floor and held it out towards him. As he took it from her, she could see this hand was wet with blood, his own blood. She reached out and touched his shoulder.

"Thank you." she said softly, turning away so he couldn't see the tears in her eyes, but he wasn't looking. She knew he was going to fight to the end to make sure her, his sons, and his friends got away safely.

"Danny, can you hear me?" Sally was standing in the unlit doorway looking back at the two figures standing opposite one another. Two adversaries bound together by harsh words and evil deeds.

JJ's heart leapt when he heard the familiar voice in his ear. Marty had been right to hold him back but now, now it was time to act. He would get to rescue his beloved after all.

"I need you to guide me out of here and back to the others. I haven't got time for explanations so don't ask. JJ's dad rescued me and he's buying me time to get away so where do I need to go."

Danny was on to it in a flash.

"I hear you Sal, loud and clear. Head down to the main doors, keep close to the wall, and then turn left and head for the children's playground. There's no movement at that end so you shouldn't come into contact with any of the bad guys but be careful nonetheless."

Before Sally could respond she heard a loud and excited voice in her ear.

"Sal, it's me JJ. We're heading back to meet you. Follow Danny's instructions and we'll see you at the fence. If you have to stop then wait for us to get to you. Thank God you're ok. I love you."

There it was. Finally. A public declaration of his feelings for her spoken for all to hear. Sally didn't respond. She wanted to but somehow the timing didn't feel quite right. Instead, she took one last look towards the man who had saved her, turned, and disappeared into the shadows.

Chapter 48

The faint sound of the gunfire Caroline heard in the atrium was very loud and very deadly out on the street. Jake had crossed the tarmac and was moving forward, darting from parked car to parked car, constantly scanning the opposite pavement for any signs of movement or shadowy figures waiting in ambush. Marty, well aware of JJ's mental state after having heard Caroline boasting about having captured Sally, had decided it was better to let Jake go alone. He needed to keep JJ near to him so he could keep him under control, stop him from taking any rash action that could get him killed.

Marty counted to ten and decided Jake would have gotten far enough for him to make his move.

"JJ, I want you to move out to the edge of that car. Position yourself so you can see anyone who tries to cross the road. If they do, I'm relying on you to see they don't make it to Jake, OK?" Marty's whisper was barely audible. JJ nodded and took up his position, squinting to see if there was any sign of Jake's progress.

Outnumbered and outgunned, Marty knew shock and surprise would be his much-needed best friends when he took the fight to them, which was exactly what he was about to do. There were two possibilities he had to consider. Either they were military and under the command of an officer or NCO, or they were mercenaries like the Cleos he had encountered earlier in which case they would be more unpredictable but less competent. As the pavement ahead of him was quiet and still Marty opted for the first scenario. He pictured how they would set themselves for the ambush. Standard practice, he thought, they probably think we're amateurs and no real threat to them, so they'll set up in three groups with the largest in the middle. He was counting on his experience and intuition but there was always the possibility he could be wrong. There was only one way to find out.

Automatic rifle in hand Marty stood up and walked down the street just as if he was returning home after a few drinks down at the local. The difference being he was as sober as a judge and about to unleash hell on anyone stupid enough to challenge him.

The Sergeant had caught a glimpse of Jake on the opposite side of the street and touched Private Allen on the shoulder signaling to him that he needed to make ready. Then out of the corner of his eye he saw something moving towards him. He turned and stared as a huge figure looking like the Angel of Death emerged from the shadows and into the half-light of the Sergeant's night vision. The second it took for the Sergeant to shake off the shock and surprise and evaluate the threat was half a second too long. Marty moved swiftly forward and hit him square in the face with the butt of his rifle, The sheer the force of the blow shattered the Sergeant's left eye socket and sent him falling silently to the floor.

The inexperienced young Private froze. Unable to react to the unexpected he met with a savage blow to the side of his head. He fell forward onto his rifle, his eyes and mouth wide open as if about to plead for his soul. Marty looked down at the young man. If there had been another way, he thought, such a waste of a young life. Sorry son, but you just happened to be in the wrong place at the wrong time and in the wrong war.

As Marty was making his move, Jake spotted the Major's group and concluded the same as Marty, this was the middle of a standard military ambush which meant two further up and two further down. He could see the middle group had split into two and taken up positions either side of a parked car. Jake darted forward and immediately heard the loud shout.

"Fire." came the Major's excited command.

Jake hit the pavement face-up and stared at the night sky, his rifle clasped in readiness across his chest. Then came the noise of metal on metal, breaking glass, and the whistling of bullets as they went high and wide of the car. Someone over there doesn't quite know what to shoot at, he thought, bloody amateurs the lot of them.

"And where the hell are you Marty, my old friend?" he muttered to himself. "Get a bloody move on, eh." He laughed out loud as he rolled over and edged forward so that he could just see across the road.

"If you want something doing, do it yourself." He whispered as he switched his rifle to single shot, took aim and fired two rounds in quick succession. He heard a cry of pain, loud and clear like a footballer's howl in an empty stadium. The gunfire abated and he heard someone calling out.

"Major. We're both hit. I think Private Jones is dead."

Jake could hear the shock and panic in the trembling voice. Thank you for the intel you idiot he thought with a tinge of sadness that they'd sent boys to do a man's job. Boys that were about to end up dead once Marty caught up with play.

"Shut up Private. Pull yourself together. We're in the middle of a gun fight. What were you expecting, a bloody picnic? We've got them pinned down so let's keep it like that."

The Major was expecting his experienced Sergeant to cross and move in from one end and the other two further up the street to do the same thus trapping the targets in a three-way shooting gallery. He'd give them the choice. Surrender to him or be wiped off the face of the earth. Gun-ho and as eager for glory as he was, he so wanted it to be the latter. A victorious parade back to her Ladyship with his captives in tow.

It wasn't a miscalculation as such on the Major's part that both options had already been scuppered by Marty. He could have had no idea who he was up against, but he was about to find out. About to suffer the consequences of his over-confident underestimation of his opponent's skill and expertise.

At the same time as the Major came into Marty's view JJ saw two figures a way down the street making a dash to cross over to Jake's side. He instantly opened fire knowing he had little chance of hitting either of them but hoping it would draw Jake's attention to the situation. Without further hesitation he followed suit and sprinted across to get between the two parked cars opposite him. It's high time I joined the fight for real, he thought, as he gasped to regain his breath, his senses heightened by the flight or fight adrenalin rushing to his brain. These were the people who had captured Sally and most likely hurt her in the process. They deserve everything they've got coming to them. Let's deal with them and then we'll go get Sally. His thoughts moved momentarily to the whereabouts of his father. He'd be somewhere out there, and JJ was sure they'd meet up on the way to rescuing Sally.

Pressing himself against the wall JJ crouched and moved slowly forward until he got to within a couple of cars' lengths of where he thought Jake would be.

"Jake, it's me JJ." he whispered.

"Shush." drifted back the reply from Jake.

A moment later Jake fired two more single shots hitting the two figures, one hugging the wall, the other leaning on the side of a car, and watched as they collapsed down onto the pavement. He smiled. His job was done. Now all that was left was for Marty to finish things off on the other side of the street. As always, Marty obliged.

Lacking Jake's subtlety, Marty had never been known for a softly, softly, single shot approach. He was the closest to a gung-ho go in all guns-a-blazing John Wayne character that Jake had ever seen, and tonight was no exception.

Marty had observed the small ambush party firing at Jake and as large as life had strolled up to within a few metres of the Major unobserved. No rifle butt to the head this time. He knew there were two separate groups so even if he did for the first the chances were someone in the second group would get a shot off before he could get to them. Nothing for it but to blast them all to hell.

The look of complete surprise on the Major's face added another picture to Marty's mental scrapbook. Standing as the Major was, already celebrating his forthcoming victory in his head, made it easier than Marty had expected. The man-mountain emerged from the gloom, looked the Major square in the eye, and then unleashed a barrage of bullets killing the Private outright and almost cutting the Major in half across his mid-drift. The Major stood stock still with enough life left for a look of bewilderment to sweep across his face. A fleeting look of disappointment. There would be no extra pip after all.

Marty moved forward knocking the upright figure to the floor and saw the last remaining soldier facing him with his arms raised and a pleading look on his face.

"Don't shoot me. Please don't shoot me. I was just following orders. This is the first time I've ever shot at anyone. I didn't want to do it. I never even hit the car."

Jake and JJ had crossed the road confident in their belief that Marty had made it safe to do so. Jake intervened.

"Let him be Marty. He's just a boy and he can do us no harm. Look at him. He's wounded and he's terrified of us, well, of you. Besides it might be a good thing to have someone left alive to tell the tale of what went on here tonight. The deadly deeds of the marauding Marty. I can hear the story now. Passed on by trembling voices spreading fear and terror throughout their ranks." Jake laughed and then went serious again.

"Besides he can also tell us what happened to Sally. He can't tell us anything if he's dead now, can he?" There was sense and sound reasoning in Jake's words and the fear in the young soldier's eyes told them he would happily tell them everything they wanted to know.

Marty loomed large over the young soldier and kicked his gun away.

"If you want to stay alive tell us what happened to the girl."

"We found her in a car over there and the Major sent her back to the camp with two of us. No-one harmed her here. She said she was visiting her granny." He was visible shaking and wishing he had been one of the lucky ones taking her back to camp. He had no idea of the irony of his wish.

Before they could continue their interrogation of the young soldier the sound of Sally's voice came drifting over the airwaves and into their heads. Neither Jake nor Marty was surprised by JJ's reaction. His categorical statement they would be going back for her they expected. His declaration of his love for her, well, that was about time. Jake winked at Marty. Marty smiled then quizzed the young soldier about who was left in the camp. More than satisfied with his answer Marty hit the young soldier knocking him unconscious.

"Looks like we're on another rescue mission. Let's go get Sally and Brains too. He's skulking around out there somewhere and bound to be up to some sort of mischief." Marty said with a smile and a definite tone of affection. Jake laughed. JJ looked at Marty with an expression of relief and gratitude. Marty continued.

"Hold your horses for just a second. We need to pop over to Jake's car to replenish our ammo. The chances are we'll run into some more trouble, so we need to be prepared for it. We'll leave this mess as it is for someone to deal with in the morning. Doubt they'll be looking for them just yet." Marty turned and led the way across to Jake's car. Reluctantly JJ followed. Jake sauntered up alongside him.

"Don't worry we'll get Sally back easy enough. The big man has that look in his eye. I've seen it many times before. God help anyone that gets his way." Jake sped up to overtake Marty and to get to his car first.

"Clever me, eh Marty. I shot at them from behind someone else's car. Just look at that. Someone won't be best pleased when they decide to come out of their cozy old home. Let's hope they haven't called anyone about the noise you made." Jake unlocked the car and opened up the boot looking very pleased with himself.

They took what was left of the ammunition and Jake rummaged around in his bag pocketing what looked to JJ like random bits and pieces and maybe some left-over explosive. He wondered what Jake had in mind and was about to ask as Marty slammed the boot shut.

"Okay. Now it's the right time JJ. Will you lead the way, or shall I?" Marty bowed and pretended to doff his hat. JJ strode past him followed by a nodding and grinning Jake.

"Softy." Jake whispered.

"Idiot." Came Marty's immediate reply.

Chapter 49

So, this is it, thought Brains, I've reached the end of the line. There he stood with a gun in each hand and pictured the scene being portrayed on the big screen at the cinema. Liam Neeson would be a good choice to play my part, he thought. Or perhaps Daniel Craig. Yes Daniel Craig. Smart, tough, and handsome to boot. What a kick the boys and their mum would get out of that. He shook himself out of his reverie and back to the situation in front of him. He could already hear the sound of voices and boots hitting the ground running, they were getting closer by the second. By the same token Caroline's confidence in her control over the situation was growing stronger. After all she had given him the very best treatment and his programmed reaction to the command of her voice should be embedded in his head somewhere. She just had to find the right spot.

"Looks like you've come quite a way since our last little get together. Do you remember our last conversation? About how you need to think clearly before you act and how you need to get all the facts straight." Caroline's voice was soft and silky smooth, like the hypnotizing hiss of a sly slippery snake. She continued.

"Now, put down the guns and let me take care of you and those worrying thoughts of yours. Listen to me, the girl's got away so there's no more need for the heroics, is there."

She was feeling like her old self now, assertive and in total control of the situation. He was swaying in front of her, clearly hurt and his mind still in turmoil as a result of his trips to the Treatment Room. I want you alive, she thought, alive so I can make you suffer for what has happened here today. Alive so I can enjoy our final hours together, just me and you having so much fun.

"Put the guns down. Let them drop to the floor and then we can move on." Her tone was strong and reassuring. She knew her voice would be playing tricks with his mind.

No. no, no. He gripped the guns so tight he felt a sharp pain from the wound in his shoulder. Feel the pain, let it work to clear my mind, let it be my friend, he thought. He steadied himself and smiled at her. It was at that moment she knew.

"You really are something special. Even now you still think you've got the upper hand, that you're in control. I'm going to disappoint you and I'm really not sorry about that. Likelihood is, I will die here today but not by your hand and not to your knowledge. The last thing you'll see is me, alive and kicking, and maybe, just maybe, I'll find a way out of here and live a long and happy life destroying everything you've worked for."

He smiled at her again. Caroline's eyes widened as she realized the Angel of Death was coming to collect her soul. But not yet, she thought. What is he doing? He can't possibly expect me to beg for my life. Perhaps he just wants to gloat over what he thinks is his victory. Her eyes flashed back at him. The message was clear.

I'm not done for, not yet.

"What happens next is for all the innocent people you have made suffer and for the poor unfortunate you tortured in front us and for what, to make you feel good."

"What I have done was always for the welfare of the people. For the salvation of humanity. The work will continue, with or without me. You cannot stop us now."

From the look in Caroline's eye and the tone of her voice there was no doubting she believed every word she had just uttered. This was her alibi. Her justification for all she and her Society had done, and he had to concede he could think of none better. He struggled to remember the quote he had once read by a French philosopher. Something about the welfare of humanity and tyrants. Got it, Albert Camus, that's who it was. He wanted to punch the air, pleased that he could still cut through the fog in his brain.

He steadied himself once again and this time spoke with conviction.

"Maybe it's too late for me but there are good people, strong-minded people out there who I know will have a damn good try and they'll never give up until they get the job done."

Out of the corner of his eye he saw movement. Figures in the shadows drawing closer, eyes focusing through the dim light. Dull minds assessing the scene in front of them. He was running out of time and running out of the strength to fight back. Consequences, always consequences. He knew that killing her would not put an end to it, that he understood. Caroline would be gone but whoever replaced her would probably be just as bad, maybe even worse if that was at all possible. They say there is always a choice but standing there he knew there was only one thing he could do. He had no choice, and he wasn't sorry about the fact. He knew left alive she would hunt down his family and friends and torture them for sport. They both understood what had to happen next and they both smiled in mutual anticipation.

"The time has come. It's time for us to say goodbye." he said as he raised the gun in his right hand. Caroline nodded as if to give him her approval. An acknowledgment that if she was in his shoes, she would be doing exactly the same. Her eyes were bright and wide. Her mouth curled in a smile. Even in the face of death she wanted him to feel she was still in control of the situation.

There they stood, looking deep into each other's eyes. One fearless and defiant and the other summoning every ounce of strength he had left to pull the trigger. At that very moment the silence was broken by the sound of gunfire close behind them. Caroline saw a flicker, a moment of concern in his eyes, not for himself but for that stupid girl she thought. In that instant she made her move. She took a step sideways and rushed towards him. Distracted momentarily, Brains cursed to himself as he registered the blurred figure hurtling towards him. He reacted instinctively. He felt the gun recoil in his hand, the left or right he wasn't sure. He watched as Caroline, slowed by the impact of the bullet, put her hands to her chest and stumbled forwards and down onto the ground an arm's length in front of him. As she lay in front of him, he felt what little strength he had left draining away. His mind shouted shoot her again but his body couldn't obey the command. The last act had been played out. The curtain had come down and it was over for both of them.

He dropped to his knees and made peace with the world. He closed his eyes and for one last time pictured his beautiful wife and his two brave sons.

"I love you." he whispered but no one heard.

His head slumped forwards and his arms fell limp at his sides. The guns slipped silently out of his hands onto the cold hard floor. He'd come to the end of a very long day. He took a deep and painful breath and finally, he let go.

Chapter 50

On Billy's insistence Obi had agreed to take a detour to the village to pick up Billy's mum. Even with the pain in his shoulder Billy still managed to think like his dad and his logic made absolute sense. They needed to keep their base safe and so would have to swap cars somewhere so why not in the village where there was very limited CCTV. They knew Billy's mum would not be safe at home as this was very likely going to be the first place Cleos would be sent to look. Dump this car, pick up my mum, use her car to take us back the rest of the way was Billy's argument and Obi saw it made sense. Having Billy's mum around would also help my sisters, he thought.

The reunion at Obi's house was a somewhat muted affair. Danny was pleased to see them as he had found it extremely hard being on his own when so much was happening to his friends. He couldn't hide the fact that his pleasure, great that it was, was etched with concern for those who had not yet returned. Young and inexperienced, Danny and Obi looked at one another each seemingly asking the other what they should do next. They were relieved of the responsibility when Billy's mum spoke up and calmly took charge of the situation.

"Obi why don't you take the girls into the kitchen and give them something to eat and drink. Once I've sorted Billy out, I'll take them upstairs to bed. That ok with you girls?"

Jessie nodded her approval. Katie was too tired to care.

"Billy, we need to take a look at your shoulder."

That's my mum for you, as always so calm in a crisis, thought Billy. Then he remembered what JJ had told him just as they parted.

"Danny, my dad told us there was the name and contact of someone who might be able to help us hidden in the list of names you found on the USB stick. You need to look for the middle initials MA and Lang in the web address. I think the person's a doctor who could help with my shoulder and maybe with what we should do next."

Danny was on it in a flash. He needed to stay occupied to keep his mind away from other, darker thoughts. All had gone quiet since the interchange between himself, Sally, and JJ. He could only wait and hope they were already making their way back home.

The Doctor drove out into the night aware that he was now putting himself in harm's way. His senses tingled as he listened to the voice of the young woman telling him to take the next left after four hundred yards. In his heightened emotional state, he realized he had no evidence as to the age of the woman or even if it was the voice of a real woman and not computer generated. Either way he had decided she sounded young. He had experienced the same reaction when he had answered the call to his mobile phone almost an hour ago now. The difference that time was he knew it was a real person.

The young man on the other end of the call had sounded desperate and genuinely concerned for his friend. At first, he panicked. Shocked by the thought it might be someone trying to trick him into giving himself away. His first instinct was to end the call but the tremors in the young man's voice stopped him. Gradually his fear subsided as the young man explained why he had contacted him so late into the night. Explained why he needed his help so urgently.

The young man told him his friend had been shot and he had no one else to turn to. No one else he could trust to help them. The Doctor listened as a wave of mixed emotions swept over him. Damn my insomnia, he thought. By the end of the young man's short account, he felt the full weight of the burden of responsibility sitting heavily on his less than broad shoulders. It was his action, his own request for help, that had somehow brought this young group of friends into direct conflict with the most ruthless network of powerful people history would ever see. He had no choice but to help them. Though not just because of some sense of mis-guided obligation but because it was time for him to stand up and be counted. Time for him to join the fray and fight for what he truly believed in. People and their right to freedom.

By the time the knock on the door came the girls were tucked up in their own beds and fast asleep. Billy had told his mum most of what had happened and had tried very hard to be optimistic about JJ and his dad getting away safely.

"I reckon they'll have both found a way out of there and back to us. Obi heard the conversations on his earpiece and said it sounded like they were all going to get away. There's been nothing yet because they're busy and smart enough not to talk to us until everything's sorted."

She welcomed her youngest son's optimism. She too had faith, especially with Marty and Jake with them but still worried that faith alone would not be enough to bring them safely back to her.

Listening to the conversation only made things worse for Obi. He was thinking about his mum and the love and tenderness she had lavished on him and his sisters. He was struggling to deal with the fact he had left her behind and that he would never get to see her again. Never get to feel the warmth of her smile and the reassurance of her touch, both of which he needed now more than ever. Tears streamed down his cheeks as he sat remembering all the good times they had spent together as a family. Memories he would cherish forever.

Obi knew he had to find a way to tell his sisters what had happened, but he wasn't ready for that yet. He had no idea how he or they would cope when he did. He'd have to tell his father at some point soon too. Would there ever be happy times for them again? He wiped away the tears. He had to be strong for his sisters. He had to believe they had a future together.

Danny was busying himself with his computers to occupy his mind. He had watched as the sorrow and pain swept over his grief-stricken friend and decided the best that he could do right now was to leave his friend alone and allow him to come to terms with his loss. Hard though that was for him, he hoped it wouldn't be too long before his friend rejoined the fray.

The Doctor's arrival was a welcome interruption for them all. Danny had made initial contact with him, received a very wary response, and was a little unsure whether he would come to help. The Doctor had needed a great deal of convincing before he would even admit he knew anything about asking for help from someone called Johnny. Once he became convinced the call was genuine and from those who had been responsible for the attack on the Holiday Camp, he had sounded like he was keen to help. Sounded like he understood what he had to do.

"You were right to contact me. If the bullet is still in there, then it needs to come out immediately. Let's go take a look at the young man and see what we can do for him."

The welcome he had received on his arrival at the house warmed his heart and soul. These were good people who cared greatly for each other. Brave people who deserved a much better future than the one they face now he thought to himself before focusing on the task at hand.

Putting on his best doctor-patient bedside manner he took a closer look at the wounded young man and gave him his well-worn reassuring smile. The young man smiled back in an obvious attempt to hide his pain. The Doctor winked at his patient and then turned his attention back to his mother.

"Please would you be so kind as to get me a bowl of water and some soap. Sorry if I sound a bit like someone from the movies but I do need to wash my hands first. I promise you once I get the bullet out, he'll be as right as rain and back on his feet in no time at all."

The Doctor had seen the worried look on the woman's face and thought it best to give her something to do whilst he got to work on her son. In truth, he had all he needed right there in his black bag.

"Looks like you've been in the wars my young friend, but nothing we can't put right. Want to tell me how it happened?"

The Doctor sounded genuinely interested which indeed he was, so Billy jumped straight in eager to tell of his heroics.

"Two of us got caught in a crossfire and had to fight our way out. You probably think I was unlucky because I got shot but that's not really the case. I don't feel I have any right to feel sorry for myself. I'm a casualty of war, plain and simple. I think everyone needs to be far more concerned about the others who are still missing. We should have heard something from them by now."

The Doctor nodded as he gently pushed the needle into the young man's arm.

"I understand. You feel that you're here and alive so why all the fuss. Well, it's my job to make sure you stay that way so let's talk later after I've patched you up. Ok."

The young man looked away and nodded slowly in agreement. His eyes glazed as the injection took effect and numbed the pain.

"I think we're all ready now so shall we get started. Let's see if we can get the worst of it done before your mum gets back. This shouldn't hurt a brave lad like you too much, if at all."

Thirty minutes later Billy was still a little groggy. The bullet was out, his shoulder was strapped, and his arm was in a sling.

With his patient now on the road to recovery the Doctor

listened to Obi and Danny's more detailed account of the night-time activities. He was shocked by Obi's version of events and deeply saddened to hear that good people had died. He was not sorry to hear about what had happened to Dr Sterbenson and his team. What upset him the most was that some of the youngsters' friends were still missing in action and although he felt responsible for that, he was pleased they had taken the fight to her and hopeful they would all return very soon.

"I'm very sorry I got you involved in all this but what you and your dear friends have done so far will slow them down for sure. It's a start but I doubt it's enough to stop them from achieving their depraved and unholy vision. It's a powerful Society spawned from evil that has taken hold of every walk of life, both here and abroad. Bringing it down won't be easy but I'm up to giving it a really good try. Especially as I know I should have done more and done it sooner." The Doctor's face reflected his feelings of regret and anguish at his inaction.

"Count me in." Obi said with the force and conviction of a man on a mission. Danny smiled. His friend was on his way back to being his old self or perhaps a new self with added resolve and a thirst for vengeance.

"Me as well." answered Danny. "But I'm not sure what we can do on our own."

"I do know of others that would join us. However, we would still be a mere few against the many. They command and control just about everything and almost everybody. Because of that the people will continue to follow and obey. They preach salvation and they could have no better alibi than the very welfare of humanity. Somehow, we will have to find a way to expose them for the tyrants that they are."

"Easier said than done." muttered Danny.

Obi, now up for the fight and keen to get started, put it into perspective.

"What's the alternative? I know we're not superheroes but what is the world going to be like for us if we do nothing? Soon we'll have JJ and the others back with us, I'm sure of it. No offence Danny, but with Sally's brains we're sure to come up with a plan and when me and Marty get back together the world had better lookout."

Danny smiled to himself. Seems I've got some strong competition for Obi's affection, he thought, but then again, it's not hero worship I'm after anyway. He smiled openly this time.

"None taken." he replied. "I look forward to seeing the deadly duo in action, but just remember one important thing Obi. No capes!"

Billy and his mum chuckled at the Edna Incredibles reference. The doctor smiled. There was hope for the world yet.

Epilogue: A Safe Haven

The office space was a little smaller than Obi's living room, but it served Danny's purpose just as well. Better, Danny decided after he had installed his own devices and made himself at home. He liked the idea that he would be able to work uninterrupted.

They had moved in under the cover of darkness. Thankful that they had found a new safe haven. At least for the time being.

The converted farmhouse belonged to a friend of the Doc, as Danny now called him, who was working abroad as a missionary doctor in West Africa. He had asked the good Doctor to water his plants and feed his cat whilst he was away. With no nosey neighbours they could come and go quietly without drawing any unwanted attention. It was an ideal hiding place from which to plan their next move. They had all agreed they would continue the fight to the bitter end no matter what. Obi had left them in no doubt that he would go it alone if he had to, but he soon calmed down once they reassured him that they were all in this together.

Danny was in his element working his way through the blue book. He had set up a safe communication network between himself, the Doc and some of the Doctor's like-minded friends. Information and data were flooding in by the minute. At Billy's suggestion, which he had intended as a joke, Danny had given all the contacts including himself and the Doctor, codenames. Billy had offered his contribution to what he considered a highly amusing discussion about what they should call each other.

"How about double O one to whatever? I bagsy number seven." Billy hummed the theme tune and made the body shape of the silhouetted figure from the title sequence. Then for extra effect blew down the barrel of his finger gun.

"Wow, that's original, Billy. Be careful you don't overwork your one brain cell. Perhaps it would be best to leave the thinking to us and we'll leave the comedy to you. How does that sound?" Danny could see the funny side but what they were doing was some very serious stuff now. After listening to the accounts of what had happened at the camp, he dreaded to think what would happen if anyone was identified and caught helping them. He felt the burden of responsibility to keep everything untraceable fell squarely on his shoulders.

"Only trying to help. Using code names was my suggestion after all."

Billy broke into a fit of hysterical laughter. Danny and the Doc resumed their serious search for sensible codes names.

Billy's laughter permeated through to the kitchen where the others were drinking coffee and reflecting on the events of the last few days, contemplating what their next steps might be. They were still just a few but they were convinced they were the few that could make a difference.

On the morning after the rescue mission Obi had found the courage to tell his dad what had happened. He hadn't been able to sleep because he needed to share everything with his dad and especially how he felt about having to leave his mum behind. He had decided to call him up on his mobile at six-thirty am. A time when he knew his dad would already be up and about. The conversation was difficult for both of them. Overcome by emotion Obi had struggled to get the words out and his obvious distress raised his father's desperation to be there with his son, to encircle him in his strong arms and hold him close whilst they shared their pain. Clive could sense his son's anguish and Obi sensed his father's resulting anger, frustration, and despair. By the end of the call Obi no longer felt alone in his grief nor in his quest for revenge. He knew his dad would be up for anything they asked him to do and if they weren't sure what, then his dad would come up with his own plan to cause the maximum disruption. A plan that would be just as good if not better than theirs as his father was right there in the middle of it. It would be mission command working at its best.

The coffee morning planning meeting was interrupted by a loud cry from Danny. He was sitting at his computer and becoming very agitated.

"Another one of those speeches has just flicked up." he shouted to the others. "I've been monitoring all the channels as I knew it would happen sooner or later. It looks like they've spawned a new President who is about to introduce themselves."

They all winced at his play on words.

"You'd better get in here and gather round to watch and listen.

Doc, you especially as you may well know who's speaking." Danny waved his arms as if to draw in the group to surround him and his screen.

To everyone except the Doctor they were watching and listening to an unknown hooded figure who had without any doubt assumed Caroline's mantle as SPAWNs President. It was very evident from what he was saying that he was all too aware of what had occurred at the Holiday Camp, using it to establish his position at the top and to whip up fervour against the perpetrators of what he described as a callous act of terrorism.

The Doctor's face went pale. He let out an audible gasp as his brain sifted through the audio and visual signals coming out of the screen, bombarding him with all the data he needed to draw the right conclusion. He knew exactly who it was and how it would shape the future.

"This is not good. Not good at all. That, my dear friends, is a man with intentions every bit as bad as Caroline Bramney's. A man who is no lesser evil than the woman he has seemingly replaced." He was speaking to them all now and they were all listening to his every word.

"That makes it even more imperative that our fight must go on. What you have done has paved the way for others to follow. Your actions were never going to put an end to it as that was never your intention, but it has forced them onto a new path where they will be weaker and more open to attack, but not for long. This time the mission is absolutely clear. We must find a way to stop them, once and for all."

To Be Continued

in

NO LESSER EVIL

Printed in Great Britain
by Amazon

45463783R10202